TOMORROW'S SUNRISE

SLAVE CITY

First Printing: September 2022
Shawline Publishing Group Pty Ltd
www.shawlinepublishing.com.au

Paperback ISBN 978-1-9228-5015-7
eBook ISBN 978-1-9228-5023-2

 A catalogue record for this work is available from the National Library of Australia

TOMORROW'S SUNRISE

SLAVE CITY

BETHANY R. MINSTER

Dedication

This book is dedicated to all my family and friends who believed in me and my creative imagination. My love for all of you grows stronger. I promise to make you proud.

Acknowledgements

Dad, Mum, Liesel, Bianca Pezzutto, Tammie Pike and finally Allison Higgins out of all of my loved ones you believed in me the most. Even when I didn't. You saw something in me. I love you all.

Prologue

Before the world grew dark and the land turned against its people, humans were on the verge of annihilation— over population and the dramatic increase for the need of food and source of fuel, turned even the most generous humans into beasts of desperation for the inherent need to survive. Little did they know it would only get worse from there. While citizens fought and slaughtered themselves the icecaps began to slowly melt, releasing pockets of ancient, deadly viruses that would swiftly and efficiently cut down the weak and the young. Hospitals and medical facilities became over run and quickly empty, the need for cures for mysterious diseases was just too great for the scientists, doctors and developers to handle. Countries once again on the precipice of turning on each other. None of them knew, however, that it would be for the final time. Fighting for the last of the earth's resources little did they know that their bombs and missiles would crack open the surface and awaken the creatures of Myth, Fable and Mysterious that lived beneath, soon they rose to the surface, some showed they meant no harm to the humans and created alliances from which new species soon arose from. Other creatures saw the humans more savage side, creating new borders and with them new enemies. As humans reverted back into their more baser instincts for survival threatened and frightened by the new beings that emerged from the crevice's their weapons of mass destruction had created, they began attacking purely out of fear, inherently creating enemies of a different calibre.

The battles for survival gave rise to the humans with the most power, influence and land, only out of desperation did those who struggled to keep what little they had accept them as their leaders of the new world. Little did they know that something far more sinister truly ruled them. Creatures of great dark power and influence from whom gave birth to the end of the world and rise to their own.

Chapter 1

'How long has it been, Farrah?'

I was staring out of a fogging window and into a vast world of barren nothingness. I didn't expect to see anything, but it's comforting to feel elsewhere. However, you always have to return to the jarring reality that you're unfortunately stuck in.

So when DeeDee asked me 'how long has it been?', I responded with a glassy-eyed, 'What?'

'I was asking how long it's been since you started working here?'

I didn't like questions in the morning, even if they were simple ones.

'Fifteen years,' I answered, returning to folding my masters' clothes in the insanely humid laundry. The length of the room was slightly bigger than my sleeping quarters, but the same couldn't be said for the height of it.

Fifteen years… I can't believe it'd only been that long. I thought for sure it had been at least two thousand. Or maybe that's just what it feels like when you work for abusive tyrants, such as Mr. Drake and his family.

They were a family of five; Mr. and Mrs. Drake, James the eldest and only son, Rey the eldest daughter and middle child, and finally little Freya.

When I first arrived, I remember the night and the breeze going past me was very slow and humid. I remember the feeling of being carried past the great door and gazing up at a beautifully painted ceiling as if it were the gates of Heaven. Being carried down a skinny, dimly lit flight of stairs, through a dark passageway, into a small room, and placed gently on a hard mattress. The next thing I remember is weeping uncontrollably, but I can't for the life of me remember why. It's been the same humid, sticky feeling every night since. Unsurprising, as we are in the middle of the wastelands which are always hot and muggy, made worse by us always working and constantly being berated for nothing.

Yes, I've wasted fifteen years of my life working for a tyrant and his monster family, and for over half my life I have been stuck on a seemingly endless loop, replaying the same day over and over. It always feels pointless to reminisce over the years gone by since I didn't love any of them. Even worse, I know I can never get those years back.

'Thanks for that,' I said, sarcastically.

'Huh?' DeeDee's brows knit as she folded another sheet.

DeeDee was a petite young woman with a strawberry-blonde bob of hair and a face full of freckles. To me, she was one of the most beautiful girls I'd seen since I'd gotten here. I don't care much about my own appearance, but DeeDee says that I have striking green eyes and long, wavy warm chestnut hair. She insists I am what the ancestors used to call 'classically beautiful'. Ms. T says that it's a pity that I have 'resting bitch face', whatever that means.

'Thanks for making me remember the wasted years of my pitiful life.'

'I don't see it like that—remember Little Freya being born, and that time Rey found out that her crush liked you instead? That was hilarious!' she giggled.

Rey is a beautiful girl in her own right; her appearance has caught the eyes of many potential suitors. Princelings, courtiers, generals, captains, you name it. Her beguiling beauty and ice-blue eyes became the talk of almost every city. However, the same could not be said for the putrid, foul soul that lived within the enchanting shell. Her vanity and rancid personality grew and grew as she became older. In the knowledge of her inherent beauty, she turned into the miniature version of the monster that gave birth to her, and inadvertently chased away every suiter that came along and never understood why.

'I guess you're right. We have had some good times.' We both giggled as we continued folding the laundry.

'And don't forget the day we met. That's my favourite,' she said, smiling at me with a slight blush brushing from cheek to cheek as she tucked a stray piece of hair behind a freckled ear.

'Mine, too,' I gave her a little smirk before shoving the massive stack of folded clothes onto the pile she was clutching in her sweaty skinny arms. Ignoring her playful glare, I turned off the clanking washing machine and picked up the rest of the baskets.

'To be honest with you,' she stopped us at the doorway, eyes meeting mine. 'I have really enjoyed our laundry talks every day.' I couldn't stop my unabashed smile, and she succeeded in evening out the blushed-face score. She gave me a quick huff, grinned, and we both emerged from the tiny muggy laundry shack with piles of clean linen and clothes.

Having practiced over the years, we knew how many steps it took to get to the stairs that led to the veranda, where to awkwardly jump over the nearby ditch, and how many stairs are on each staircase and which creaky ones to avoid. It only took about three minutes to get from the laundry to the back door of the manor, which was a cinch for us, even when we were sight-impaired due to the clothes in our faces while we're doing it.

Still, something about today felt off, like either or both of us would not make it to the door with the linen kept clean. Unfortunately, I was correct on the second guess.

As DeeDee was waddling carefully up the dodgy worn-down stairs, I heard her grunt and everything turned black when I hit the ground.

It only took a few seconds for me to take the undergarments off my head to see the blazing red sun pierce my eyes. My head hurt and I felt my elbows starting to burn. I looked towards the stairs and saw Mrs. Drake and her usual vicious scowl set on DeeDee, who was half lying on top of me. We both squinted, looking at her in apparent confusion, and I noticed her daughter, Rey, and one of her snobby friends snickering at us.

DeeDee tried sitting up, hand rubbing her stomach. Mrs. Drake must have pushed her for her to take a tumble like that. Anger boiled inside of me, but I simply kept a passive expression whilst clenching the dirt underneath.

Mrs. Drake remained at the top of the stairs, her hands on her hips.

'How dare you forget! I told you yesterday that Ms. Fayela will be staying with us this weekend!'

DeeDee stared at her, disoriented, then wobbled to her feet like a drunk, arms out just incase.

'My apologies, Mrs. Drake. I'll prepare a room right away,' she said, finally standing, brushing the dush and dirt off of her apron.

'It's too late now! Ms. Turner is almost finished preparing one. No thanks to you!'

'My apologies Mrs. Drake. Please, how can I make it up to you?'

'Clean those clothes properly and don't be so clumsy this time! There is still a big stain on them, right there!'

'Yes, Mrs. Drake, right away, Mrs. Drake.'

'Pardon, Miss,' I interrupted, 'but where is the large stain? I can't seem to see it.'

Mrs. Drake's silver lips curled into a smirk as she lifted her make-shift, hand tailored dress. She sauntered down the rickety stairs that groaned in pain with each step. When she reached the bottom, the lady wiggled her large hips, hands shaking under her skirts, and started pulling her undergarments down. All the while, her eyes in a fixed glare with a poor DeeDee, who was unsure and nervous of what was going to happen next.

Mrs. Drake crouched down, and soon a familiar potent smell started to emanate from her. Yellow fluid splashed down from under her dress and onto the lightly dusted clothes. Bursting out laughing from the deck above, Rey and her friend were watching on with as much shock on their faces as ours, until they leaned into each other and their eyes creased .The ladies eyes still fixed on DeeDee when the last trickle landed, Mrs. Drake lifted up her undergarments.

Standing over my dear friend with hands on her hips and a big evil grin stretching her old, tired face. 'Are you blind? That one right there.'

'Oh yes, now we see, pardon us, Miss,' DeeDee mumbled, disconnecting herself from their eye contact. She bowed repeatedly until Mrs. Drake and the girls went back into the manor snickering and snorting away.

'She didn't tell you a guest was coming, did she?' I said lowly, making sure that Mrs. Drake wouldn't be able to hear me. DeeDee just looked at me and shook her head before picking up the dirty clothing strewn on the ground. I bent down to help DeeDee pick up the rest of the clothes we had tirelessly and pointlessly cleaned for most of the morning.

'I wish you would just tell her straight up she is mistaken, so you don't have to put up with that bullshit!'

'Well... If I did, then how would I be able to make what money I can for my brother back home?' she finished with a worn smile.

I released a large breath. 'Well, at least I don't have to do anything else today.' I clung to her scraped arm as she was turning back to the 'Laundry Shack'.

'Yes... I'm sure... It was really my fault... I should have watched where I was going.'

I released her arm, unconvinced, and let her return to her duties.

Just before supper, my last duty was to make sure that the

water tank was running and that there was plenty of clean, uncontaminated water in it. After all, we don't want the family to melt from toxic chemicals in the water system do we? Slumping down the concrete stairs and into the hottest room in the entire house, I found the water tank stone-cold and silent (which happens from time to time). I checked the gauges by giving them a tap and watched the needles bounce up and down a little. Grabbing the nearby pole, I gave it a big swing, whacking the old girl and creating a little echo in the room. The tank rumbled back to life with her usual jangling hum.

Tired and weary from the day, I meandered down the passageway and into the kitchen, where I would usually find Ms. Turner preparing food. I still hadn't recovered from this morning's fall—my muscles felt as if they were burning off of my bones—but maybe a full stomach would help the process along.

As usual, I found the busy cook looming over a massive steel pot currently seated atop the stove, the narrow mutant propped on a little wooden stepping stool originally bought for the youngest daughter to play with her oversized dollhouse, but who'd long since grown tired of dolls.

Ms. Turner was ancient. She looked so old, in fact, that you wouldn't even be able to fathom her age, it's a marvel how such a thing could even still be breathing. Hunched back included, she was barely standing at four foot five (and shrinking like cling wrap), her skeletal body wrapped in tanned leathery skin. Even so, she shuffled around the house and cleaned it like the best of us, while still managing to look after the other staff members like a mother.

'Are you just gonna stand there looking tired, as if you did things today, or are you gonna peel those vegetables for me?' I heard her scratchy voice echo out of the pot she was hip-deep in, her tail keeping outstretched to keep her from falling in.

I smiled. 'Yes, Ms. Turner.'

'How was your day, dear?'

'You ask as if it would have been any more interesting than the days and weeks and months before,' I answered sarcastically, reaching for the peeler. The very act of holding it made my arm sore. The old woman's groan was amplified.

'What else is there to talk about? The weather?' she retorted as she climbed down the stool. Making her way around the island to the grimy kitchen sink, she started another task (she never stops). Her long bare tail gracefully trailed behind her, pink and naked, with many silver marks all the way along it. Battle wounds from the youngest Drake child's dog, Winter; a little rat who tormented us servants just as much as the overly privileged family does. Every morning whenever DeeDee or I prepare their beds with fresh clean linen, the little beast jumps up when our backs are turned and does a little piddle, then scampers off smiling, proud of her work. When we walk up and down the halls, she hides behind the doorway we are about to pass and zooms past us, causing us to tumble and whatever we are holding crash on top of us. I hate that little shit.

'Is this all there is to living now?' I asked, not really expecting an answer. She gazed out the kitchen window framed by mold and sighed.

'You know you ask this almost every time? You're young, and your personality is too big for just cleaning up after others. Heck, you could even have your pick in men with your looks those gorgeous green eyes. You know, if there were any around.'

'Yuck. No thanks. What does that have to do with anything, anyway?'

The old woman laughed. 'What I'm trying to say is that you're meant to be a leader. You have such spirit; I've seen you grow over the years, my dear, standing up to the Drakes, not taking any nonsense. I promise you, when you're as old as me…' she sighed, 'you'll be a good caretaker of this manor, too.'

She carried a large bowl of broth from the sink, waddling over to the stove as it sloshed.

'Great,' I said flatly, taking my anger out on a defenseless potato.

'What's great?' a familiar voice came from the doorway.

'Oh, Ms. T just told me that when I become an old crone like her I get to 'inherit' her duties as caretaker of the manor. So dreams really do come true!' I said with forced cheerfulness, continuing to peel. I noticed too late that the 'old crone' had taken up her large wooden spoon to whack me on the upper-middle part of my back. Hard.

'Ouch!'

I heard a deep laugh next to my ear. 'As long as it's not me, that's fine,' said my good friend Miles as he placed his large, rough hands on my shoulders.

'Ew! Your hands are dirty!' I exclaimed, looking at the dark prints he left on my sleeves.

He just smirked when I glared at him, his hand moving past my face to reach for a cactus apple on the island.

Miles was a tall, young lad of beautiful sienna-coloured skin and dark brown curls with eyes the same colour of the clearest sky—that's what DeeDee says, anyway. He was the caretaker of the manor like his father before; whenever his father needed to fix something, Miles was always by his side learning and helping his daddy. His mother died during childbirth so he never really knew her, but every chance he got he would ask his father to tell him a story about her. His father would always say that she was the most beautiful, intelligent, and kindest person he'd met, who always looked on the bright side of life even in these dark and uncertain times. He'd say she was so excited to be a mother and was eager to meet Miles, knowing he'd be the perfect son.

Miles's father died of sickness when he was twelve years old, which was around the time I came into the picture (reluctantly). I don't think he ever mourned for him. The day after they buried him, Miles began picking up his work as if nothing had happened— although he never smiled like he used to with his daddy. When

DeeDee came along two years later, his whole attitude changed. Chatting more, smiling more. The three of us became best friends ever since.

Clambering noises echoed from the main hall's stairs, as if a beast was pounding down them. I paused and watched the entrance to see who or what it was, jumping when I saw DeeDee emerge. She was huffing and puffing, leaning on the doorway as if she planned to sleep on it.

As usual, whenever DeeDee entered the room, Miles clammed up and became shy. As I continued peeling, I noticed his posture straighten as he chucked his half-eaten apple core aside and 'casually' crossed and re-crossed his arms a few times before settling on the 'manliest' stance.

I smiled, charmed, despite myself.

Ms. Turner looked over her shoulder, gesturing to DeeDee with her wooden spoon, 'I thought that was a heffalump coming down the stairs.'

'Ha-ha-ha,' DeeDee said, pushing off the doorframe and falling onto Ms. Turner's back to give her routine cuddle.

'How are you, dear?' Ms. Turner asked, stirring the contents of the pot. The salty aromas of beef and onions were filling the room.

'Exhausted and ready for a bath,' DeeDee answered honestly, rubbing her sweaty, freckled face.

'That's all right, take the rest of the night off and have a bath,' suggested Ms. Turner, tapping the edge of the pot with the spoon. She gave DeeDee an understanding smile.

'Are you sure? Thanks, Ms. T.' She gave her another back cuddle as Ms. Turner refocused on her stew.

DeeDee noticed Miles standing on the other side of the kitchen island acting a bit strange.

'Are you okay, Miles? You don't look well,' she asked, genuinely concerned.

'Huh? Uh, yes, I'm fine.'

Listening to their conversation, I found myself grinning

'Yeah, he's fine, he just caught something,' I smirked, giving Miles a quick glance.

'I'm sorry to hear that, Miles. Well, I hope you feel better soon.'

'Yeah, ah, thanks.' He coughed into his hand.

'I think I'm going to go rest now. I'll see you guys tomorrow,' she said, waving goodnight.

As soon as she left, I looked at Miles. He shot me a scowl.

'Wipe that grin off of your face.'

'I'm sorry, but when are you going to tell her?'

'Let's see, today is Wednesday…so let's say never.'

'Come on, you've gotta tell her sometime.'

'No, I don't.'

'What happens if someone else wants her as a maid? One of Mr. Drake's associates, for example?'

'Well maybe it will be gone by then.' He recrossed his arms, more relaxed this time.

'Yeah, okay. And maybe the wastelands will turn into a forest overnight—oh, and maybe we won't have to work here anymore! You've been infatuated with her ever since she first got off that truck thirteen years ago. It's not going to stop… You need to tell her.'

Releasing a long sigh, he grabbed some bread and patted me on the shoulder before going up stairs.

***

As usual, Ms. Turner and myself prepared the dining table for supper. We work fast, thanks to our years of practice, and hurried to our places by the end of the table farthest from its head, just as the family started to enter. Rey and her friend gave me another snicker. To which I responded with an eye roll of exhaustion. Nudging my side, Ms. T led me to the place we stood by every night as they enjoyed their undeserved posh supper.

'I hear you and Lord Baymont are planning to expand the company,' Mrs. Drake said once everyone was seated, striking up the regular evening small talk.

Mr. Drake, sitting on the other end of the table enjoying the beef stew, wiped his moustache.

Little Fraya indiscreetly passed pieces of gross sucked meat under the table to the little monster waiting patiently beneath. She must have decided she's vegan...*again*.

'Yes, he and the others of the board are actually coming to dinner next week to discuss plans and finances needed.'

'How exciting.' She sipped on her wine.

Rey perked her head up from slurping and munching on the bits of vegetable in the stew. 'So will Mr. Anderson be attending, Father?' she asked, hope in her eyes. Listening into the conversation, as usual, I watched her with a smirk. He's the one that flirted aggressively with me instead of her, and seeing the look on her face as it was happening was priceless.

'I would think so, he is the Head of Employment.'

A smile and slight blush bloomed across her cheeks as she sipped some wine. James, the eldest Drake child, started smirking as well. Their mother cleared her throat, reclaiming the focus.

'He is quite handsome, dear, and his family are of a high standing like ours; no disease or half-bloods. Very good husband material for a lady of your stature,' Mrs. Drake said, taking hold of Rey's arm. The young Drake's face was turning an almost violet colour from extreme embarrassment.

'Mum!'

James burst out laughing to the point of tears, only stopping at the sight of his mother's terrifying glare. I had to bite back my own giggles, hiding my smile behind my hand by pretending to wipe my nose. Ms. Turner elbowed me, giving me a warning gaze.

Ms. Turner once told me that James looked a lot like his father when he was young, sandy blonde hair and big, charming brown eyes. A handsome young lad with a pleasant personality to match. However, Mr. Drake had always been a serious man; his father before him used to beat him whenever he misbehaved. He was groomed to take over the family business and produce a son who would do the same and so on. However, due to his difficult upbringing, the master never wanted his heir to be brought up the same way he was, which is why he is more lenient towards young James.

'Yes, we will be inviting him along with the others of the council, as well as their wives. Which means, Ms. Turner, you will need to plan and organise starting tomorrow,' Mr. Drake turned briefly to our corner. 'It will be this time next week. And, as you know, we only get supplies once a week, so I need the list in my hand by the morning. Think grand—I would like it to be as if we are celebrating Christmas! After all, a big occasion has cause for extravagance.'

Ms. Turner nodded her head obligingly.

As if she didn't have enough to do on a regular basis.

Having settled the matter, the room fell silent, other than the small clinking of cutlery hitting plates and bowls.

Chapter 2

Rarely are the doors of the grand dining room opened, and one can anticipate the absolute best when the Company's renowned council convenes. The room is framed with crimson walls, imposing ivory carvings, and two-story-high scarlet curtains, currently tied back by shimmering rope to reveal an unimpressive view of the barren desert. A varnished dining table dominated the centre, decorated with delightful china plates, golden cutlery, crystal wine glasses, and a veritable feast laid out carefully. Each juicy dish filled the room with beautifully reminiscent smells from every remaining city in the world.

The doorbell chimed, signaling the arrival of the first guests. Before DeeDee could touch the door, Mr. and Mrs. Drake, as well as their two older children, briskly walked to their invisible marks. Ms. Turner and I followed suit, placing ourselves on either side of the dining room doorway. Mr. Drake gave a nod to DeeDee. She nodded in return before opening the door, and was immediately greeted by a tall man with pale skin. His jet-black hair was combed back, and his bronze, brooding eyes stared down at her dismissively.

'Lord Karn! How are you, old friend?' Mr. Drake greeted him with open arms, grabbing his shoulders, which seemed to give the Lord a bit of a surprise.

He cleared his throat. 'I am well, Sam. The trip here is a bit too long for me, though. I almost feel sorry for you and your family,' he said with a deep voice, face straight.

He strode further into the dining room, and as he passed me, a deathly chill went down my spine. I followed him with my eyes, and it felt as if the air around him was stale.

Ms. Turner made a hissing noise, getting my attention, and gestured ahead. I straightened, refocusing. I couldn't cause trouble, not tonight.

More guests began trickling in, some I recognised from the many years I'd worked for the Drakes—like Mr. and Mrs. Haroldson, who seemed to look different every time I saw them. Mr. Haroldson, for instance, would age a decade or two in the span of a year, and Mrs. Haroldson would have visited at least a dozen plastic surgeons in that same span of time, thinking no one would notice. DeeDee and I call her Lady Blowfish.

Most of these people were your typical high-and-mighty types that didn't seem to bother talking to the likes of me. That is, apart from Lady Farrow. She was the only decent person among the obnoxiously wealthy. Coming from a more humbling standing, she was still just as angelic even surrounded by her loathsome peers. Her eyes matched her golden hair which fell gracefully around her slender, delicate face and onto her bare shoulders, showing off her fair complexion which was the envy of every other lady of her stature. She didn't really have conversations with us, but she asked us small-talk questions, such as 'how are you?' or 'how old are you now?' And always gave us corner smiles that showed she saw us as more than just tools.

She was joined by her husband, the Head of Development, and their nephew, Benjamin Anderson, the secret love of Rey's life. Unfortunately, he didn't reciprocate those feelings. In fact, he had eyes for another, and that person just so happened to be yours truly. Sadly, like Rey's feelings for him were unrequited, I didn't feel the same way he did.

He, Lady Farrow, and her husband passed me and Ms. Turner

on their way to the dining room. As Lady Farrow gave her usual friendly smile, her nephew shot me a wink from a slightly blushing face. 'Hey, Farrah,' he mouthed.

And as quick as a roll of my eyes, he was gone.

'Ben!' James beckoned his friend over. Mr. Anderson gave a nod as he joined him and the other younger men.

Rey and her mother greeted Lady Farrow, both giving her a kiss on either cheek.

'So, um, Lady Farrow, did you come with anyone else?' Rey asked with an innocent face and a drink in hand.

Lady Farrow answered with a smile, gesturing behind her. 'Benjamin is over there with your brother.'

Rey's face quickly changed shades, nearly matching the dark copper-coloured hair of her crush. It's always very amusing to watch a proud postured young lady turn to a little girl, terrified of the big bad elephant in the room everyone knew about.

Almost all the guests had finished arriving before dusk and were now in their own little clusters, chatting away—apart from Mr. Haroldson, who quickly made a beeline for a lounge chair after saying his greetings to the host family. He was out cold in under a minute, which is to be expected from a ninety-four-year-old man trying to keep up with his young gold-digging wife. While he slept, she kept busy by sling-shotting herself at all the young lords of the party.

The final arrival was a tall man of golden hair and eyes the colour of light bronze, walking with a cane he didn't really seem to need but carried only to accentuate his meticulously tailored suit. I carefully observed him, and as soon as he passed, he shot me a steely glare. His stride did not slow. The only greeting he gave was the strange stench he left behind: coal, oil, and just a hint of what I could only assume was mud.

So there we have it. A room of gorgeous upper-class Lords and Ladies, men and women who think themselves as powerful as gods and were as ridiculously as wealthy as fat kings and Queens.

With all guests accounted for, Mr. Drake gave us the nod to close the doors. He sharply rapped his wineglass with a silver fork, effectively garnering the room's attention.

'Good evening, everyone. It's nice to see that you've all arrived safely to our humble abode in the middle of nowhere. May I please direct your eyes to the beautiful feast our staff has prepared for us this evening, and you will find your place settings. We can continue our conversations there.' He finished his announcement with a smile, waving his arm towards the extravagantly laid-out dining table.

Ms. Turner and I were waiting nearby with wine bottles in hand, cloth slung over our arms and lips stretched from cheek to cheek. As expected, the oldest person, Mr. Haroldson, and by far the most spry, is the first one to find his seat, his unimpressed trophy wife in tow. After some shuffling around, people were finally seated, eyes greedily taking in the bountiful display. With one word from Mr. Drake, the feast began, and everyone started digging in. Everyone, that is, apart from poor, shy Rey, who was 'unfortunately' placed next to her indifferent crush.

I wonder who would have such cruel humour as to do that to a fine young lady of her stature?

Smirking at the floor, I dared peek at Ms. Turner. She was giving me the worst death stare; the type where you can see into the pits of hell through the person's eyes. I returned the gesture with a proud grin.

I refocused my attention on the table and caught sight of the blonde man who'd left behind that foul smell. He was watching me with smiling eyes, taking a slow sip of his wine. It didn't seem to faze him that I was meeting his gaze; he just continued his unabashed observation. Mr. Anderson, who was seated directly opposite him and thus could see what he was doing, did not seem happy.

'How is your mother, Benjamin?' Mrs. Drake asked, chewing on the tiniest bite I'd ever seen.

'She is the same, unfortunately,' he answered, trying to hide the agitation on his face.

'Such a pity. What does the doctor say?'

'He says it's cancer of the lungs due to the toxins surrounding our town. Many of our people are quickly falling ill. There are not enough healers to take care of the masses, but fortunately, we have our personal family healer, Winston, so we don't have to worry.'

'Yes, that is fortunate. It is also fortunate that you were born into wealth, so your family has more access to cleaner oxygen.'

'I'm sorry to interject, but why is your mother one of the worst of the whole town if she is married to the mayor?' Mrs. Haroldson said flippantly, chest thrust a little too outward as she went to grab a bowl of peas.

Before Mr. Anderson could open his mouth—

'She was a whore, wasn't she?' Lord Karn answered from the other end of the table, stunning everyone to silence.

Mr. Anderson recovered quickly, clearing his throat. 'Yes, "was" being the operative word. As some of you know, my father prefers "working women", rather than women from a place of power.'

'The apple doesn't seem to fall far from the tree when it comes to desires of the flesh, does it, Anderson?' Lord Karn crooned, smirking under his wine glass.

Mr. Anderson coughed and sputtered out his last sip of wine, turning the same crimson colour as the poor girl about to cry next to him. His watery eyes darted towards me, which a few people at the table caught, including the man who had been staring at me before. I had to bite my tongue hard until it almost bled, trying not to look furious at the insult thrown to both of us. *How* dare *he?*

Murmurs erupted around the table.

'Leave the boy alone, Karn,' Mr. Drake interjected.

'It's all right, Anderson. I just like to stir people's cauldrons, if you know what I mean. No hard feelings. You should be proud of being in the position you are in. If you were my bastard son, I would have left you on the streets with your mother.' His comments sounded more and more like insults thrown to a very agitated Mr. Anderson.

The only sound in the room was cutlery clinking on plates.

'May I be excused? I suddenly feel very tired.' Rey's chair screeched as she stood, and the look of embarrassment smeared across her face said it all. For the first time since I had worked for her, I felt sad for Rey Drake.

'Are you all right, dear?' Her mother crossed the table to her.

Pushing in her chair, she took a breath and lifted her head. 'Yes, Mother, I am fine. I'm just tired, and I feel the need to retire. May I?' she answered with a thin smile.

Mrs. Drake looked at her with concern, as well as to Lady Farrow. 'Yes, dear, you may leave. Goodnight, and—' Rey was gone before her mother could finish.

Mrs. Farrow cleared her throat loud enough to attract everyone's attention. 'I hear you're leaving to train for a position in Lord Cowan's security squadron at Buson, James.'

'Yes, it's fortunate that Father has such beneficial connections.' James swung to face the man on the other end of the table, raising his wineglass with a smile, as did Mr. Drake. It was the man who'd arrived last, the same man who had been staring at me all evening.

'To be completely honest James, I need a new officer. I transferred the last one to the mines…The last overseer had an unfortunate mortal accident.' He mumbled the last few words under the lip of his champagne flute.

'My soldiers are a bunch of half-drunk horny beasts who seem more focused on handling what's in their pants more than the untamed citizens they are supposed to maintain…I would rather someone I could trust keep their mind clean and take care of their personal business in their own time, that's why your Father recommended you.' He confessed with a gentle smile and lift of his flattened glass. Which was returned in kind.

'Are you sure I am up to the task? I don't have any training of being a soldier, never mind being a leader of a squadron of them.' James answered with a shaky tone and tightened brows.

Managing to pull his head up from the mountain of meat and gravy he had in front of him and clearing his throat. 'You're the son of a Lord, you don't have trouble bossing these people around, do you?' Mr. Haroldson answered rather gruffly, half-heartedly gesturing to myself with a flick of his cloudy eyes.

'Well…no.' James answered.

'You were born to lead, boy. Soldiers and common folk aren't smart enough to know what to do with themselves, they need us to tell them what to do, otherwise they will just wither and waste away like our ancestors. Trust your gut. And if that doesn't work, forceful intimidation is pretty effective.' Lord Karn answered calmly, in-between comfortable bites.

A snicker of laughter slowly simmered throughout the table, as whisperings of memories were told.

'Very well. I will try to do my best, Sir.' James answered, slightly uncomfortable with a hint of confidence in his voice.

'Just don't make me regret it.' Lord Cowan replied lifting his glass to his partially opened lips once more, returning his cold dagger-shaped eyes directly on me. A creepy smile spread across his face just before he took his last sip allowing the sparkling liquid to drain quickly into his mouth.

What is with this man and his incessant staring? It's getting on my nerves.

'My, what a scary face that servant is making,' Mrs. Haroldson commented, aghast.

Shit. I hadn't realised I'd let my emotions appear . Unfortunately, I was in the Lady's line of sight, just behind the handsome young Lord she was feeling up with her feet under the table, her hand pinching a lock of her loose off-white coloured hair.

'Girl!'

I snapped my head towards Mr. Drake, whose expression was just as foul as the one I'd had. He forcibly relaxed his face with a sigh. 'Please, go, and get the board room ready for us men. We will be… meeting soon.'

With a quick bow, I scurried away to the boardroom to prepare.

It was only a few minutes later before I was completing my final task of centreing the cigars on the small meeting table. When they were perfectly aligned, I placed clippers in my lower apron pocket for later. The unassuming furniture piece was surrounded by grand, high-backed evergreen-coloured chairs, with thick cushions and polished legs.

The first of the men meandered in, continuing their conversations from the dining table in low murmurs. They seemed to be deliberately avoiding me, but keeping me in their line of sight. I never wanted to disappear so much in my life after the intense conversation earlier. While I made my way to one of the dark corners, I overheard voices picking up, conversations becoming looser, and I felt myself breathe steadily again. Now it was just annoying, not awkward and annoying.

The men nursed glasses in their hands, some brimming with beer, others with wine. I hid by the chairs furthest from the doors, hands clasped in front of me.

Once everyone had found a comfortable place to be, Mr. Drake snapped his fingers at me and pointed to the door. Even when giving the command, his focus never left the two Lords before him, one of whom was that strange blonde man, Lord Cowan.

This time he gave me a creepy side smirk, making bile rise up my throat. I forced myself to swallow back the rancid taste.

The room was lit only by a single blazing fireplace and a few candles scattered throughout the already grim decor. The men's dark silhouettes all took their seats, finally beginning their meeting.

I tuned in and out of listening to their dull conversation, catching only a few words here and there. Most of my inattentiveness was due to the fact that I was exhausted and had been on my feet for at least twelve hours. Every passing minute proved a test of my abilities to stay awake.

'You! Girl! Are you deaf?! I said give me another drink! Now!' an overly aggressive and slightly inebriated Mr. Haroldson startled me alert. He turned to Mr. Drake, flinging out his arm dramatically.

'Can't you afford smarter servants, Drake?' he sarcastically asked as I approached his chair.

'Sorry, sir.' I placed a tray of a crystal bottle of Snake Venom (the most potent alcohol around nowadays) with a clean glass beside it and a small bowl of sphere ice cubes I had to prepare earlier today.

'Anyway, as I was saying… My men in Esata and Harlen were able to acquire many "workers", but unfortunately, the tap of young blood is about to run dry in those cities. They were only able to acquire crippled and old ones.'

The man he was talking to was the same one who had been creeping me out most of the night. He sat across from Mr. Haroldson in an identical chair, sucking on a pipe with his legs crossed as though he were the master of the house.

'I see. What about Kraznia?' he asked, casually sucking in another puff of tobacco.

'The Icelands! Are you insane!' This one simple question not only made Mr. Haroldson look terrified, but everyone else as well, making all small talk obsolete and silencing the room.

'You do remember what happened the last time we sent in not only his men but your soldiers as well, Cowan, to that godforsaken place, don't you?' The master asked, making everyone shudder at whatever memories lay behind their agitated looks.

'I'm not saying we target the big colony. I'm saying we target the smaller, weaker colonies that are closer to the border. There are only women and children there and, remember my friends, we did get a few of their men,' he said, still sitting casually yet rocking his elevated leg in what I could only assume was mild nervousness.

'We captured them at a great price,' Mr. Haroldson retorted louder than before.

'True, but as you know, not only the men but the whole species have unnatural strength and healing abilities which were beneficial for harvesting and spiked our revenues. Isn't that right, Mr. Williams?'

Everyone's attention turned to a young man about the same age as James and Mr. Anderson, but didn't look as princely. He was a mousy fellow with jet black oily hair and glasses that looked like they were made of two different frames fused together. He was so skinny that I didn't even see him pass me when the dinner party started. He seemed like a very unassuming fellow who was frightened of the attention he was getting.

'Yeaa… yee… yess. That. That is true, sir,' he answered timidly. Then, as soon as the attention was off him, he scampered back to his little spot at the bar.

'You see. Even if we don't get men, we still will profit from taking the women and children.' Lord Cowan relaxed back into his chair and took a victory puff with a slide of a grin going up his other check.

'How am I to do this when most of my men would rather being devoured slowly by one of those ghastly Greavors!?' He questioned, frustrated.

The whole room fell silent in thought.

'Surely you have some spare bodies Cowan?' Karn questioned from his darkened corner, a glint from his sly grin gleaming off of his exposed tooth.

Cowans whole body tensed at the simple question balling his rested hand into a white fist, and cocky face went pale, falling silent as the whole room waited for his response.

'No actually.' He humbly answered.

'Another riot occurred in the tunnels, every time the workers get closer to the collapsed pocket those creepy powers these creatures use get inside their simple, weak minds and somehow influence them with those damn visions and false memories. It creates a mass hysteria, every time one bumps into another it spreads like wildfire, they turn into animals tearing each other apart. The overseer got in the way of a gun. That's why I need your son to be the new officer of the guards'

Murmurs rumbled through the small cloisters of distinguished yet rotten men.

'Then what do you suggest we do?' Mr. Haroldson asked the room, which was answered with stumped silence.

'We could go hunting for the desert folk again, remember they are the natural enemies of the Kraznians, and with their mystic powers over nature we could learn and have them teach our soldiers how to control nature themselves our soldiers would become unstoppable against the Kraznians. But if we take a small force of desert folk under our control to Kraznia with the promise that they could return home once they fill a certain quotar.'

Silence filled the room once more while the other lords considered the intriguing proposition.

'Very well. I agree, but only with those terms. I am only letting a small squadron of my men go with them and only to the smaller villages. Agreed?'

Lord Cowan relaxed his demeanour and a smile turned into a grin, showing his teeth in satisfaction.

Shocked as much as I was about the conversation that just took place, I knew I couldn't get myself involved; that's too stupid, even for me.

Besides the desert folk know how to keep themselves hidden in the sands and if they needed to, they could easily take down any foe that threatened their peace, they had been doing it for years.

The only thing I needed to focus on was waiting patiently in the darkest corner of the room and coming out when asked for a beverage or to clip a guest's cigar. Drinks, cigars, staying awake. I could handle that.

I knew halfway through that I was being stared at, but luckily not by the creepy blond. Mr. Anderson wasn't so comfortable. He generally did it in small glances, trying to appear as if he was looking behind me.

Don't get me wrong, he was quite a handsome fellow, but any attraction I would have felt was instantly killed due to the unspoken rules against men and women of power. It was highly frowned upon to do such unsightly things with the people they deem as "lower" class.

And the fact that I secretly despise those who think of themselves higher than others just because they were born into rich homes. The only "hard work" they know is signing documents, telling others what to do and finding faster ways to make more money.

As the men gravitated out of the room, I began to clear away their dirty ashtrays and stray glasses. I didn't realise I wasn't alone.

'I'm sorry about before,' a solemn voice from the bar said.

Startled, I jumped straight up from cleaning a side table.

Benjamin appeared from the dim lighting with a sorrowful face, his thick quaff of auburn hair deflated and out of place.

He walked slowly closer and closer until he was able to touch my tense forearm. He was clearly just as drunk as the others; he still had a chilled glass of scotch in hand and gazed at me solemnly with his sad puppy eyes.

'What do you want from me?' I responded curtly.

'I want you to forgive me for the trouble my attention has brought you,' he said, gently caressing my upper arm with two thick fingers. He forced his way closer with smaller steps towards me, so close that if he wanted to, he could kiss me.

'And I—I want you. I've always wanted you,' he finally admitted.

Oh God*! Give me a break.*

I stepped away, putting my hands up to block him from coming closer again.

'Look. You're drunk, you don't know what you're saying.'

'Yes, I do! I want you, Farrah! I don't care what our stations are! Everyone knows my feelings for you!' He strode confidently closer, arms wide, smiling admittedly. His face looked as if something had finally been lifted off his pathetic shoulders.

'I don't feel the same way about you. In fact, I never have, and it's because of your station and you can't change that. Besides, you're better off marrying Rey. She loves you just as much as you love me, and the lords won't make fun of your family anymore if you do. You need to sleep it off. You'll feel better in the morning and most likely won't remember this ever happened.'

I *will though.* Yuck*!*

And with that, I made my escape through the doors, leaving a sad and speechless Benjamin Anderson alone in the darkness of the drawing room.

As the moon rose higher, beckoning the darkness and calling awake the stars from their sleep, the guests finally retired to their rooms.

Ms. Turner and DeeDee arrived soon after, and we cleaned whilst dreading the onslaught of daft requests from our newest snobby guests. Like Mrs. Haroldson, who asked if she and her husband could have an adjoining spare room and if we had any sleeping remedies on hand for Mr. Haroldson, who had already fallen asleep with his clothes still on, looking like a dead fish flopped on the bed.

It was about an hour later when the meeting had ended, but I remembered that after the meeting a few of the men had gone to the balcony for a smoke. I wandered over to the ashy remnants of the cigars and discarded glasses.

Seizing the chance to admire the beautifully displayed night sky,

I took a deep breath of the cold clean air.

'Gorgeous night, isn't it?'

Lord Cowan was standing by the glass door, finishing a cigar.

I jumped, fumbling the ashtray I was cleaning, which he easily caught with cat-like reflexes.

'Y-Yes, fortunately one of the few things I'm allowed to enjoy.' I warily took back the offered ashtray.

'What is your name?'

'Farrah,' I answered hesitantly.

'I'm envious of you, Farrah. I would love to see it like you do, where I live—'

'Unfortunately, I don't always get to see it. I'm not as important as you, apparently,' I interrupted with a harsh stare. 'I also know that your ancestors gained wealth and power by terrorising those who had barely anything to give but the few things they had in their bags and whatever land and remaining worthless money or jewels they had on hand, for the promise of protection which was rarely given.'

He scoffed. 'Well, obviously you don't know me as well as you think you do. My servants wouldn't have the nerve to say such things to me.'

'Well, I guess I'm glad that I'm not one of them. I don't think I would be able to stand you staring at me like a rapist every time I see you.'

He returned my snappy remark with a chuckle.

'Quite a few of them seem to enjoy the attention. Granted, they're… well, off the streets.' They don't hold a torch against your striking beauty and wit.' A sliver of lip slides up his cheek. *Is he… smiling?!* 'It's no wonder it doesn't faze you.'

He reached out to brush my cheek.

I dodged it like a bullet. 'It doesn't faze me because your sad version of flirting, to be frank, sir, creeps me out. I feel sad for your servants that they have to deal with it.'

Again, he chuckled. I wanted to break his stupid smile but thought better of it.

'I must go back to my chores. Us servants have dreamless sleep to catch up on. After all, we lower-class people aren't smart enough to dream of better days.'

Slapping on a fake smile, I picked up the last few glasses and walked away, leaving him on the dark balcony.

What a creep.

***

My body was barely functioning as I dragged my feet up the stairs after yet another day of pointless work. Half asleep, I wondered if it was my imagination that I could hear strange noises coming from down the hall. Against my body's wishes, I followed the sound, and discovered the origin at the Master's office.

Curiosity got the better of me, and I cautiously peered into the dimly lit room. I gasped, finding the Master and my best friend.

Mr. Drake's hand held her back down, pressing her cheek to his desk, the bottom half of her dress on her back. Tears were rolling down her salmon-coloured face, lower lip snared between her teeth.

I could hardly believe my eyes. Rage flooded my body, but before I could do anything, DeeDee's expression changed to shock. She met my gaze, and her head slowly started shaking. Though she dared not speak, her face said it all.

Gritting my teeth until my head thrummed in pain, I forced my body to move away from the door. Anger, sadness, revulsion, and regret filled every ounce of my being. When I returned to my room, I couldn't sleep; I didn't want to. I just sat, brooding over what I saw.

The next morning, I was cornered by DeeDee, her eyes wide and face pale.

'Please, don't say anything,' she whispered.

I couldn't even look at her, I felt so uncomfortable.

She grabbed my tense arm and whisked me down the stairs, past the kitchen and a busy half asleep Ms. Turner, turning tightly into the cold brick tunnel that held all our humble quarters and straight into her room, not before slamming the door out of panic almost chopping my hair in half.

Once we found ourselves away from the pricked ears and wandering eyes of the house, she explained herself, eyes watering the whole time.

'It's not what you think… You know that I have a twin brother at Buson. Well… he is always very sick, and we only have each other.' Her fists clenched. 'I begged the Master, pleaded with him, that I would do whatever it took for my brother to stay well and be cared for. I don't earn enough for the medicine he needs just as a slave. So the Master suggested that I be his whore. And he promised my brother would be taken care of as long as I please him and never say no.' As she said this, she inadvertently rubbed her stomach.

'There's something else, isn't there?' I asked slowly, keeping my eyes on hers. I could always tell there was something wrong when it came to DeeDee. Whenever she was silent or avoiding eye contact, that's when I know something is wrong. And for the past month or so, something had been very wrong. Her sudden disappearances and need to go to the bathroom so frequently and how tired she always seemed to be. She was silent for a long moment before she shoved her face in her hands.

'Farrah, I… I'm with child,' she broke into sobs.

I was taken aback, speechless.

'Please, Far,' she pleaded, her hands reaching out to grab my arm, 'promise me you won't tell the others—especially Miles!'

I responded with a smile. 'You like him, don't you?'

She blushed, looking down.

I took her in my arms and started to slowly pat her hair. 'Your secret's safe with me.'

I held her until I felt her whimpers die down.

'Here, I have something to show you,' she exclaimed, breaking the calming silence

Clambering off the old lumpy bed, she got down on all fours and reached under it, pulling out an old shoe box that looked like it was falling apart. Climbing back up next to me, she opened its flimsy lid. As she did, I was met with an astonishing amount of letters, images, and bundles of money crammed into it. I couldn't hide my shock.

'My god, DeeDee! What's all of this?!' I asked, gingerly picking out dozens of letters and photos, grazing over them with bewildered eyes.

'I've managed to save everything I could from my past. Even a few pictures of my brother,' she said, smiling reminiscently at an image of a small boy and girl who, to me, look almost identical, both smiling so happily with not a care in the world. The girl's arm was slung over the boy's shoulders so proudly.

'What's his name?' I asked, changing to a lighter subject.

'Francis, he's the only family I have left… After our father died, he grew gravely ill and so I had no choice but to sell myself as a maid to the Drakes in order to pay for his medication and treatments. It was either leave and never see him again or let him die alone. I couldn't let him die,' she answered, rubbing the image of him softly with her thumb.

'I would love to meet him one day,' I replied, holding her shaking hand.

As I let DeeDee reminisce, my eyes caught the sight of something suspicious. Upon closer inspection of the letters, I noticed that one of them was dated just last week—the day before the dinner party, no less. What drew my attention, though, was the name of the sender. Lady Farrow.

'How did you get this?'

'Oh that. That's from Lady Farrow. I get lots from her,' she responded fondly.

'Lady Farrow writes to you!?'

'Yes, in secret. She uses an assumed name so that the Drakes don't stumble upon it and find out. She and her husband have plans to buy me. And she says she knows someone who can help me with my… situation. When the mail gets here, I always make sure I'm the one to get it so that I can take it out of the bounded stack of bills and such for the family and sneak it into my apron pocket. Clever, huh?' Her smile grew.

'You were just going to leave me alone here!'

'No! No! I was asking her if you could come as well.'

She took something out of her pocket. Opening her hand, she revealed crumpled up bills.

'Oh my God! Does the Master pay to do… that to you!' my mind raced at the thought and my stomach churned in disgust.

'Only a few coins! When he leaves to make himself a drink. I find the time to… you know.'

'Steal!'

'No! I'm not *stealing*… I'm merely helping him with his blood-money issues.'

I burst out laughing, finding this so hilarious that I can barely hold my pee in. I smacked the lumpy 'mattress' in agony.

'Shhh…,' DeeDee held a finger to her lips, her brows furrowed. 'He'll hear you.'

'I can't believe it, you've been stealing from the Drakes! That's amazing!' I wiped my tears away as I calmed myself down.

'I thought maybe I could save enough for all of us. You, me, Miles and Ms. Turner.'

'You mean… run away together?' I said, double-checking I heard her right.

She nodded. 'I have just enough so that we could leave and go to stay where Lady Farrow lives. The city of Prona. We could steal the family car and drive straight there, taking with us anything we need.'

It was clear that she had been planning this for a long time. I took her hand in mine, then nodded, agreeing to her plan. Even if it was stark raving mad. At least it was better than what I had; nothing.

***

Before we had breakfast or were given any morning chores, the household servants, including myself, were forced to form a procession to see the guests of the night before off.

One by one, they casually strolled by, most of them ignoring their inferiors as they walked out the door to their respective vehicles of copper and wooden design, decorated with stripes of iron and metal filigree from nose to tail. The more human guests, however, gave a little nod and smile as if to say 'thank you for your services'—this included Mr. Anderson, who added his usual shy blush to his charming smile.

Thank god. He doesn't remember.

Mr. Drake and Lord Cowan walked out of the door looking like a dynamic duo. My master's arm was slung over his friend's shoulder, a wide grin on his face. As they glided past me, Lord Cowan's amber eyes met mine, sending a nervous shiver down my spine. Stopping at the doorway, Lord Cowan turned back to face him with a big smile just as my master grabbed his shoulder to form a more aggressive handshake. When they did, our eyes met once again, and his smile shifted until I could see the points of his canines.

Something bad was about to happen. I could feel it in my soul.

Chapter 3

A crackling voice was blaring from the makeshift radio, and all of us listened intently to the foreboding news.

'Warning for all those in Dead Man's Land: an acid rainstorm is forming at Memorial Crater, causing one of the worst toxic depressions we have seen in a long time. Please prepare your homes for one of the largest storms recorded as a Category S. We have not seen one of this magnitude since the desolation of Port Carina fifteen years ago.'

Frightened silence swept through the room, the staff glancing at each other with pale faces and open mouths. The tension was broken by the clearing of a deep throat.

'You heard the man. Prepare the house and begin erecting the pylons for the shield; and kids, go to the safe room, ' the Master commanded, as he crossed his arms.

Miles and I locked eyes from across the room, obviously thinking the same thing. Being the fastest workers in the manor, it'd be more efficient if we set up the defenses together.

Moving quickly, we ran outside and prepared the pylons and rigged the field, hardly saying a word as we did so. Miles rushed to clear away any debris covering the shafts from which the pylons emerged, so they wouldn't get stuck when they rose. As for me, I rushed to the side of the laundry shack where a large box of electrical wiring for the whole manor could be found, including the switch for the pylons hidden behind a sketchy mess of wiring. Making sure Miles was at the ready and out of the way, a quick flick of the stiff switch began the alarm, warning everyone to get inside the shield before the pylons hit their apex.

I watched as the pylons slowly rose, waiting at the switchboard just in case they stopped. I jumped at the feeling of Miles tapping me on the shoulder. When I turned to him, I noticed his gaze was not on me, but over my shoulder, to the horizon. His face was slack with shock. I followed his line of sight, and my body stiffened.

Hardly ten miles away, a massive storm was bursting outwards, quickly consuming the sky. Green hues of toxic air mixed amongst the swollen gray clouds, casting the ground beneath it in a sickly light. As it moved, it was clear the storm was alive and angry, ravaging everything in its path with swift, deadly force. Fossilised trees crumbled away and became swept up in the unforgiving currents of the wind.

I swiftly turned back to face a petrified Miles, whose gaze still hadn't left the dark horizon. I nudged him and pointed towards the house with my head, gently reminding him if we didn't hurry, we'd be locked outside. The wind was starting to turn up the sand, dust blinding us as tumbleweeds and grit scratched against our skin.

Running toward the manor, shielding our eyes from the sheets of sand, we stumbled up the creaking stairs and burst through the back entrance. We took a second to catch our breath, turned, then pressed our palms against each door and pushed. The wind was strong, and it took Miles and I working together to get them closed. Just before they clicked into place, I swear I saw something small and dark flash past us.

'Did you see that?' I said, backing away from the doors.

'See… what?' Miles was struggling to catch his breath. There was still sand in his eyes; maybe he couldn't see anything, or maybe it was just my imagination.

'Nothing.' I shrugged it off, following Miles into the downstairs kitchen for a much-deserved drink.

DeeDee and Ms. Turner were busy boarding up and securing the insides of the manor. Of course, most of the security was used on the rooms that held the family's valuables. They had just started boarding up the cracks and gaps of the back door when a shrill cry rang out, making everyone rush to aid whoever it was.

'Where is Winter?!' It came from little Fraya. Turning around, I saw the cute girl with tears in her eyes.

'Are you sure you've checked everywhere, Fraya?' I asked, bending down to her height. 'Maybe she's just hiding somewhere from the storm. Did you know dogs can sense danger before it comes?' I thought that throwing in a fun fact would make her feel better, but she still looked up at me with teary eyes.

'I've checked everywhere,' she sniffled. 'All of our favourite hiding places, and I can't find her.'

God, it makes me feel so uncomfortable when someone cries.

The wind outside started getting louder, rumbling like a stampede of angry bulls, making me nervous. Wait, that dark shape that passed me… I knew it wasn't my imagination!

I looked at Miles, who stared straight back, already knowing what I was about to do. I cut him off, 'I think I know where Winter is… Let me go outside and check, okay?'

'Farr! The storm is almost on us! You can't go outside! You'll die!' DeeDee exclaimed, shaking.

'You have to save my Winter!' Fraya squealed, stomping her little foot down. 'Otherwise I'll tell Daddy you let my best friend die!'

I stepped back, shocked that I was being blackmailed by a little girl. Though I suppose that's what you'd expect from the upper class; even the youngest saw us as disposable.

I patted DeeDee's arm to reassure her. 'I'll be okay. I promise I'll be quick.'

I knelt down to eye-level with the youngest Drake, trying my best to keep my face straight and swallow the absolute disgust I felt for privileged people like her family.

'Don't worry, I'll get Miss Winter back for you, Fraya.' Her tears vanished and a big grin replaced them.

Ms. Turner tapped on my shoulder holding something rather ominous looking in her skeletonized fingers. 'Here use this.' She held out an old well used gas mask scratches and tiny cracks poked and marked the visor practically turning it into a blinder. The respirator was half squashed in. It's not much but it'll help.'

I nodded, taking them from her. 'You guys should go into a safer room. Once I open this door you could all be in danger.' They gave me a last look of concern before rushing to the dining room and closing the doors.

Why are you doing this? Farrah, you idiot.

I sighed, strapping the virtually useless gasmask tightly around my head.

'Okay, come on,' I whispered, steeling myself. My fingers wrapped around the handles of the double doors that led to the loud rumblings of the oncoming storm.

The sky had taken on a threatening greenish grey dullness since the frighteningly short time Miles and I were last outside. Violent ephemeral gusts of sand thrashed and tore a fresh path for the great looming beast that roared impressively towards me. Scurrying tongues of eradiated grains and smaller debris whipped against me, my skin stinging in pain as if it were being cut a million times. Every time I sucked in a big breath the excruciating sensation of hot glass mixed with an odd tasting flavour much like gas swam down my exposed throat, ripping it raw. Radiation had been pouring in past the weak holes in the shield. Delicate webs of yellow sparkled and sparked against the dark green-grey shrouded background. Every time a large object riding the sandy waves struck, the shield turning into smaller pieces of shrapnel that rained down around me as if I were in the middle of a war zone. Trying and failing to shield myself with my bare scorched arms, I peered between them as best I could, struggling to see past the scratches and marks on my visor. I could have sworn that I could see something rather odd waving in the current of the sandy sea, almost like a clump of fur.

Winter?

The dome continued to spark and zap like a giant bug zapper. My heart ached in fear and beat against my tightened chest like a hammer. If I left to save my self and left that damn rat out on its own, I'd never hear or feel the end of it. Against my bodies compelling wishes, I forced it onward towards whatever it was that caught my eye not paying attention to the giant fucking branch that was about to impale me. My stomach dropped like a stone and ears rang like a siren while I sucked in a gulping breath all I could think to do is drop. My outstretched palms crunched down on something corky, and the crunch of wood as it crumbled and snapped beneath my weight crackled in my ears. Slowly racing my face to only lock eyes onto a dedicated corpse of a beast that must have been uncovered by the storm. Remnants of its fur fluttered and danced in the wind. Almost all of it had been uncovered. The creatures giant bear like head lay gently only inches from where I knelt. It was the body of a Giant Dune Bear, a great and noble beast of the desert plains, companions of the desert folk a wandering tribe of humanoid creatures, known for their almost onyx colour and recognizable for their almost glowing yellow eyes and tall, slender figures with protrusions of bone on their chins and ridges along their ears and scalps. They once lived in the canyons until they were driven out by an army of soldiers that came from beyond the sea with their masters one of whom I know serve.

Driven out of their ancestral home and forced to find a new one within the still standing buildings and ruins of the old world. This poor creature must have died of dehydration or old age and they had to leave it behind. A small mound of smooth sand stones uncommon in this area lay by its belly half covered by loose sand. Atop the small mountain a beautiful opalescent black stone shone in what little life was left behind with a small spiral of scripture spiralling from the edges of the stone to its centre. A ritual stone made for the deceased to give them safe passage to the next life. Guiding my hand over it's rough, thick, straw like fur following what's left of its body as it rose and fell from head to it's very long tail that once trailed gracefully behind it. Strangely finding my-self calmer and more relaxed if only for a second. Something momentously large collided head-on to the roof of the shield, erupting in a frightening ear-splitting explosion, creating a magnificent and rather frightening light show weakening the shield immensely, allowing a plume of gas pour in and with it two massive predators soring in on the hunt for dinner. A high piercing ear shattering screech rattled my bones and shake the shield, destroying the calm serenity of my mind. Scavenger Hawks.

Eyes of all consuming pits of darkness surveyed the interior of the dome with effortless ease, scanning for anything that moved. Flesh had decayed and sluffed off of their heads and parts of their mighty bodies. Even now feathers fluttered and waltzed in the gusts of dust. I was going to have to fight for my life. Keeping my own eyes glued on the dangers circling above and senses on high alert I guided my hand blindly, pushing through the loose sand like a ship through calm seas to its nearby target sitting motionless behind me. Feeling around, my fingers touched and grabbed hold of hopefully something I could use in self-defence. Using the advance of objects colliding and exploding into the shield, I managed to quickly and smoothly yank out the bone from the weakened and degraded socket quickly. But obviously, not quick enough.

Hearing the crack and pop of the bone, one of the bird's heads jerked to my direction, with a loud and shrill screech it twirled its powerful large body into my direction. Aiming directly at me. With a graceful and tight spiral motion and a blink of the eye it was on top of me and it's claws lifted me up by the legs with ease as if I were a twig and launched back up into the toxic air with one powerful and deep push of its powerful wings, rising higher and higher, sawing meters above the hard unforgiving ground.

Flailing and twisting about, desperate to reach something to find something to grab onto, while it still clutching tightly onto the one thing that could save me. Swinging back and forth, getting closer to its decaying torso. I didn't even notice the second ugly beast silently swooping in closer to steal the prize. Me. It began to nip and scratch at me and the bird that had successfully won in snatching me first, grabbing at my outstretched arms as soon as I swept up and pulling, it was now or never. I quickly swung the bone and crunched down onto its toes, forcing it to yelp and let go then with my second swing smacking the other bird in the ribs so hard it released me before smashing straight into the shield instantly turning into burnt bone and flesh. The remaining bird glided below me while free falling to my imminent and likely death. Fortunately landing on its wing frightened it and we both tumbled onto the harsh dry earth. Cracking my mask on impact, hitting the ground so hard I gasped and sputtered coughing a spray of blood. The bird flailed and flapped in its own pain, snatching the discarded bone from a few feet away, I confidently strode to it's head. And without hesitation lifted my weapon above my head and smashed it down on its bare skull. Over and over again until my arms ached and it finally grew silent. Wheezing and coughing, the radiated sands flooded my mask and lungs. I spun to find the laundry shak only meters away. Dropping the bloodied, fractured bone from my loosening grip. I raced to the only shelter practically kicking the door down. The walls shook in fear of the gailing winds and storm above, while I crumbled in a heap in exhaustion and pain. The last thing I remember seeing was a tall figure standing above me in the doorframe. Before finally resting my sore eyes and worn, overworked heart.

Chapter 4

Warmth encased my body, and the air smelled pure and sweet. Harsh red light was all I could see at first, but it slowly dissipated into a soft blue. Strange noises filled my ears, sounding almost like...small animals.

Don't be stupid, most of the animals died during the Final Hour. It's probably my imagination. Whatever, stop thinking, enjoy this moment while it lasts.

'Farrah? Farrah?' someone called.

That voice...is so familiar. Why does it make me feel... happy?

Sitting up slowly, I waited for my eyes to adjust. I couldn't believe what I saw. Green rolling hills, a blue sky, and a golden sun. I looked down and noticed that I was sitting in a field of grass.

'I must be dead.' I paused a moment, realizing it was me who spoke. My voice was higher pitched, almost nasally.

Why do I sound so weird?!

'Darling! There you are.'

I noticed a woman approaching, though the sun's glare made it impossible to see her face. When she reached me, she bent over so that her head came close to mine and her body shaded me from the sun. Arms outstretched, she lifted me up effortlessly. Her touch felt so familiar. Her dress was so simple and gracefully folded over her form down to her ankles, flowing in the warm breeze. The material was soft to the touch, just as her skin, the fabric a vibrant red.

I could see her face clearly now. Every feature was as gentle as the gold sunlight, and the colour of her eyes was as brazenly green as the rolling hills surrounding us.

'What are you doing out here, my darling? Daddy is almost home!' Her smile was warm and kind, her soothing smile paired well with her honeyed voice. I took in a deep breath to steady myself and immediately smiled at the scent. Her smell was so pleasantly familiar.

With me in her arms, she walked back to a green iron garden table with two moss chairs all of the same ornate design.

As she gracefully sat down and placed me on her knee, a large, thick book caught my eye in the middle of the table. Its cover was a rusty red leather with gold design and a few marks here and there suggesting that it wasn't new, fastened closed by a latch which seemed to be trying with all its might to keep the spare pages that were peeking out inside. A large quill lay on top, the feather grey although in some spots white, and the stem coloured in gold.

It seemed to call to me, coaxing me to pick it up.

I reached out slowly, as far as my little arm could, but the lady's hand quickly stopped me by grabbing my wrist firmly. Looking up at her face quizzically, I saw she seemed concerned and even somehow sad.

'Not yet, my dear. You're not strong enough,' she answered, as if she knew what I was thinking.

What's that supposed to mean? It's just a book...right?

An odd sound distracted me from the kind woman.

A rumbling noise puttered up from beyond the hill and rolled towards a beautiful quaint house I swore I'd seen before. The building had large windows with ruby red roses framing them, ivy stretching up the trellises and in between dark chocolate exterior, with a small chimney topping off the reddish-brown tiled roof like a crown. From the crest of the hill came a makeshift car only the powerful could have. It squeaked into park and a handsome, well-tailored man stepped out, smiling right at us with pure joy in his eyes.

'There are my girls! Are we ready for supper?!' His voice boomed across the distance as he waved extravagantly.

The woman's smile beamed as she strode through the field, holding me close.

Once we entered the house, the man's face finally came into view. I was met with eyes as blue as the sky, and a smile that showed all his teeth—even his canines. His hair was charcoal black and neatly combed down his scalp, meeting with a clean-cut beard of the same colour. His large hands reached out for me as he took me into his chest, and I got the feeling of being so safe in his arms. He softly caressed my head and pulled his face into mine, making our foreheads gently touch.

The air around us began to turn into a thick white fog, and the loving family faded away.

No! I don't want to leave!

This time, the voices echoed in my ears—it sounded like the man and woman arguing.

The same man was there, but he seemed very angry and stressed. He paced back and forth, rubbing the back of his neck as he argued with the crying woman, who was shaking and holding herself. He seemed to be trying to convince the woman about doing something.

'We cannot do this! She is our daughter! We are a family now! We are finally free!' Her voice was shrill as a banshee, making my chest violently constrict and throat close up.

'When they find out what she is, they will take her away and turn her into a monster! Is that what you want?!' the man snapped back, spitting at the poor woman as he did so.

'You can't believe that! They won't take my baby away!' she argued, her hands quickly forming into tight fists. The man rubbed his face, exhausted, before calmly walking back to the woman and holding her.

'It's our only way to protect her. She has to go.'

Taking her in closer, he rubbed his grieving wife's back softly.

'It's the only way she will be safe. The only way we can safeguard the future for the last of our kind.' The man's eyes wandered towards the ajar door to the room, his sad eyes connecting with my scared ones, as if he knew I was there watching. As if to say 'I'm sorry'.

The image again faded as he continued to hold the blubbering woman tightly, rocking her from side to side, hiding his face in the crook of her shoulder and fighting back his own tears of sorrow.

A brilliant flash of light suddenly blinded me before I had time for my eyes to adjust. A woman's blood-curdling screams rattled my head, soon followed by a man's.

This dream was different from the others.

The sky was on fire, smoky and red.

My heart was racing, cheeks damp with tears, and I was terrified. My hands were sticky, not from the tree I was hiding behind. No— the stickiness was red and smelled of something metallic. Blood.

Was I bleeding? Looking down at my sweet pale pink-and-white dressing gown, I found larger stains of blood splashed and smeared all over; but nothing hurt aside from my breathless chest. It's not my blood.

The woman screamed again, but this time she screamed something inaudible. My attention snapped in the house's direction. The once charming house; with the large windows and ivy stretching up the trellises, and the proud brilliantly coloured flowers that also called it home. The house that, for some reason, I felt so much love for began to smoke and was quickly set ablaze. As I watched on, large black silhouettes began to march out; one of which was clearly the woman being dragged by two monstrously shaped creatures. Once they stopped, she dropped to the ground and watched her home burn.

Someone came out from the shadows behind her, another monster, and talked to the man who was held between her and the burning house. The monster held something sharp. He seemed to be asking something of the man, but I couldn't quite tell what.

It stepped between him and the broken woman, pointing the sharp dagger-like weapon towards her, threatening the man. The man started shouting, twisting and squirming to get free, but to no avail. As he did, the monster turned towards the woman and began stepping toward her, agitating the man further. Suddenly he stopped, and within a split second pivoted and tossed the weapon like a dart towards the man.

The world stood still as the weapon reached its target, perfectly sinking into the man's chest. As the man's body fell to the, the woman's scream rattled my bones and made my ears ring. The wailing continued as she was dragged away by the monsters. I was screaming and crying too, the feeling of my soul being torn apart was so agonising that I couldn't breathe, I couldn't even move.

Without noticing it, a large dark hand cupped my wet face and a grabbed me from behind.

'It's all right, little one. You're safe.'

It was the last thing I heard as the strange sensation of falling backwards consumed me, making me feel sick. I tightly closed my eyes until the sensation stopped.

Chapter 5

'Farrah? Farrah, dear, are you awake? Can you hear me?' The familiar voice coaxed my weary eyes open to a welcoming sight: Ms. Turner.

There's a blinding pain in my head as bursts of colour scattered and danced all along on the ceiling.

'There you are,' a shaky sigh of relief passed through the old lady's lips.

However, it felt like that sigh was not only for me. I strained to lift my heavy head to face her.

'How long have I been out for?' I slowly forced my poisoned body up, waiting for a response.

'Almost two days, dear,' she said, gently taking hold of my hand. Her face of sorrow could mean only one thing.

'Ms. Turner? What's wrong?' She averted her sad eyes. A sinking feeling hit my chest.

'Tell me what happened.' I demanded sternly, my mind quickly racing through all the possible, horrible scenarios it could think of, every one worse than the other.

Her glassy, red eyes looked everywhere else but me.

'When you left…' she finally began.

'DeeDee panicked, frightened she would lose you…We all were.' Her poor hands began to tremble.

'The poor thing worked herself up so much she became sick. Miles took her to bed; he couldn't stand to see her like this…so he put it upon himself to save you for her sake.'

'When she finally woke, she demanded to come with him, and he refused, accidently blurting out how he felt…When he finally came back with you in his arms, they embraced each other like lost loves…It was beautiful. The master must have heard us, because the next thing we knew he was standing at the end of the hall staring right at us…I had never seen such darkness or fury on his face before.' She finally confessed, wiping away the tears and snot from her face.

That's who saved me. I thought it was a dream.

'What did he do?' I hissed between gritted teeth.

Where was my *DeeDee*.

My aching body was forgotten as I stood and demanded to know where DeeDee was. Within seconds I was gone, images flashing in my mind of the worst possible scenarios. I strained to push my body down the hall to where Mrs. Turner said I'd find her.

The cellar.

A burning sensation filled my chest, forcing me to a stop. Leaning on the wall for support, I forced my lungs to cough up the rest of the poison I had breathed in during the storm. As I inhaled, I was overwhelmed by a metallic smell that usually only accompanied one source. My heart stopped and my stomach slowly sank.

I reached the cellar door, finding it slightly ajar. Pushing it open, I briefly recoiled from the increased potency of the metallic smell. It was nauseating, and my mouth grew sour; every time I drew a breath, the taste of death clung to the back of my throat, making me want to gag.

Each step down the cellar was another step to the unfortunate and dreadful truth awaiting at the bottom. Tears were already falling down my face, and I could only try to brace myself for whatever I would find.

The cellar was dim, damp, and the floor was covered in a pool of a thick crimson liquid. My eyes slowly followed the strange liquid's edge to its epicentre, my heart pounding with each passing second, until my gaze finally settled on the body of my dearest friend.

Every inch of me started shaking with fury, sadness, and emotions I couldn't even name. I was standing over an almost unrecognizable body, but I knew it was my DeeDee.

Deep slashes covered her once-perfect skin—arms, legs, face— but it was her stomach that brought my hand to my trembling lips. A giant chunk of flesh had been carved out of her lower belly, intestines left to spill out into the thick pool. I turned away in horror, taking in big, desperate breaths of the stale polluted air. Then, I saw it. A small bloody form laid beside her, lifeless.

I splashed down to my knees, struggling to breathe through the tears and smell of blood.

Picking up poor DeeDee's head, I laid it gently in my lap. There were cuts and bruises covering her beautiful face, her wavy short hair matted with blood. I started stroking her limp hair it was as if she were just sleeping.

'Oh DeeDee, I'm so sorry,' I whispered, struggling to breathe. 'You didn't deserve this.'

Rage swirled up in my chest and filled my entire body.

'Those uptight bastards will pay. With pain and blood,' I sniffled, struggling to fight the tears that welled up and blurred my vision.

'Aaaargh! Please, no!' A voice wailed through the walls.

I carefully rested DeeDee's head back down, promising to return before racing up the stairs. Needles filled my chest after each breath and every muscle was stiff, but everything in me screamed to run faster.

It didn't take long to discover the source of the wailing, it echoed clearly down the dimly lit hall toward the wine cellar.

Crouching outside the cracked door, I peeked inside. I could barely see Miles at the centre of the room, tied up like an animal, bloody and beaten. Three men surrounded him. It was clear that one was the Master, sleeves rolled up his thick sweaty forearms.

Pressing my ear against the splintering wood, I can just make out what they were talking about without alerting anyone to my spying.

'You think you can steal from me?! You think you can take what you want without me finding out about it, in my own house?!' Lord Drake roared, preparing to whip poor Miles's already shredded flesh. He paced the length of the room, clearly angry and tired.

'I'm your master. I gave you everything you needed! And you think you deserved more!' Another vicious strike from the whip, spraying droplets of blood back onto the floor and ceiling.

'She was my property! A piece of shit like you has no right!' Another slice, making Miles wail in pain. The men watching on laughed, enjoying the show.

'Like father, like son,' one remarked with a voice I did not recognise. It was a man wearing a soldier's uniform with greasy brown hair.

'Exactly. Your father assumed your mother was his to keep when they came. He learned quickly.'

'They were already together. Married,' Miles mustered his strength to retort, knowing it was his turn.

'What did you just say, boy?' the Master ground his teeth in frustration.

'She was not yours! Neither was my DeeDee!' Miles screamed, egging the master on with his lip curling into a sneer.

One after another, over and over, the Master taxed the bloody whip and struck ferociously.

Miles continued to smile at him through the pain.

I winced, unable to watch as the horror continued. Witnessing one of my dear friends being tortured was indescribably painful.

The Master rested on a stool to take a swig of wine, chugging it down as a small trickle flowed down his sweaty neck.

'Your mother learned to enjoy it.' He wiped the residue off his slippery mouth, showing Miles his wine-stained teeth.

'She came to me voluntarily. Even began smiling as I thrust my cock inside her.' He got up and walked over to Miles and gruffly grabbed a tuft of his sticky blood matted hair, forcing his head up. Leaning over, he hissed in his ear. 'She begged for it.' A grin stretched across his blood-splattered face. His evil eyes looked directly into Miles's terrified ones, sauntering back a few paces to where he laid his weapon.

Miles was speechless, but the Master continued. 'She came to me so frequently that it was more than when she was with her "husband".'

This made him and the other two men burst out laughing.

Miles still sat there, looking more defeated and depressed than ever. The laughter quietened down into a sickening silence.

'The last time she laid with me, she told me she was pregnant.'

Miles's head shot up in shock and confusion. I leaned in closer in disbelief, accidentally making the door creak slightly. It came to the attention of the unknown soldier nearest to the door, whose head turned towards me. We locked eyes, and he gave me a sickening smile as if to say 'you're next'. My nausea worsened, but I didn't leave. I couldn't.

'When she gave birth to a son. We agreed she would tell your father that it was his. You can imagine his confusion and unrest when he knew they hadn't been together in two years.' The Master took a seat again, crossing his legs, and lit a smoke from his pocket.

Miles's mouth seemed to twitch, blood dripping from his lips.

'What was that, boy?'

'I said, YOU'RE LYING!' Miles screamed, face filled with rage. He jerked his body this way and that, as if rabid, screaming and wailing in anguish. I covered my mouth, tears welling in my eyes. The other men watched on, amused.

It took him a while to settle down, eyes focused on the Master with indescribable animosity.

The Master continued calmly sucking away at his cigarette.

'Little did I know that my wife, Mrs. Drake, would take offense to this and do what she did to your mother the night you were born. With you in her arms, even. We told your father he could tell you the truth, but he opted to lie and tell you she died of an illness,' he said nonchalantly, still sucking away without a thought to what he just said.

All these years.... Oh, Miles.

'I'm just sorry it had to come out this way, my boy. But I still have to teach the others a lesson.' All three walked closer to Miles, surrounding him. The Master leaned down and growled to a sobbing Miles. 'Not even my blood steals from me.'

And with that, he gestured for the soldiers to untie him and head toward the door I was peeking through. *Shit.* I tried to scramble to my feet but tripped back onto the floor.

'Hello. See something interesting, do we?'

I turned around. A dark figure stared down at me with shadowy eyes. His black hair hung limply around his face, masking everything but his shiny teeth that gleamed at me in satisfaction. He snatched me up just as the door to the wine cellar swung open and the other menacing men filed out, holding a barely conscious Miles between them.

'Look what I found snooping around,' said the inebriated soldier, as he swayed slightly.

He must've been in charge of guarding the door.

The Master looked at me, displeased, before stepping forward.

'Looks like we have someone else to help us demonstrate lessons tonight,' The Master said with an evil look in his eye.

The hungry wolves marched a barely conscious Miles and I in single file to our fates that awaited us outside.

The night lit up as a stream of torches walked from the house, held by a small squadron of soldiers that must have arrived while I was unwell on Cowan's orders.

They didn't seem to care that a couple of innocent people were about to die. Unfortunately by law, the owners of a servant were allowed to inflict their own justice, so it was really an everyday thing to see this. All their attention was pointed towards us, which seemed to put devilish smiles on their faces. As we stumbled up to our forced positions, the four men stretched our hands as far as they could go, making them meet the prepared ropes that hung from the large crosses. The drunk soldier looked me straight in the eyes and shoved a knot of cloth into my unwelcoming mouth, tying it as tight as he could. Beside me, looking half dead and without hope, was Miles. He didn't bother with him.

Circling us like a hungry beast around defenseless sheep was Mr. Drake, covered in what we both knew was not his own blood. His pitch-black eyes burrowed into Miles murderously; yet he smiled, pleased with his work and eager to continue. The light of the torches glinted off his sharp teeth.

I noticed his devilish glare snatch a quick look at me, then just as quickly cut back to poor Miles.

His smile grew bigger. The small crowd of servants and soldiers behind him drew undesirably closer against many of their wills.

'I'm glad to see that so many of you have arrived to witness this. As your master, I do not ask for much. My family has given you a place to stay and kept your bellies full. And what do you do?' He pointed a knife at Miles, almost piercing his eye. My anger rose, body shaking and hands clutched so tightly that my palms began bleeding.

I can't do anything… Miles.

'You betray me. And treat me like a fool. Pursuing something you could not have, and forced my hand to destroy something beautiful.' As he was saying this, I noticed the silhouette of Mrs. Drake in the light of the house, standing on the patio with her two eldest, watching on uncomfortably. Looking closer, I could see a large cut slashed across her lip. Her face was red and eyes welling as she clutched herself in her own arms. Of course he would say that he did it, otherwise the others would make him kill his wife as well for the injustice they felt against her for viciously murdering one of their own.

His voice raised even higher and he reeled his arm back, ready to strike.

One quick slash was all it took to take the life of my best friend.

Tears streamed down my face and an uncontrollable wail forced its way out of my already broken self and passed the bloody cloth.

Miles's body hung limp and lifeless on the cross beside mine.

'And you! You think you can corrupt my love? Force her to leave her home?!' The testosterone-fuelled ignorant beast redirected his attention toward me. Sauntering over, he held out the knife caked in Miles's blood.

'Don't think you get away so lightly,' he says, roughly grabbing my face with one of his large hands. 'It would be such a waste… to let such a pretty flower like you fade away so quickly.' His grin returned to his blood-stained face.

He lifted the butt of the knife as high as he could, then with all his might brought it back down upon my head, causing me to black out.

Chapter 6

My face was so swollen from last night's beating that it felt like the skin was about to peel off. Fortunately, I blacked out on the first blow.

Miles... DeeDee...

My eyes had swelled too large for me to cry anymore. Not that I wanted to; even with my heart constricting in pain.

Those bastards are going to pay, tenfold.

'My, what an ugly look for a woman. You're lucky your new master has already paid for you.'

A man with wiry hair waltzed up beside the cage I was stuffed in. Skin as dry and cracked as the earth beneath us, stretched across his body, his tanned face etched with cracks that suggested too much time spent in the sun. This made it hard to guess his age, but he was definitely older than me. His eyes were like poised daggers, the sharpened look a predator would give its prey before it struck. The type of man most women would avoid or hide from. But what he didn't know was that I wasn't most women.

'What are you, mute? Or stupid? Why are you just looking at me?'

Getting increasingly agitated by my silence, more wrinkles appeared; and he gritted what few teeth he had. He snatched my chained wrist and pulled me against the side of the cage, slamming my bruised, puffy face against the bars.

'I'll make you talk, one way or the other,' he growled, followed by a long sniff of my blood-caked hair. His slivered lips grew thinner, stretching across his creepy face.

I stared back with unfazed, disinterested eyes.

'Leave her be, Mandez. She's already damaged goods. We don't want her more soiled by your filth.'

His leathery face turned into a scowl before he whipped around to face the young master.

'Yes, Master James,' Mandez answered, bowing half-heartedly before leaving in a huff.

James continued to my cage without breaking eye contact. After a minute of heavy silence, he spoke.

'What happened last night... a few of us felt it was not right. What my father did to you, I mean.'

'And the others? What about Miles, or DeeDee?' I responded in a raspy voice, having given up on my manners altogether.

'DeeDee deserved her fate; that stupid whore thought she could become a part of the family with her bastard child. And Miles, that idiot, thought he could save her; and worse, love what was not his,' he said, rubbing salt into an already deep wound. It only made my lust for vengeance grow stronger.

'But you did not deserve such a vicious beating. People like you cannot help their feelings and actions.'

'People like me?' My swollen eyes narrowed as I sneered.

'The kind of people who are more animal than human,' he said earnestly.

'James!' someone barked.

Our eyes unlocked from each other; the moment interrupted by a chillingly familiar voice. A voice I'd been fantasizing about hearing beg for its life the next time we met.

Mr. Drake stood on the edge of the deck that was only a few paces to the left, ushering his son over to say goodbye to his family that were standing close by.

At the corner of the manor, I spotted Ms. Turner, her slight form pressed against the wall and creeping closer toward me keeping a wary eye on the distracted masters.

I noticed a square object under her apron.

What is that?

The old woman stayed within the shadows, watching as the family exchanged practiced formalities and exuberant goodbyes. The moment all of their backs were turned, she scuttled over like an armadillo running on its hind legs. As quickly and quietly as she could manage, she shoved something into my cage. It landed atop the pile of bloody rags, effectively hidden.

Without saying a word, she reached through the bars to grab my hand. She squeezed them gently, her eyes starting to swell and become red.

I responded with a genuine smile; hoping to communicate the thousands of things I wanted to say with this one gesture.

She squeezed my hand a final time before briskly returning to the mansion.

Unfortunately, her departure caught the eye of the man that brutally and mercilessly murdered my friends. Mr. Drake sauntered over, hands in his pockets. He casually leaned against the rusty cage, eyes looking elsewhere. 'That boy could have lived, you know, you could have gotten between them and put a stop to it.'

I knew, as much as I wanted too, saying anything would only make things worse, so I just kept my mouth shut.

'That boy thought he deserved what wasn't his property. He needed to learn. People of your status do not need those pleasures.' He turned to face me. No light shined from those dark, dead eyes. A shiver seized my spine, but I forced my face to remain docile.

'We give you everything you need. And yet you people have the nerve to want more. Ungrateful cows get what they deserve.'

And with that said, he returned with a turn of his heel to his shameless family. I switched my gaze to his psychotic wife, who was watching us with a devilish grin of her own. As if to say, 'you will never win'.

They say that an image is worth a thousand words. The last image I remember of that day was while I was being driven away from that nightmare. When I bring it to mind, the diverse amount of feelings and emotions come to me in a flash. What had happened, why I left, who I left; and every word fueled my rage. The only thoughts I had now were of vengeance, and of how gratifyingly slow it would be.

The wind picked up, and as it did, the dust and remnants of the past city that laid beneath us were carried with it. Covering myself with my rags, I found the opportunity to look at what Ms. Turner had given me. A book, an old one, and it looked oddly familiar.

The red cover was charred and scrappy at the edges, however I was able to see and feel an imprint of what felt like a shield in the middle of the cover with two snakes entangled at the bottom.

Opening the crackled cover, a photo of DeeDee and her brother, the one she showed me, slipped out.

I promise you, DeeDee, I will return this to your brother.

Turning a yellowed aged page, I saw a short, hastily written scribble. Unfortunately, the charring had found itself into the pages and burnt most of the words away. All I could make out was:

My Darling Girl,
It's important that you find M….
Daddy

The rusty old truck stopped abruptly, forcing me against the back part of the cage.

'We're camping here for the night. Set up.' The man who ordered the others seemed bored. He gave me a quick glance and sighed. 'And get the girl out for a piss. Ten minutes, Got it?'

With a tired screech of the cage door, the reluctantly obliging soldier reached in for my chain and yanked. I winced at the pain of the gnarly sunburn on top of my already injured neck and resisted as if I were a stubborn animal unwilling to get out myself. I had to admit it was nice feeling soil under my feet again, even if they were cut and sore.

As I looked around, I noticed, in the red light of the sun's last rays, we were surrounded by large smooth grey walls and some noticeable structures. It was obvious people had been here before, however there were no bodies, no skeletons; nothing to say that humans walked these lands except for the crumbling remains of these once-great buildings. Small holes scattered in various areas, some in rows and others in clusters up and down these great structures. Fresh carvings lay atop of them, a story or historical recording of some kind depicting the desert folk fighting against the new comers, soldiers forcing them out of the canyons of their home. Looking around by my feet old tools and descicated herbs lay quietly, half buried and methodically laid out along the edges of the ancient concrete walls. It was clear that this was one of the desert folks camp sites. And once, one of the last standing refuges for the innocent. Now it was a true refuge, filled with only eerie silence occasionally broken by the crunch of dust under our feet.

It was sad to realise that, after we die, this is the only thing that shows humans were once a flourishing species. Goes to show it truly doesn't matter what you do, over time it'll be like you never existed.

'Hey! You gonna just stand around or you gonna piss?' the man behind me yelled, yanking the chains connected to the rusty collar around my neck. 'I'm not gonna wait forever!'.

I shot him a glare. He was average sized, with a torso ending in a bit of a beer gut. Like many of his fellow companions, he had cracked, weathered skin, suggesting many years of working in the blazing sun. The dishevelled state of uniform instantly portrayed how he felt about his job. Dead end.

'All right. If you're not gonna do anything, I'm taking you back. Piss in the cage, for all I care.'

Again, he yanked on my collar as if I were a dog, and we both trudged on with only the rhythmic clanking of my chains to accompany us on the short walk back.

The fire roared and crackled just beyond my isolated cage. Soldiers of the convoy began roasting an ottampi—a small vermin-like creature with the head of a mole and body of a lizard—whose flesh was infamously foul-tasting, but the proteins within could sustain you for up to two days.

As the men huddled together around the fire to feast, I noticed that James was more isolated from the rest. After all, why bother being friendly when his influential daddy got him a job as an officer without needing to be a soldier yet.

Whisperings hissed around the fireplace, carried by the warmed breeze, while they gave the poor boy dirty sidelong glances.

One whisper carried a little louder. 'I can't actually believe that spoiled snowflake is going to be an officer before me.'

'Clang, clang!' the bars beside me rattled. I turned, noticing a familiar worn leathery face staring back with a bowl in his hand. Mandez.

'Your new master wouldn't like it if his pet turned up dead,' he said, grimacing, before placing a bowl through a space between my bars.

I didn't trust him; he could've done something to it. My suspicions grew with the deepening smirk on his face and the snickering of the other men behind him. He slid it closer to me and walked away to the cheering squad by the fire. I could feel their smiling eyes on me as I picked up the bowl, giving it a sniff and skeptical glare. Odd shaped balls of flesh stared back at me from a bath of viscous foul-smelling liquid.

I lifted a small spoonful of the disgusting-smelling broth to my lips. I knew for a fact that they'd done something to it, but I also knew that I've been starving ever since I left that shithole and I couldn't afford to be picky.

After a hesitant slurp, I was overwhelmed with the sensation of sandy grit grinding between my teeth, and a grotesque taste that I've never had before swimming down my throat. It took everything in me not to spit it back up or make a face.

Having gone through that, I was even more averse to trying the balls of flesh, yet I still scooped one up on the request of my growling stomach. Like a snail on the move, I forced it closer and closer to my unwelcoming mouth. Taking the tiniest, littlest bite, I was greeted with a squishy, rubbery feeling as my teeth slowly pierced into its creamy texture, overcome by saltiness.

I found myself chewing and chewing, unable to break the piece down any further. Finally giving in, I swallowed hard. It was more pleasant than the fluid, but not by much. However, the peanut gallery nearby found this hilarious, bursting out laughing so hard that they began to cry—one of them even falling off his log.

'Was that as good for you as it was for us?!' said the leathery-faced Mandez, holding his sides.

The uproar began again, this time everyone but an uncomfortable James laughed. He couldn't even look me in the eye.

'It wasn't bad.' I lied. 'What is it?'

'I'm guessing your first oral experience!' This made the men laugh so hard that one of them that was sitting on a rock by the campfire fell over backwards, almost pissing himself with laughter.

Of course, ottampi balls... Men.

'At least ottampi balls aren't STD-riddled sultanas,' I spat before I popped another one in my mouth, eyeing him as I did so.

My remark made James laugh, if only a snicker, as well as a few of the others. The wrinkled man's laughter stopped, his face souring. That reaction was all I needed to sleep like a baby that night.

Little did we know that tomorrow would be one of the worst days of our lives.

The day grew hotter as the sun rose higher. The searing breeze whistled through the thick rusty iron bars of my cage, scorching me like a raw steak and causing my wounds to fester more. There was barely any life to be seen or heard of in the barren wasteland; apart from a small caravan of desert folk on the horizon just past the invisible sea possibly in search of their next camp site accompanied by the sound of our truck's engine grinding along, loud enough to keep them at a wary distance, and worn tires kicking up dust clouds on the invisible road.

On either side of me there were always a pair of 'witless warriors' on motorbikes, just in case I made an incredible escape attempt. What would be the point, really? Any direction I go in, I'd die from dehydration, hunger, or some scary-ass desert beast would eat me like a sand gobbler or giant lizard.

However, as I sat in the cage of scolding hot iron bars, I noticed that one of the soldiers keeping me company was the one that I mocked last night. There's nothing more humiliating to men like him than a woman insulting your junk in front of your friends.

However shrivelled or diseased they may be.

Now and then, Mandez would glance at me, clearly irritated, then look forward. It made me a little joyful knowing that he was still pissed off.

Gazing out into the distance, I noticed a few dark specks clashing with the orange dunes of the desert. On closer inspection, I realised they were slowly moving. A Hermit colony!

I'd never seen any near the manor, although DeeDee swore she saw one once on a really windy day. Ms. Turner told us they were like her—mutated humans—and became that way because of a gene handed down from unfortunate souls that survived the bombings of the Great War. Their ancestors had lived close to the radiation and, unfortunately, survived the side-effects. The mutated humans were cast out by every town and city they sought shelter in; a decision made not only by the rulers, but by the disgusted civilians as well.

They started their own colonies, looking after each other, and doing whatever it took to survive. Living off of ottampi, building shelters on their backs from scraps to shield themselves from the harshness of the desert sun. They roamed around like turtles, and whenever they found a safe place, they crouched down and crawled into their handmade shells. They didn't speak to any outsiders, only those like them. They were a reclusive people, much like the desert folk.

I was so immersed in watching the Hermit colony that I didn't realise the wind had completely dropped. A dark blanket of cloud had sneakily crawled its way towards us, and below it, a massive wall of sand. I'd never seen anything like it. Great flurries of sand barrelled towards us, picking up speed. The Hermit colony tucked themselves away, bodies disappearing into the storm. Grabbing the burning bars, I rose up as high as I could, eyes affixed to the sandstorm.

'Aaahhh… guys?' I said, trying to warn the soldiers.

'Shut up, slave,' one of the soldiers barked, clanging against the bars.

'Guys!' I repeated ignoring his stink eye and this time smacking my hand on the roof of the truck's passenger compartment behind me to get the driver's attention. *Anyone!* But where could we go for shelter out of a storm we couldn't run from? Terrified out of my skin, I kept shouting, even knowing it might be in vain.

'Hey, meatheads!'

'What!' Mandez said, looking at me, then following my line of sight to the imminent cloud of death racing towards us. His eyes turned as big as mine as he started screaming, 'Go! Go! Go!'

It took a second, but the old rusty truck began to roar with excitement, smoke spewing out the exhaust as soon as the other soldiers saw the danger. Those on their handmade copper and iron bikes began to rev up as well. It was useless.

The storm was on top of us and within a second the splintering winds consumed us. It instantly blinded me and most likely the others, but they still went on pressing down their squeaky pedals as hard as they could.

One by one, the side vehicles disappeared in the unforgiving storm, and soon enough the truck I was trapped in began twisting and turning uncontrollably; causing me to ping-pong around my confined area.

The front of the truck hit something invisible, toppling over and getting caught up in the strength of the storm until it was rolling like a tumbleweed. My cage door flew open, and the moment the truck finally stopped I was flung out of my death trap. Eyes closed against the sand, I stumbled to my feet and ran. My chains jangled and banged against me. I couldn't hear anyone else, and I didn't know where I was going, but I just kept running.

Chapter 7

I woke up and immediately felt my body scream in pain. Looking at my arms and legs, I saw them covered in scratches, bruises, and scrapes. Memories from yesterday came flooding back to me as I slowly regained my bearings—the soldiers, the storm, the darkness. Looking around, I saw Drake's men lying unconscious in the abandoned house I blindly stumbled upon—at least, what was left of them, as I could see only five that survived the storm. The others must've perished or found other shelters. I carefully got up, feeling an intense pain on my side. Finally on my feet, I could better observe my surroundings and noticed the doorframe of where a door once stood, possibly the one I had to break down to get in.

I walked out onto a tiny old deck. We seemed to have found refuge at an abandoned mining town.

The sun's harsh rays scorched the sand and burned my fragile skin as I stood at the edge of the deck. My eyes were still sore and watering from the dust and sand trapped under my lids. I was able to just see the outlay of the street and where the remains of the miners' houses once stood. Some were just the foundations and frames leftover, but many were just piles of sticks. Very few houses were still somewhat standing, with their own battle-wounds from the many years of desert storms.

A chill went up my throbbing spine as the wind slowly picked up; the type of shiver that lets you know someone, or something, is watching you. An unnatural whisper brushed against my ear, but only for a second. The next thing I knew, the breeze dissipated along with the whisper, and the heat of the sun warmed my body as it did before. The feeling of someone watching me disappeared as well, but I was still wary of my surroundings.

While my eyes were still adjusting to the brightness, the aftermath of yesterday's storm appeared before me. One of the convoy's vehicles emerged from the dust cloud a few meters away. I could just make out bodies of the soldiers that disappeared during the storm. They laid as if they were rag dolls, their limbs pointing in directions they shouldn't be.

I flinched at the sound of low groans, instinctively holding my hands in front of my face. Nothing happened, but the groans continued. I lowered my hands and hesitantly followed the sound to the motorbike, which rested on its side just a few steps away. Hobbling over, I saw the face of the man who had played that cruel, disgusting joke on me. Mandez. His dark eyes locked with mine—they were filled with fear. He was trapped, unable to move with his leg pinned beneath the bike.

The smell of gas reached my nose, and I realised that a large puddle of it was forming near the engine. All I needed to do was walk away, and time would do the rest. No evidence, it would just look like an accident. It was an accident.

A person like that did not deserve to live.

Just walk away. Just walk away and pretend you didn't hear anything.

'Help me. Please,' he pleaded, groaning in pain. I was prepared to turn around and walk away, but something seemed to stop me. It was as if *she* were watching me from afar. I could almost hear DeeDee's voice coaxing me, telling me that this wasn't who I was. That I wasn't the type of person to just leave a helpless, injured creature stranded.

I clenched my fists and swallowed what anger I had towards him. *Fine.* With a low growl, I trudged back, almost stomping to show my displeasure.

Lifting a light piece of old wood nearby, I shoved it under the bike. I wasn't entirely sure I'd be strong enough, but I hoped I'd be able to leverage the motorbike off and leave enough room to crawl out. I pushed. The metal beast groaned, barely moving. I closed my eyes, shoving with all my might. Every muscle cried in pain.

'Aaah! Go! Hurry!'

The inhuman scumbag scrambled and clawed at the hot sand around him, only his arms working.

Not even looking if he got free, I dropped the bike.

Opening my eyes, I looked down and saw a thick trail of crimson leading from where he was trapped to where he now sat. Blood gushed from his leg like a running faucet. I didn't even know that much blood could come from a person.

God, he's going to bleed out at this rate.

'Tear off a piece of your jacket,' I instructed.

'W-What?'

'To stop the bleeding. I'll use this piece of wood—wrap it above the wound and I'll twist as tight as I can to stop the flow. It's going to hurt.'

Saving the bastard who looked at me like I was nothing more than meat was my only choice; either that or I'd have his death on my conscience. Besides, it would be obvious that someone tried to help him, and I would be the only possible suspect due to the fact that I'm not wearing shoes. My footprints were everywhere, along with small traces of blood my feet left from the unknown shards of smaller rubbish hidden amongst the sand.

I needed to get him back into that house.

I found longer planks of old wood sticking out of the sand nearby and, using Mandez's sleeping mat from his satchel on his bike, I cobbled up a make-shift stretcher and assisted the wounded animal. I dragged him towards the house in a zigzag-like pattern, trying to find as many bumps and ditches to drag his mangled ass over, just for a laugh. As Ms. Turner would say, it's best to find the bright lights in the darkness.

I managed to haul him onto the deck of the house but froze when I heard people murmuring inside. At least two more had woken up.

'Don't move, it doesn't look good,' a worried young soldier said to another, his friend lying down and wincing in pain. I couldn't be certain, but it looked like the man he was talking to had a broken leg and a nasty wound on his head. The blood was dripping down half his face, effectively blinding one eye.

I gently placed the groaning animal out of the way of the sandy elements and walked further inside.

'You survived, I see,' said a third soldier I hadn't seen before, pushing himself towards me from the corner of the room. He wasn't as battered as the other two, but he still had a few cuts and scrapes.

'Yes, I'm lucky the door opened from my cage.'

'Seems like you have an angel on your side.'

'Where is young Master Drake?' I said, ignoring his comment. 'Did he survive?'

'We haven't seen him yet. He may be among the dead,' the younger soldier said, injecting himself into the conversation whilst tending to the groaning mess beside him.

'Go and look for him, slave,' growled the standing soldier. 'He's still your master until we reach the city.'

I begrudgingly accepted his order. After all, it wasn't James's fault that I was here. No, that fault laid with his father.

'Get some water too while you're out there; it's hot,' he added, tossing me his water canister.

Too tired and withered from the events of yesterday, I was unable to restrain myself.

'Would you like me to go to the market while I'm out? Is it someone's birthday? I could pick up a cake.'

Dirty glances answered my rhetorical quip, which was to be expected. I'd do the same.

'Get your master and some water, or I'll tie you to one of the posts outside and you can be dinner tonight,' the tall man hissed, dagger eyes matching his sharp tongue.

I returned to the blazing sun and sand-infested winds, shielding my eyes with my stronger arm. Sand hit my skin like needles, and I could hardly see, but I pushed through.

I tried to distract myself from it, combing my mind for anything that didn't have to do with sand or blood. An unexpected memory popped in.

Every year the matriarch of the family, Great Aunt Hilda, would visit for a few days, inspecting the cleanliness of the house and to make sure that proper relationships were held between the family and its servants. DeeDee was still new and had never met nor even heard of this dreadful woman before and was never told about how 'particular' she was when it came to every little thing. Whenever Aunt Hilda came over, it would put everyone on edge, even the family. She had this annoying ability to find fault in every single thing—from the clothing everyone wore to the manners and casual behaviours that apparently didn't fit their station; and she always made it her duty to rectify them. One of her biggest alterations was changing everyone's clothes so that the family wore all white whilst the staff wore brown and beige (her way of visually stating the hierarchy of the household). She always wore extravagant wedding gowns that covered her from neck to toe, and always bleached her hair white as a sign of her purity, as well as nude makeup with a vibrant splash of ruby red lipstick that extended far beyond the edges of her tiny pursed lips.

One unfortunate day, DeeDee was the one chosen to be her personal maid and expected to be always by the old crone's side wherever she was called upon, tailing her around everywhere she went. She carried tools to dust and clean whenever the old bag pointed something out. Poor DeeDee was always overwhelmed and flustered, and that one day when she was cleaning and gently spreading out sheets on Aunt Hilda's bed for the third time—meticulously making sure that every wrinkle was flattened—she was so drained and tired that she thought it would be all right to just take a little nap, just five minutes rest while her temporary master was berating the Drake family at the breakfast table for the simplest of things. She crawled into bed, not knowing that she was about to start her period. Two hours had passed and DeeDee was sprawled out like a starfish, with blood smeared everywhere, like the beginning of the abstract painting in the library, the master said no one was allowed to touch. The doors burst open and a ghastly scream erupted from the room, echoing throughout the entire house, causing everyone to stop what they were doing.

DeeDee was dragged out by her hair by a fuming and red-faced Aunt Hilda, disgust and anger filling her face as she dragged the poor blubbering girl into the drawing room and commanded that everyone join her. She sat in the middle of the room, and everyone, even the family who stood at the front, nervously watched on, frightened of what was about to occur. Three feet away she sat, stern-faced and tense, holding onto the poor new girl's wrist with all her might, causing her fingertips to turn almost purple.

'I am ashamed to see what this household has become,' she began. 'Not only have you allowed your children to dress like common folk. You and your… wife have allowed this entire estate to turn into a household of anarchy and ridiculous frivolity. I will not allow it any longer.' Her voice sent cold shivers down everyone's spine, causing the master's face to grow pale in fear.

'You have also allowed your servants to run around the house like wild animals. And worse, treating this place as if it were theirs! What would your father say if he were here, Samuel?' she barked, looking at him as though he were a helpless child in trouble.

'I have seen enough and can no longer hold back my honesty.

Consider this an example of what is to come.' She raised her voice, yanking at the poor girl's arm so hard that she forced her to flop over her lap.

She then violently forced the girl's pants and underwear down so that her bare bottom was visible, causing her face to turn scarlet with embarrassment. Magically whipping out a stiff stick, Aunt Hilda raised it in preparation, shot the silent, shocked audience a deadly look, then struck down hard, leaving a red strip on the plum cheeks of her yelping victim. As he watched on, Mr. Drake occasionally let out a tiny cough, covering his mouth and bright red cheeks, agitating his wife who continued to give him the side eye as the disturbing show in front of us continued. Not everyone was as interested and 'excited' as the lord, the children Rey and James uncomfortably watching on, cringing. The rest of us—Miles, Ms. Turner, and myself—turned away, unable to watch.

Later that evening, DeeDee retired early, ashamed and uncomfortable about the day's unfortunate event. Feeling bad for her and angry at the stuck-up old bitch that embarrassed her and everyone else, I snuck into Aunt Hilda's room in the knowledge that she would be knocked out after dinner and stole all her clothing—every single thing she had. I took them to the laundry shack outdoors as silently as I could, a devilish smile stretched across my face, amused by the plan I had made.

Morning arrived, and just before breakfast, a terrifying shriek of horror rang throughout the house that woke up the drowsy family from their laziness. Once again, everyone flocked to the same room as before, led by Mr. Drake, who burst through the doors, allowing everyone to flood in and spread out. There, by her dressing table, staring her frightened and shocked self in the mirror, was a balding Great Aunt Hilda. Silent, with a gaping mouth and equally wide eyes. I was just as shocked as well as amused; so amused that I found myself struggling to hide my laughter and teary eyes, turning my face away and into my shoulder, unable to stop the shaking. Mrs.

Drake gave me a nudge to shut up and raised brows of seriousness, only to turn back and let out a little chuckle of her own.

'What on earth happened?' Mr. Drake asked, feigning concern.

Aunt Hilda swirled around, instantly turning her face into a demonic one, every single one of her wrinkles showing as her brows furrowed and her eyes narrowed, looking at all of us as the culprits. Without a word, she huffed off and stormed to her cupboard. The knowledge of what was about to greet her made me squeak, clasping onto my mouth as tight as I could to hold anything else back. As the doors opened, a potent waft of concentrated manure greeted us, causing everyone to gag and step back. Everyone, apart from me. Every one of her garments, all once beautifully pure white dresses, were now brown and smelling of cooked shit.

Watching Great Aunt Hilda walk out of those doors wearing a shit-stained dress, bald headed and red-faced, was one of the best days of my life living and working for that family. As she rode off as fast as she could, even Mr. Drake gave me a side wink of approval. I never really found out who caused her to go bald, but knowing Ms. Turner, she always knew how to cook up devilishly evil things in those kitchens to take the family members down a peg or two. Someone's small arm wrapped around my slack one. I didn't even need to turn to look, I could smell the sweetness that always followed her around. DeeDee squeezed my arm and brought it into her chest. From that day on we were as close as sisters and always had each other's back.

When I'd been running through the storm the first time, I remembered passing what looked to be a well. I walked in the general direction of where I thought it was, hoping I wouldn't get myself lost. Uncovering my eyes just for a moment, I took a quick scan of my surroundings and spotted a silhouette of what could have most likely been the well. I covered my eyes again and altered my direction slightly until I reached my target. Squinting through the wind, I saw an old wooden bucket resting on the well's edge, secured to a rope. My eyes followed the rope to a wheel fastened to the ground, and I quickly made my way over. My muscles ached as I turned the large, rusty wheel, lowering the bucket as far as it'd go. The wheel stopped abruptly; it wouldn't go further.

I leaned over the bricks to see if there was an obstruction. I could still see the bucket, barely, bordering on the darkness. The rope was still slack, allowing the bucket to swing. Leaning a little further in, adrenaline filled my body, and my heart began racing faster and faster.

A gust of frigid air burst in my face, sending shivers down my spine.

All the voices in my head told me to run, except one. The breeze curved around my face and around my ears. I could almost hear something, but it was faint. It sounded like…

A moan from nearby broke my concentration. This could wait.

Heading towards the direction of the noise, I noticed a silhouette of a fence through the bellowing sandy winds.

I walked around it to find the source—James Drake.

'Oh, god!' I exhaled, hurrying closer.

The young master was splayed beneath another soldier. The other soldier was definitely dead, but when I touched him, he was warm. His eyes were still open. In fact they seemed to be as wide as they could get, his pupils so tiny that the blue in his eyes almost consumed them. It was as if he saw something terrifying, and, following the corpse's gaze, they seemed focused on the well. Something was definitely wrong here. I helped heave the corpse off, and another louder moan squeezed out of James's scratched lips.

'Fuck,' he muttered. A large gash cut across his forehead, providing a thick flow of blood down his face. That wasn't the worst of it, however. A large, rusty metal rod was lodged straight through his side. I heaved the young master across my back, then trudged back to the hideout where the others were, not really caring if I was being ladylike or delicate. His once golden hair, was now covered in blood, dirt, and sweat, swayed from side to side, making it even more difficult to see where I was going. I barged through the doorway with a stumble.

I found a suitable place to rest the young, wounded master down, but as I pulled away, I caught eyes on me. A few more soldiers had joined us, some in better shape than others. There were too many to fight off; I'd have to choose another time to escape. Although the question was, where would I go?

'Where's the water?' asked the same soldier from before.

'There wasn't any. The well was as dry as a bone.'

The soldier's head jerked up, as if something clicked inside his tiny pea-sized brain.

A foul, angry look fell upon his face as he clenched his fists.

What's with that face?

'God, what happened to the young master?' Our locked gazes were interrupted by the other soldier tending to the others.

'Don't know. I found him this way,' I replied.

'All right, well, we need to start a fire to cauterise the wound and stop the bleeding. We can't do anything about his head injury with what we have. We'll clean it and put a bandage on it until we reach the city. But until then we just have to wait and see.'

'Yeah. If we survive this place,' said a soldier who must've arrived before I returned.

'We will. We just have to hold on,' reasoned the soldier tending to James. 'The city guard will realise we haven't arrived and they'll send help. We just have to survive at least two more days.'

The rest didn't look so certain.

'Gather the others to survey the area,' he continued.

'You're not my superior,' snapped the tall soldier.

'Look around you—our commander is dead, and no one else is stepping up.'

There was a brief pause before the angry soldier scoffed. 'Fine. Come on.' He stomped out, taking three others with him. All of which had minor cuts and abrasions such as me. I studied each as they passed.

One in particular, a large hulk of a man who seemed to be shaved naked from head to toe, looked as if this wasn't his first test of survival—scars of many sizes glistened like silver in the sun, battle wounds covered his ginormous arms, which seemed to be more for definition than defence. Another man strutted behind him as if he were going out to the bar with what, from far away, looked like an odd smile on his face, but closer inspection turned out that in fact it was just another large, jagged scar from the corner of his mouth to the lobe of his ear. He seemed to be hobbling more than the rest, dragging his left leg as if it were broken or gravely injured, though I didn't see any blood and he didn't seem to be in that much pain. The final soldier to come out, however, had scruffy mud-brown hair, a scratch over one of his eyes which forced him to keep it closed, and had a fresh wound on his arm which was wrapped in a piece of torn cloth. One after the other they trudged off forcefully into the harsh sandy winds, disappearing into the dust until the next time we saw them again.

Every attempt at a campfire was quickly snuffed out by the harsh winds, so we settled on lighting a torch indoors. It was enough. As the fire burned away, the young soldier held his sword above the dancing flames. We glanced at each other, growing unease in our faces, both terrified at what was to come next.

The sword gradually began to glow bright red, indicating that it was almost ready.

'When the sword is hotter, I'll need you two to help me,' he said nervously, taking in a trembling breath. 'You need to pull the pole out—not all the way, so I can cauterise the hole in his back first. Then we can move on to his stomach. You need to hold him still, too; he's going to feel it.'

We all drew a shaky breath.

He grabbed the hilt of the red-hot sword as the larger soldier took a crouched posture, steadying himself, his large, tanned muscles flexing and veins bulging in readiness.

'Okay, slowly roll him to his side—and make sure the pole doesn't touch the ground.'

We both nodded, acknowledging the fact that the four-foot-long pole was already about a foot out of his side and prepare to do as instructed.

The soldier beside me had the job of pulling the pipe out, as he was presumed to be stronger.

Grabbing the pole with both hands, he took a deep breath and readied himself.

'Remember, not all the way,' the young soldier confirmed. The other man nodded.

I also readied myself, hands firmly pressed on James's shoulder.

'One... two... three... grrr!'

'Aaaaaaaarrrgghh!' Everything happened at once. As the pole was being pulled through, we could all hear a very loud and disturbing scraping sound, followed by the gush of warm blood flowing out of the hole it made. Soon after, we heard a sizzling sound and could smell burning flesh.

Poor James was screaming in absolute agony, making noises I never thought a human could. I looked down at his sweaty, anguished face and felt my heart wrench.

'I'm sorry,' I whispered.

'Okay,' the young soldier said, huffing, 'Turn him on his back—make sure it's slow.' He grabbed a piece of cloth, folding it into a square.

I took James's shoulder and rolled him gently onto his back, then pressed down to keep him in place.

'All right,' he continued, wiping away sweat and blood from his forehead. 'Last time. One, two... three!'

The standing soldier grunted as he yanked out the bloody pole. A stream of blood began rapidly spewing out of his second wound, and another agonizing wail came out of poor James's crying face. It was followed by the second sound of sizzling flesh and the smell of cooked meat.

I felt sick.

'He's lost a lot of blood,' the young soldier said wearily. 'I know that I'm O-, which means I can give him mine. Let's get him to the table so that I can begin the transfusion.'

The larger soldier and I both listened and, with a simultaneous grunt, lifted the young master as gently as we could. As we carried him, the soldier who instructed us through this ordeal rushed to get supplies from his little med kit that survived the storm.

We laid him on a makeshift bed on the miraculously still-standing wooden table. I'd never seen James so pale and weak.

The soldier that helped us wandered back to his corner to take a nap.

'You sure know a lot about medical things,' I observed, curious.

'Yeah, well, I always wanted to be a physician, but my father wanted me to be a soldier like him. Guess who won,' he responded, eyes focused on his injured patient. 'Didn't mean that I couldn't stop reading, though.'

'Huh.'

'What?' he said, shooting me a quick glance.

'Nothing.' I shrugged.

It seems even men of his status don't even really get a say in their lives.

Curiosity getting the better of me, I continued to stare at him, which clearly agitated him. My eyes zeroed-in on his uniform. The name sewn on his chest pocket said: MICKA G.

'Go and look out for the others,' he said, refocusing on James. 'They should be back by now.' I nodded grudgingly, exhausted from the day's events, and made my way out of the room heavy-footed.

Chapter 8

The winds of the raging storm had finally settled revealing the horrific aftermath of smoke and death it callously left behind. Soldiers' bodies and limbs lay distorted and torn from each other, half buried in the now calm sands. I couldn't just leave them like that. Picking up a piece of nailed wood nearby I managed to find a secluded plot of land in the skeleton of a house and began to dig, cracking the earth like a stone inch by exhausting inch and dragging their bodies into their sad little unmarked graves. Granted it would have been easier to feed them to the sand gobblers whose mouths lay patiently open and waiting. Their teeth exposed like animal traps waiting to feed the hungry fat slimy lizard creature beneath.

'What do you mean, "what"? Did you forget your position here? You're still a slave! Stop playing around in the dirt and find those men!'

Startled by his newfound leader attitude, I jumped to my feet.

'I'll go with her,' said someone behind us, 'make sure that she doesn't run off.'

Loud thuds made their way closer to the doorway, until a large, muscular, dark brown-haired soldier emerged, paranoid dark eyes looking straight at me.

'Thanks, Hudson. Try to find them before nightfall. I'd say you have about two hours.'

The man who answered to the name 'Hudson' nodded, his

large hand gripping my arm. Shoving me out the door, we headed towards the centre of town.

The glowing sun turned the sky a vibrant orange, coating the discarded buildings like thick paint. Our mahogany shadows stretched out before us, the tall shapes reminding me of the sand kings said to roam the area.

They're usually harmless, however, the stories say that they'll attack people they feel have ill-intent for others. They can sense negative energy emitted by humans.

Surveying the beauty before us, I started having a feeling of being watched. Out of the corner of my eye, I glimpsed of Hudson staring at me with a foul look on his face.

I turned my head to meet his gaze, but his eyes quickly flicked forward. However, as I slowly lowered my head back down, I noticed his fists clench.

What is this guy's problem?

'Just try it, slave.'

I responded to his bizarre comment with a look of confusion.

He spoke again as if he knew what I was about to ask.

'Run as fast as you can, but no matter how far you get, the elements and desert monsters will get to you before we do.'

His face tightened, dragging a corner of his slim lips up higher than usual.

'Personally, I would love to see that happen. It means that we don't have to drag you all the way back to the city.'

I didn't say anything in return. I knew that's how they felt about people like me. Soldiers and guards believe themselves to be better than people at my level. They think of us as disease-ridden low-lifes, and that we get better than what we deserve. That's why Micka behaved the way he did. Having picked up the gauntlet of leadership, he needed to show the others that he understood his place and mine are very different.

'But for some reason, the Lord of Buson wants you as one of his maids. I don't get why; he could easily find someone else off the street.'

Stopping in my tracks, I had to wonder the same thing.

The warm, dusty breeze picked up and I felt something hit my foot. Looking down, I discovered an old newspaper. They stopped making these some time ago. I reached down to grab it.

It was an article warning the nearby town of soldiers coming to enslave the healthy and able. It detailed the number of soldiers suspected, what weapons they were carrying, and how many citizens were speculated to be taken.

'I gotta go piss. Go on ahead,' Hudson said nonchalantly, clearing his throat.

With my eyes glued to the decaying article, I ended up striking something with my shin. I fell down, hard, the air leaving my lungs on impact. The paper flew out of my hand and back into the swirling winds.

Gasping for breath, I weakly propped myself up to survey the area.

It seemed to be the edge of the town; the ground rising into a small cliff, not much higher than one of the houses. I slowly found my feet, wiping the dust off of my sore knees. I took one more deep breath before walking up the slope. Maybe there was something in the distance that I could use for shelter, or maybe there was a hiding spot to get away from these barbarians. Upon reaching the top, I was astounded.

The earth I was standing on wasn't shaped naturally. No, it was a by-product of our ancestors' destruction. I'd heard stories about how big the craters were when the Great War ended, but I'd never imagined seeing one with my own eyes. My jaw dropped, and my eyes were as wide as they could go. It was so massive that I couldn't see the other side, and it was so deep it was as if a mountain had been cut out of it and plonked somewhere else. Indented lines of sand trailed around the bottom, then disappeared to the edges of the immense crater, indicating the presence of a leviathan helminth—which were essentially giant worms—and once it had claimed something, it would protect it with a fierce animosity against any other leviathan helminths who dared to cross into it.

The hairs on the back of my neck rose, and the feeling of not being alone snapped me out of my trance.

A frigid gust of air breezed past me, forcing me to hug myself for warmth. It was a familiar feeling. I scanned my surroundings, then spotted a strange shimmer against the desert dunes. Rubbing the sand from my dry eyes, I saw the strange warp emit an odd light. As the light grew brighter and larger, it shaped into a figure I could recognise.

The figure of a woman looking out into the vast beyond.

Squinting through the light, I could make out the details. She wore ragged clothes that draped around her lean figure, hiding almost everything but her head and hands. Her hair seemed to be of a different entity entirely, the long dark strands swaying gently this way and that in the translucent ripples that surrounded her. Her hair masked her face, but when the strands were pushed aside, I saw it was beautiful and elegant—that of a fine lady. Even though her eyes were alluring and slender, I could sense they were sad as they looked into the great crater that lay before the both of us. Her feet were not touching the ground—in fact, they were nowhere to be found. She was just hovering there, staring down as if she was grieving.

As I watched, her demeanour changed. Her eyes became spears, and her head snapped up. Then she turned to me.

Fuck!

What was once a graceful, yet ghostly woman turned into a terrifying monster in mere seconds. Her hair whipped around as if made from a horde of angry snakes. Her eyes, pitch-black and scowling, bore right into my frightened ones. Her nose scrunched up, turning her slender mouth into a threatening snarl. She looked like a lion preparing to strike a lamb.

My eyes frantically searched for a path to freedom. As I did so, I realised I wasn't keeping watch on the bringer of my death. Looking forward, my heart froze. She was no longer across the crater. No, she was right in front of me, nose to nose. The same terrifying snarl was on her face, and, like a viper, her hand struck at my throat.

'I told you to leave this place!' Her voice scraped the inside of my ears, the haunting shrill echoing through my skull.

That was the voice I kept hearing.

'You and your companions are *not* welcome here!' her grip on my throat constricted, forcing me to uselessly claw at her cold wrist. 'There is no one left to take!'

What? My eyes widened. *She thinks I'm with the soldiers.*

With all the strength in me, I whisper, 'I... am not... one of... them.'

Her snarl deepened, showing her disbelief.

'You are with them! You are one of them!'

'No—T-They took me,' I struggled to choke out. 'My... master s-sold me.'

Her face softened slightly as her eyes trailed down to the shackle marks on my neck, wrists, and ankles.

Her grip loosened slowly, gradually, until she released my poor self. I fell, gasping, my hands rubbing along my neck.

She floated a safe distance away, her face calm.

'You are not one of them,' she admitted. 'My apologies.'

'It's all right. I understand,' I said, continuing to rub my neck. I felt curiosity getting the better of me and cleared my throat. 'When you said there is no one left to take, what did you mean?' She looked sorrowful again, turning her back to me and looking out to the crater before us.

'Long ago, this town was happy and thriving. Filled with laughter and good people. This came at a price. Every year, they would come to steal our food and take our men and boys away as slaves. It was the price our forefathers agreed on when the town was young.'

She wrapped her arms around herself, her voice beginning to shake.

'They would take them away from their mothers and wives. And when there was no more to take, they demanded something else—all the women and girls who could be mothers. We refused, but it was all in vain. They returned; then began killing until they got what they wanted. They took the girls and lined them up. As they killed each one of them, they'd ask over and over again for us to surrender. They made us watch as they killed our babies. We couldn't take it anymore. So we revolted. Most of us were killed. There were too many.'

She sobbed uncontrollably.

'They killed my baby!' Her hair coiled and slithered.

'I'm so sorry.' I walked towards her, cautious in the knowledge that she was not human. 'What happened to you?'

Taking in a few breaths, she answered.

'I was the last one to survive the massacre. I was broken, alone. I couldn't take the emptiness, the sorrow, the memories… I let it all consume me. My spirit, as you see it now, tore away from my body. I watched myself turn into a creature some knew to be a Griever. Unlike others, my soul was not completely transformed, which is why you see me like this. My body roams the desolate town, ravenous, feasting on anything it can to survive.' She turned to look at me, eyes filled with regret. 'I know I can't ask you this; we don't know each other. But I cannot be free with my family in the next life until my body rests...'

'I will help you kill your monster. I promise.' I gave her a genuine grin (which was rare for me) and we looked out into the vast beyond. I'd made a promise, and it was one I intended to keep.

Chapter 9

I jumped, startled by the sound of a bone-shaking, gurgling scream. I hurried out of the cabin I'd been hiding in, stopping as I reached the middle of the road. The brisk breeze of the night air swiftly passed me caused me to shiver. It sounded as if the noise came from one of the nearby abandoned buildings—the larger one, possibly a great hall or hotel. Surprisingly, it was almost untouched by the elements, aside from some large holes in the walls here and there, and the roof was crumbling inwards, but all in all, it was in far better shape than many of the others. The same scream erupted again from within the creaking building.

The missing soldiers, maybe? Why were they screaming? I felt a chill shoot down my body when I dared to wonder: Is it the Griever?

Finding my courage, I picked up a rusted crowbar and slowly and quietly trudged towards the danger, holding my weapon in preparation and ignoring my mild terror. Closer and closer I approached, reminding myself of the promise I had made to the spirit. I crept to the dark looming building, eyes searching for any signs of movement. I gingerly stepped up the creaky steps towards the front doors, grinding my teeth at the loud straining sounds each board made after a long time of being unused. The final step screeched the loudest, making me cringe. If it was too loud for me, I knew something else heard it too.

I was right. Above me, I saw ragged curtains on a second-floor window flutter quickly, followed by the sound of scratches against glass.

I gulped down my terror and tightened the grip on my weapon. *You can do this.* I took a deep breath and entered the dark house of horrors.

I gently pushed the great doors with a creak. A brilliant blue awaited me. It seemed to shower through the windows and empty panes of the building, every feature of the old building baked in the glow, making the whole scenario creepier. A single flight of precarious stairs lay before me, looking just as bad as the ones outside. Surveying the rest of the surroundings, I found twin rooms to the left and right, and a small, shadowed doorway above the stairs.

I looked warily at the stairs with the flimsy railing. I really didn't want to, but I had to take the riskier path in order to get to the second floor where my battle awaited me. Again, I walked softly and slowly, trying to make as little noise as possible in the dead silence that surrounded me. I arrived at the more supportive landing of the second floor and was immediately overwhelmed by the feeling of something watching me; every nerve in my body alerted me that danger was near.

Fresh blood painted the floor and splattered high against the peeling wallpaper. I followed the trail, seeing it as an obvious sign of where the soldiers were, although I knew there was a chance it could be a trap.

A weak moan came from up ahead.

I have no choice. I've made it this far. *Fuck!*

I turned the corner into a massive room with two large windows, the moon illuminating my surroundings with a light-blue hue. I could clearly see everything, and by the small town flag sitting on the desk and other ostentatious decorations, I had a feeling this must have been the mayor's office. Not much furniture remained, but a large desk was shoved at the far end, along with two old wing-backed chairs that had their backs to the entrance. A large fireplace was nearest to me on the opposite wall, and next to that, two bloody corpses lay crumpled in the corner. I froze. Their faces and bodies were mangled and torn apart, with huge scratches and bites taken out of them; they were so disfigured that they were hard to differentiate one from the other—only their uniforms were clear.

Not even *they* deserve that.

A weak moan diverted my attention to one of the wing-backed chairs. Walking closer to it, I noticed a bloody hand draped over the armrest. Circling around, it became clearer that it was the third soldier. My hand went to cover my mouth, eyes widening. His abdomen was torn open, intestines spilling out, and, like the others, he had bite marks and chunks taken out of him. It was a miracle he was still breathing.

Holy shit!

He began to mumble something. I edged closer so that my ear was by his bloody lips. I was just able to make out his last words.

'It's... watching.'

Scratching and gurgling sounds emanated from above. I slowly tilted my head back to see a hideous humanoid creature clinging to the ceiling like a spider. Its head turned completely around, ghostly dead eyes staring straight into my shaken soul. Features on the creature's face were similar to those of the ghost woman's.

This must be her other half.

Drool tumbled from its rotten mouth. And like a fly, it dropped down to attempt to land on me with its arms spread and claws wide. I dodged at the very last second and landed on my heels, holding my weapon high and preparing for a fight to the death. The Griever did the same, allowing me to get a full picture of its horridness.

Cooked crispy skin, brown and tight, stretched over a skinny body that seemed to be wasting away—I could see every bone in its dominating stance. As it prepared to strike, it unhinged its bottom jaw, stretching it unnaturally wide. It was terrifying.

A nasty sound forced its way out of the creature, screeching like nails on a chalkboard. It was so painful that I was forced to cover my ears, causing me to drop my weapon. Like a bolt of lightning, the Griever struck fast, lunging straight at me with skinny arms and razor-sharp claws wide open. With the image of the creature closing in, I snapped out of it and rolled out of the way at the last microsecond.

Quickly surveying my surroundings for anything I could use, I spotted something behind the creature. Beside the fireplace lay an old rusty fire poker. The dangerous question was how I was going to get it. Without thinking, my body took control and I ran straight at the creature. It did the same towards me, and within the blink of an eye, my body vaulted over the thing and to the fireplace with a flawless landing. I rapidly picked up my new weapon, terrified out of my mind. Turning around, I poked and prodded at the air in an attempt to provoke it into making the first move. It obligingly ran at me, and I sprinted towards the wall by the doorway. Once again, my body took charge—planting a firm left foot on the wall, I flipped over the beast, and then, with all my might, I struck the beast in the back of the shoulder. It pierced the thin flesh, pinning it to the old crumbling wall.

It kicked and squealed in pain like a pig, releasing its horrifying cries. I backed away, adrenaline pumping through my veins and heart pounding, prepared for it to come at me again. The Griever squirmed and attempted to grapple at the handle with all its might, but it only succeeded in losing energy. Within minutes, it became silent, then motionless. I took the fire poker out of the creature with ease, allowing the lifeless thing to fall in a pile of bones and skin, leaving a streaky line of old brownish blood on the old wallpaper.

I did it.

'Well, that wasn't too hard,' I declared valiantly, lying to myself.

I strode out of the room and turned to the stairway, grappling the railing with a free shaking hand. Just as I was about to make my way down the stairs, I heard a familiar noise behind me. Before I could look, the creature leapt on top of me, pressing me to the floor with the fire poker held tightly along my chest. As we struggled to get leverage on each other, neither of us realised we were rolling onto an unstable surface. The rooted railing by the top of the stairs collapsed, frightening the Griever and giving me the chance to get out of its loosening grip. As we fell, I managed to squeeze out of the creature's grasp and flip it over so that it was the first to land. I took hold of the fire poker and struck it into the chest of the surprised creature just as we slammed into the floor. Right where the heart would be.

Again, the Griever wheezed and squirmed for freedom, but quickly lost energy. This time it seemed different. Fear actually seemed to be projecting from its face, its eyes as wide as they could possibly be. I felt for sure it would be the last time; the creature seemed to be slowly pausing in its cries and screams as its body finally began to decay and crumble, beginning from its fingers and toes, and making its way up until it was as if the creature was never there to begin with. After years of torment and anguish, the woman, the last of her people, finally got peace. I imagined her with her family and friends up in the heavens, happy and grateful for my help. The creature was dead, and I stood victorious— although a bit confused by how I had managed it.

'How the hell did you do that?' a familiar voice from behind startled me. Hudson. The broad-shouldered man stood by the door of a darkened room with a gun raised towards me. His eyes were filled with mixed emotions. Unsure of what he would do next, I raised my hands to indicate that I wouldn't fight him. His big dusty boots stomped closer, his weight making the floorboards creak and groan.

Wait, was he watching? Why didn't he step in and help?

He stopped just a foot away from me and stood over the sandy ashes of what was once a vicious, terrifying creature.

'It's dead, I swear,' I promised, taking a quick glance at the weapon pointed at my stomach and back at his serious eyes. There was a double-clicking sound as he set his gun to shoot. Terror set back into my chest and I couldn't breathe.

What's he doing? The danger's over.

'Hudson?'

His eyes fixed on their confused target. I backed up slowly so as not to set him off, my hands still raised. He began to close the distance, determined not to let me get away.

'What are you doing?'

'No one is here to see. They'll just think it was an accident,' he responded robotically.

'You don't have to do this. I won't tell anyone, I swear,' I said, trying to buy more time. I was running out of floor and before I knew it, I was up against a wall.

Hudson was inches now from me and responded with a quick backhand to my face, leaving a mark behind.

'Shut up! It's not personal... It's just business.'

Sweat beaded on his forehead, and I was getting the impression he was trying to convince himself more than me. 'W-What—'

'No! Don't say anything... After this is done, my family will be...' He didn't want to do it.

'Hudson, listen...you don't have to do this.' I was begging— as much as I despised doing so—but it seemed to stall him. He mumbled to himself, looking down and wiping at his sweaty brow.

Maybe this was my chance. I inched sideways as slowly as I could to get out the door, which was only two feet away, planning to run like hell.

'No!' he yelled. I made a mistake. Now his conscience seemed clear, ferocity glazed his eyes as he pressed the gun into my bruised chest.

'If you have to do this,' I cut him off, 'then at least tell me why.'

This stunned him, his eyes looking me over. I didn't think he'd answer, but then:

'I was sent to assassinate you by a man with money. He said he would pay handsomely for your death. That money will free my family from the debt I made.' His nostrils flared in preparation. His mind was made up, thanks to the thoughts of his beloved family. He raised the barrel of his gun to my face and pressed it hard to my cheek. It seemed to be taking forever, but then—BANG!

I almost pissed myself. Blood sprayed and splattered all over and around me. I opened my eyes to an equally shocked and motionless Hudson, thick blood trickling down his relaxed chin. He held his chest in a futile attempt to close the wound. Blood quickly soaked his shirt and coat as it ran down his body like a river. When I stared into his eyes, I swore I could see them grow dimmer, as if a light inside him was going out. With a few brief moans of pain, the poor, dying man stumbled and stammered to the ground. For the next few moments, he fought against his body's urges to die, struggling to lift himself back up to finish the job he was paid to do. Watching him turned my fear into pity and sadness. Kneeling over, I reached down to calm his shaking body, looking into his frightened eyes. I wanted to show him it was going to be okay, and that I forgave him—after all, if I were in his position, I would do the same thing.

Floorboards groaned behind us. I turned around, ready to defend myself—only to find that I was face to face with the only soldier I least expected.

Micka.

The gun was smoking from the shot fired, and the barrel shaking in his clenched fists was still pointing forward.

I raised my hands once again, showing cooperation.

'It's okay...you can put it down now,' I said, calmly. Slowly, I stalked towards the potential new threat in an attempt to disarm him.

'Why was he trying to kill you?' he asked.

In the knowledge that honesty may be the only way I got out of this crumbling place alive, I softly replied, 'I don't know… he only told me he was enlisted by a stranger of higher standing. He didn't know his name.' I paused. 'Did you follow me as well?'

'I followed him and hid in one of the old rooms,' he said, callously waving around the gun he forgot he still had.

'Is James still alive?' I asked; not that I really cared.

'Yes, he's fine,' Micka seemed to be more relaxed.

'Do, um, do you mind if you…?' I gestured for him to put the gun away.

'Oh, um, I don't think so…' He smiled a devilish smile and grabbed for something behind his back. It rang familiar as he flung it at my feet.

The shackles.

'One of the men went back and retraced your steps when the storm hit and found them in a pile of sand by the truck… put them on.' He said, waving the gun from the shackles to me. His face was now stone cold. 'A convoy of men was spotted not far from here. We are going on with the journey to Buson.'

I really didn't want to be an animal in a cage again, but this seemed to be the only way I was getting out alive. Obliging, I gingerly and slowly slipped on the chains, and once again became a prisoner. As if I had ever stopped.

I was escorted at gunpoint back to our temporary holding; the fleet of vehicles was not far outside of the disintegrating town. From a distance, I could see trucks and motorbikes of different styles and designs that'd been rebuilt with mismatching parts.

As I was being guided to the fixed truck with the cage strapped to its back, something caught my eye. A corner of the red leatherbound book poking out of a small dune. In a desperate attempt to retrieve it, I pretended to trip on top of it, quickly smuggling it under my rags.

'Stupid slave! Get up!' grumbled one of the new soldiers, covered in soot and grease.

'Sorry, sir… My legs must have given out.'

'Get in there!' he shoved my already sore, worn-out body as if it were a sack of potatoes, causing me to stumble and bang my head onto the back of the cage, making them chuckle.

Out of the corner of my eye, I witnessed two of the new men carrying James on a wooden plank out of the building and plonking him onto a small trailer linked to one of the motorbikes.

I was shoved into my new cage, the door screeching shut behind me. The fleet of soldiers and guardsmen had almost doubled in size thanks to the survivors of the storm. I found it somewhat amusing that they didn't have enough vehicles to go around, so a few of them had to share seats with the motorbike drivers.

Knowing that I was leaving one desolate, remote desert for a desolate, remote prison for god knows how long quickly turned my cheeky smirk into a solemn frown.

Chapter 10

We were travelling through the vast terrain of graceful rolling sand dunes, escorted once again by a fleet of soldiers—now larger in size. The iron-barred cage I sat in was aboard a large rusted truck with four large pipes, two on either side, all billowing out an excessive amount of black smoke that wafted back into my cage, causing me to gasp for clean air.

The scenery that passed us rarely seemed to change, but now and then orange and yellow pillars of stone would emerge from below the dunes, pushing themselves as high as they could. More and more kept appearing in different ranges of distance and height. It became a more pleasant sight, rather than creepy old decaying towns or—God forbid—lone Manors. Soon enough, the silent men escorting me became elated and sighs of relief seemed to break out through the party. For them, this sight brought comfort to their eyes and fond memories to their minds. For me, this sight was not the same; seeing it meant more suffering and eventually a painful, but gratifying, death.

Looming ahead of us, the pillars of orange and yellow became merged in a great big magnificent clump. High cliff faces rose before us, and I had to admit it was an incredible sight of nature to behold. They formed the Great Ravines of Buson, which hid the city well within the maze of golden stone and cold grey rock.

I quickly checked to make sure no one was watching me— fortunately, they were all too focused on what lay before us.

Discreetly unveiling the book I had managed to keep safe, well, for the most part, I opened the cover just a smidge so that I would be able to see DeeDee's image that Ms. Turner gave to me. Sneaking a peek at DeeDee's face, even though it wasn't the one that I remembered, still gave me a little smile and helped keep my nerves down. I patted it fondly as she did her brother's when I first saw it, as it gave me comfort.

I promise, DeeDee, I will return you to your brother. Even if it is the last thing I do.

As we made our way through one of the great ravines—the passageway to the city—the vehicles of rusted iron and steel caused the walls to come to life, shaking with the roars and growls of machinery and steel. We were growing closer to my new 'prison' when the soldiers began to murmur and chuckle, talking about what they were going to do when they got home; go to the tavern, go to the Bagnio (whorehouse), and so on.

Before we knew it, the chasm opened up, revealing a small plain of sand that acted as the doormat to the city of Buson. What stood beyond it was one of the largest chasms, and in-between was an impressive iron and steel gate. The Great Gate of Buson, with its tallest dark spires and towers peaking over the top, which appeared to be the viewing stations for the guards to protect the city against invaders and other potential threats. We slowly made our way over the sandy plain, but stopped as a shout echoed across the golden canyon. There was a brief pause, and then our caravan leader shouted back.

Within moments, the impressive hulking gates—the path to my inevitable doom—opened up with a sound of screeching that echoed and vibrated all around us. We passed through a dark, cloud-smothered city that, to me, appeared to know no colour or light. When we reached the convoy stop, they let me out of my iron cage—but not out of my neck brace or shackles. They were used to lead me around like a dog, clutched by one of the new soldiers who rescued us from the crumbling ghost town.

The buildings that lined the streets appeared to be houses salvaged from the Great War, stacked on top of the other like crumbling boxes of wood and steel. They leaned hazardously this way and that, with bridges and walkways perilously weaving in between them. Above, cables and wires hung in a chaotic fashion, crisscrossing each other from building to building, some taut but many slack and simply tied together. The ground quickly transitioned from dry sand to a sludgy mud-like mixture of lots of presumably unpleasant things. The people that roamed around were dirty and unwashed, wearing nothing but thin rags. All seemed awfully timid around the soldiers, yet many cast curious glances.

Whispers occurred between a few of them as they looked on at a safe distance. As we made our way down the sludgy street of brown and grey, I noticed small, slightly raised wooden platforms scattered here and there, and when we turned the corner, I found out what they were for. Small crowds formed around at least four more platforms that were being used by others in chains, their faces sad and broken and their eyes were lifeless. It wasn't just humans, though—creatures I had never seen before in rags, their crimson skin bruised, their tall statures altogether different and intriguing to look at.

Chains…chains…chains…

That one word and thought filled every crevice of my mind. A scowl covered my face and my sunburnt hands clenched into fists, causing hot sticky blood to ooze out of my palms.

'Farrah!'

I looked down, confused. James had grabbed my wrist, alerting me to his presence. I locked eyes with one of the men I most hated in this world. His frail body was slumped and limp on the makeshift stretcher he came on.

'I said this is where I leave you. They are taking me to the infirmary.'

I answered with a blank expression.

He continued, 'I just wanted to say…thanks.'

He seemed like he was itching to say more—after all, we had grown up together. But he knew at his status that it was taboo for a person like him to form any sort of emotional attachments to people like me, and even worse to show them in front of his equals.

As he was carted off, I watched until someone else caught my eye.

Micka, his head was sunk in shame as he was being berated by a person who must have been his superior officer. The man's throbbing neck veins were visible from where I stood as he screamed at him, spit flying at poor ashamed Micka. He was a large man, full of so much muscle that his uniform seemed to be stretching tightly over everything. On top of his overly compensating body was a comically large blonde head, a square jaw, and above a set of thin lips sat a broom's head-sized mustache that billowed as he screamed and yelled. The muscular captain waved over two soldiers who were standing by, amused by what they were watching, and bound Micka's hands in thick rope. Micka's sad gaze met mine and all I could do was give him a slight smile to show that I appreciated him for not treating as the others.

While the city soldiers watched on, the remaining soldiers that survived both the storm and horrific beast stood at a distance, their heads slumped. Including Mandez, who nudged his companions and jerked his head in the direction of a rather busy-sounding building. Presumably they'd drink themselves silly until they forgot what had happened or take out their frustration on some poor street women.

'Come on, you,' commanded a city soldier with a thick, ugly accent I couldn't quite place. With a yank of the chain, he led me in a different direction, limping all the while. He looked different from the rest, almost bald, with a few black hairs sprinkled over his head, a forehead that seemed to fold past his eyes—giving him a permanent grumpy look—and a pronounced ridge across the top of his nose.

Travelling further into the muddy dirt-ridden city, we trudged our way up and over bridges and pathways, gradually climbing higher and higher. As we did so, I noticed that the buildings we were passing were becoming cleaner and brighter and colourful. The cables above that seemed chaotic and hazardous-looking before began to sort themselves out, neatly forming lines and creating large boxes above the street. It felt as though we were literally climbing up a hierarchy-ladder from dirty and unkempt to pristine and orderly.

Eventually, we found ourselves at the foot of one of the largest houses in the city. It peered over the rest and protruded out of the rocky wall. White marble steps lay before us, leading to a bright yellow three-story house with white trimmings. Two thick columns framed the entrance, revealing a tall crimson door. At its center lay a brass knocker with fancy inlay surrounding it.

The soldier gave the knocker three big knocks, and the door responded soon after with a light squeak. A small woman in a white puffy bonnet, apron, and round broken glasses peered through the opening.

Her pale blue eyes bulged in surprise and almost became watery. We remained standing by the door awkwardly for what seemed like too long. Until—

'Agnes! Why is the door open?' A shrill voice screeched from inside, making the poor thing jump and snap back to reality.

She opened the door just enough to let us in, single file. Her wide eyes stayed on me as we passed; it was as if she'd seen a ghost.

'Who's at the door?' the shrill voice screamed again.

'T-the new maid, my lady,' the small woman stammered.

The clacking of heels against polished wood grew louder as the owner of the unappealing voice approached.

I was immediately overwhelmed by a red dress, bedazzled to the hem with black beads in the shapes of different flowers. It clung tightly to a pale woman with slender legs and slightly muscular arms. Her hair was raven and her eyes were dark golden brown that seemed to criticise everything they looked at. A long nose protruded from the middle of her face, and below it, tiny, bright-red pursed lips. This woman was the embodiment of judgement. As her hand lay on her bony hip, her eyes peered down at me, and she leaned in uncomfortably close.

She looked me over, giving me a quick sniff of her pointed nose. Her lips tightened and their corners slightly rose.

With a huff of satisfaction and a slight cringe of the nose due to my stench, she finally said, 'You'll do.'

Her gaze shifted to the soldier who delivered me. 'You can go now.'

With a little bow and grumble, he unshackled my neck and wrists, then took the chains with him.

'Agnes. Take our...new little pet to your room and show her what her tasks will be.'

'Uh…Yes, ma'am. Come on.' Agnes gestured to the stairs, leading me down the hall and all the way to the back. The light grew dimmer as we walked in silence, finding ourselves at another flight of stairs. Only three steps, made of stone, and leading to an old, worn door.

Opening to a small room of the same stone as the canyon, two small cots lay by the far wall with mattresses that were so thin they might as well be sheets of cardboard. On top of one rested a nicely folded and ironed uniform, the same as Agnes's—A blue-and-white-striped dress, white puffy apron, and an equally puffy bonnet, as well as a pair of dress shoes by the foot of the bed.

Dear god, please tell me this is a dream.

A single mahogany cabinet sat against one wall, and along the next wall hung a small, cracked square mirror. Finally, a small yellowing intercom box next to the door frame that had seen better days.

'So, this is our room...' she finally spoke, her eyes avoiding mine. 'I know it's not much, but… it's home.'

'This is it? Where are the other maids?' I asked, bewildered.

Agnes returned my facial expressions with a head tilt and raised a brow in confusion.

'Ahh, yes—I think you are mistaken. You see, there are only ever two house-keepers at one time as they only give us one room and it's too small to fit any more cots in.' She paused, walking over to my bed and bent down to flatten the tiny invisible wrinkles out of my thin sheet.

'I thought there would be other maids around. Considering how big this place is. Where are they? Are there other rooms?' I asked, my nosey curiosity getting the better of me.

'The Master and Mistress...they like us maids to...contribute in group activities, and sometimes they become too, lets say, *excited* and become wrapped up in it, so much so that when they are finished the maids are taken away and are never heard from again,' she answered softly, bowing her head to look at the floor.

What the fuck kind of 'group activities' is she talking about!?

'Okay. How many maids were here before me?' I asked slowly, afraid of the answer.

'Twelve,' she answered, still avoiding eye contact.

Twelve? *Twelve maids come and gone like they're nothing?*

'Why am I here?' I asked cautiously, desperate to change the terrifying subject.

This question seemed to make her jump and clam up. Her eyes begin to well.

I looked at her levelly. 'Do you...know me?'

'I understand why you don't remember me,' she whispered. 'You were too young.'

'What?' I answered with a confused smile.

'I used to work for your family… The day your parents...' she paused, covering her mouth to stifle her sobbing.

'My parents? How do you know—? Wait, you worked for my family?!'

She took a breath. 'Yes. You were a noble, Farrah…'

I couldn't help myself but snort in derision, not really believing that absurd comment. 'You can't be serious.'

'Your parents were the nicest people I'd ever worked for. And that dreadful day when… your father was… Lucius took you to safety.'

'Who?'

'Lucius was your family's handyman. He loved you like you were his own… We both did.' She smiled, taking my hands. 'It is so good to see you again, Farrah! You've grown into a beautiful young lady… I did wonder if you still had your father's eyes… So beautiful.'

She patted my hands and turned her back, wiping away her tears.

'What happened to you, Agnes? How did you end up here?'

'They took me once they had… finished their business with your father… Lord Cowan took me and made me his own maid.'

My blood boiled. 'What! He was there? Cowan was there the day my father died?!'

'Yes, among others.'

'Who else?'

'I'm not allowed to say… I'm not allowed to tell you any of this. It's supposed to be a secret. They don't want you to know who you are.'

'The other nobles?'

'Lord Cowan knew you were still alive,' she said, slightly changing the subject. 'He has been obsessed with finding you… When he found out that you were taken to a trading town for protection, he threatened Lucius that he would kill his wife and burn the town to the ground if he didn't give you to him. So Lucius had no choice and handed you to Ms. Turner, the caretaker of your old master's home.'

I'm starting to have more questions than answers. Why did they kill my father? What happened to my mother? Why didn't they kill me? Why is Lord Cowan obsessed with me? I'd have to find out later.

'You should probably bathe. I'm sure you will feel much better after such a long journey.' She suggested, handing me a towel from the cupboard.

'The bathroom we use is opposite this one. You'll need to wait for the water to clear. The pipes are rusted. There's some soap on the ledge of the bath. Oh, and there's also a laundry shoot just outside for our clothes.' She explained whilst tucking away the loose strands of hair that had popped out.

The bathroom was just as sad as the bedroom, carved out of the natural stone the rest of the house bore into without a lint of colour and a sad little bulb that hung on a frayed wire above. A carved off-white almost yellow sink and large shard of mirror that was screwed into the stone above it. The really odd thing about the room was the small painting of the new masters posed in fine attire staring pretentiously at me, their eyes almost drilling holes into my skull.

Turning the tap to the copper bath made its pipes grown painfully and as expected brown rusted water sputtered out causing the nose of the tap to shake and clink against the copper and steel, eventually calming down as the water soon become clearer and started heating.

My clothes slowly peeled off, it felt like I wore a second skin for protection. I managed to keep hold of the book, and know cradling it like a newborn babe I swaddled it in my shedded rags to protect it from the steam and moisture. The water had almost filled to the top of the copper tub, but I couldn't wait to get in. Like a dancer, I pointed my foot to test it leaning on the edge. The water was almost scalding, but to me that was perfect. Gingerly placing my worn blistered and tender body into the tub caused the water to rise and the steam to lift and fill the room. The piece of soap Agnes had mentioned was exactly that a piece, one little well used and grounded down oval of sweet-smelling goodness. This was the first time in a long time I had felt so relaxed and moderately peaceful. Thanks to the water and steam, the dried skin on my arms and back peeled and floated away. All the dirt and crusty blood came off, revealing all of the cuts and scrapes I had sustained. But I didn't worry about them, all I could think about was the silence, it gave me a great sense of satisfaction, so much so that I scooted further into the bath took a breath and allowed the cleansing powers of the hot water and soap do its magic.

I felt like I had shed a whole fur pelt after watching all the gunk and muck slowly make its way out of the bathtub almost made me feel like a new person.

Almost.

Once we arrived, I started preparing for my first day of my new job. I unraveled the nicely folded and ironed apron and pinstriped dress. After Agnes gave me an approving nod.

'You know Ms. Turner?' I asked, finally beginning to change clothes. As I undressed, I revealed my stark tan lines, sore blister, and rashes I got from the shackles rubbing on my neck and wrists.

'Yes, she taught me all I need to know to survive.'

'Before I left, she gave me something… I think it's my father's… I managed to smuggle it in.' I unravelled the precious package that was the book I had hidden under the rags and had wrapped it in them as I was taking the bath. I handed it to her, and she looked it over with glistening eyes. 'This is… this was your father's… Now it's yours… We must hide it away.'

'But where and, for that matter, why?'

'There might be a hiding place in here somewhere… we just have to find it. If we find one, we can tear it up and place the book inside,' she said, getting all excited as she looked around. Suddenly, she paused, grabbing me by the forearms.

'Farrah, you must not let Lord Cowan or the mistress see it; they will kill you for it.' I just looked at her with widened eyes of fright and heightened anxiety.

We found a small hole along the seam of my mattress, then tore at it until there was a space big enough to fit my book. Before hiding it, I pulled out the picture of DeeDee and slipped it under my pillow. After, we shoved both the book and the leftover old clumps of grey fluff back in and massaged it down so that it wasn't that noticeable. A sigh of relief fell over both of us, knowing that the book was safe.

'What was that?' Agnes asked, gesturing towards my pillow.

'It's an old friend of mine and her brother.'

'Is she still at the Drake mansion?' she continued, smiling.

'No, she passed away a few days ago.' I answered, lowering my eyes as a twinge of pain twisted in my chest.

'Oh. I'm sorry for your loss. I didn't mean to bring it up,' she said, forcing her smile to disappear and her eyes turn big and wide out of consolation.

'It's fine, really,' I replied, giving her a subtle smile. 'I promised I would give it to her brother who is here in Buson, so that he could have something of hers.'

'That's so sweet of you. She must have been very important to you,' she said, softly grabbing my arm in comfort.

'She was.' I replied reminiscently, recalling some of the best times we had together.

'We should go back downstairs and pretend everything is normal. I'll show you your tasks so as not to draw any suspicions,' Agnes said, breaking the silence.

***

I was shown around my new prison and handed a list of chores and tasks of my own, which was unsurprisingly similar to before. Doing the laundry (only now in a larger laundry room, which was an actual component of the building), preparing baths, cleaning every room every day, and assisting with acquiring ingredients and groceries from the local vendors.

As we headed to the front door, we passed the reception room; a large white room with polished floorboards, and eggshell-white walls towering over everything with arches at the top, making it seem as though large windows should be there if it weren't built into the rock wall. On the far back wall were two large bookcases as tall as the walls, filled with books of every size and colour, and in between them hung a painting of a man that looked like Master Cowan, but older. Splashes of grey were sprinkled throughout his hair, his eyes were slightly dull seemingly unimpressed by the young maid that stared back up at him and yet they followed me wherever I went. By his feet, a mangy-looking wolf-dog hybrid snarled viciously at me. Put it all together, and it was an image that would forever haunt me.

The nearest bookcase seemed to... whisper something. Maybe not with words, but with... intentions? I couldn't explain it. Curiosity got the better of me, though, and I wandered over. My eyes glimpsed a novel that looked more familiar than its neighbours. Then it clicked—it was the exact same book as the one in our room.

'Girl!'

I jumped, whirling around. Neither of us had noticed the mistress relaxing on a pale red chaise-lounge, grazing on a small bowl of sultanas whilst reading a book.

Without another word, she simply wagged one of her pale, skinny fingers, gesturing for me to come closer.

I did so, but still kept my distance.

'What is your name?'

Her husband didn't tell her he knew me?

'Farrah.'

'Such a pretty name,' she said with a wry smile, adjusting herself to an upright position.

Holding out her hand, she continued, 'Well, are you going to just stand there?'

I glanced back at Agnes, who watched on with wide eyes, hugging onto the Mahogany door frame.

The thin woman took my hands and pulled me in much closer than I was comfortable with, then clasped my forearms and began to pull me down, forcing me to kneel. Her golden-brown sadistic looking eyes met my frightened saucer-shaped ones.

She brushed my hair back behind my ear, her long, sharp nails poking me as she did so. Her eyes seemed to be focusing on every single detail of my face, making me feel more uncomfortable and unsure where to look.

'Such soft hair, too… I've never seen a maid's hair be so soft and clean before. And I love the caramel brown shade of your hair,' she said, gently brushing my head. 'What mesmerizing green eyes you have, too… So pure.'

She caressed my cheek. There was something about her that felt more like a predator than a woman; the way she spoke, her dark, consuming eyes, and the way she was looking at me like I was food.

'Do you know what your tasks are here? Has Agnes shown you around?' she asked in a soft voice.

'Yes, ma'am,' I choked, afraid to speak out of turn.

'Good… and do you know I will be calling on you to collect and purchase items I desire?'

'No, miss.'

Her eyes narrowed and darkened, and her once-sweet demeanour twisted into a frightening scowl. A lightning-quick slap from her hand cut across my cheek, making it warm and red.

'That is your first warning. You only answer me with ma'am, or Mistress Cowan when in front of guests. Understood?' And, just as quickly as it appeared, her scowl vanished.

'Y-Yes, ma'am.'

'You are to do as I say as fast as you can. Clean as if we were hosting a party every day, and prepare a warm bath for my husband and myself every night.' She started fingering my hair again, placing the tangled strays behind my ear once more.

'If you are good, you may get a reward, hmm! Doesn't that sound nice?' she said with a smile.

'Thank you, ma'am. I shall do my best to please you.' A sentence I never thought I would say without laughing, but my sheer terror of the woman was enough to control my voice.

'Good girl. We shall get along swimmingly,' she said, releasing her grip on me at last. I relieved myself from the room and out into the blood-red passageway, where Agnes hid.

'Are you okay?'

'I'm... fine.' I wasn't really sure whether I was trying to convince Agnes or myself.

'She can be scary, but... like she said... if you don't do anything wrong, you'll be fine,' she whispered, rubbing her hand as she did so. I could see a glimmer of silver circular burn scars culminating between her thumb and pointer finger. She clearly had experience in the matter.

'Promise you won't do anything?' Agnes said hastily, stopping us on our walk back to our room.

'I promise.' Something I never said lightly.

Once we arrived, I started preparing for my first day of my new job. I unravelled the neatly folded and ironed apron and pinstriped dress. After Agnes gave me an approving nod, we headed back towards the foyer.

A startling cry pierced the walls of the house, making the both of us jump. We peered out the tiny window. Out in the sludgy courtyard, surrounded by his own kind, stood Micka—beaten and bloodied until I could barely tell it was him. At least five soldiers stood around him, clearly angry and in need of an outlet, which, unfortunately, ended up being him.

On nearby balconies and inside open windows, beady, black-hearted eyes peeked outside, enjoying the spectacle. Other 'pure bloods' cheered ecstatically as the poor soldier got beaten.

Since we were so high, we couldn't hear what the soldiers were saying, but it seemed to be their way of condemning him for something he shouldn't have done.

Letting me roam free? Killing the other soldier?

As soon as I was able to figure out what they were saying, a shot fired and reverberated across the walls surrounding us. Micka dropped like a fly, lifeless.

Unable to believe what I just witnessed as his body was being left where it lay, my mouth simply hung ajar. All I could think to say was:

'What is this place?'

'Buson… the locals call it Slave City,' she answered softly. Though there was a solemn expression in her eyes, she behaved as if that wasn't the first time she'd seen something this horrific. And I had a feeling that it wouldn't be the last.

Chapter 11

It had been just over a month since I arrived in Buson that Lord Cowan returned from his trip (from doing what, I wasn't sure, though it likely involved eating children or burning the homes of the innocent), however he never seemed to have the time to meet with his new pet, the one he had specifically hunted down for. He was always confined to his office space, and if not there, then the dining hall for meals, which he still would just hide behind a handwritten newspaper of the limited things that had been happening in the different cities. I felt like it was only a matter of time before I grew sick of the silence and stormed in to talk to him myself, asking him basically 'What the hell!', but I promised Agnes I wouldn't do anything stupid. I'd just have to wait.

I was secretly excited when I was asked to go out one day to fetch some things for Mistress Cowan, and I found myself relieved I didn't have to walk in public wearing my ridiculous maid getup.

Agnes told me that the Mistress didn't like us getting our nice uniform dirty and tracking mud in with our dress shoes, so we had to go to our separate servants' mudroom. There, a pair of clunky workman's boots, brown-green track pants, and a black jacket lay nicely folded in our own separate cabinets.

Shopping was the only sense of freedom I had had in a very long time, although the mistress always demanded that a guard follow me closely out of distrust. If it weren't for that and the guilty feeling of leaving Agnes behind, I would have bolted and hidden in a safe place until I found this Lucius person.

It actually was a good idea to wear big boots rather than delicate shoes, because as soon as I made my way down to the marketplace, I found myself sludging around in a putrid mixture of mud and god knows what else. The stench permeated my nostrils, making me recoil in disgust.

Every shade of brown could be found covering the decrepit old buildings and leaning crumbling structures. Not a spot of brightness or beauty could be seen; even the people were covered in filth.

Who am I to judge, though? If I weren't in my position, I would probably be like them—as a girl in a potato sack dress, unwashed and mangy. I'd watch on, as everyone else did, at the woman in nice clean clothes shopping for her Mistress, and judging her for being a sell-out and a coward. If only they knew the truth.

After I'd completed a majority of my tasks and stopped at most of the shops listed—which clearly were the cleanest and most refined—I made my way down a slight slope of mud. It wasn't long until I found a market square, or at least what seemed to be one. The space was filled with makeshift stands of flimsy tin propped by dead sticks that displayed a sad collection of mealy produce.

More people seemed to congregate in this area, some selling or trading their stock, others just minding their business. What was unsurprising, though, was the amount of orphans (or 'street rats', as Agnes called them) scurrying around. I would sometimes catch them watching out for each other as the more stealthy and tricky stole fruit or petty cash from the other poor people who didn't have much to start with.

I checked the last few things on my list and replayed the names over and over in my head so that I wouldn't forget. I scouted the surrounding stalls and spotted the one that had all the ingredients I needed.

'Hello, miss. How can Mino help you?' A small hunched man

with few teeth and a greasy, scruffy face smiled at me. He wore a torn green knitted sweater and fingerless gloves which showed his stumpy fingers.

'Two jojo fruits and four wild paiker berries, please,' I responded, just barely able to remember the strange names.

'Very nice, miss… Having a celebration, are we?' He tried making small talk, still giving me a gummy smile.

I answered back with a blank face. 'I don't understand,' I said honestly.

'Well, you can make many things out of these two ingredients alone, but put them together and, well…you're in a different world.'

I answered back with a quizzical brow raised. He laughed at my confused stare.

'You can make your own drug out of it, love!'

A scraggly woman with a bird's nest of hair piled on her head was leaning in, nearly falling off her stool. She tugged at her faded purple dress, impatiently waiting for her own customers.

'Would you like some deadry root to go with it? It can give it a bit more of a kick!' she said, desperately trying to hook in her last sale of the day. The woman waved a twig at me with a hopeful smile.

'No, sorry, it's not for me; it's for my mistress,' I answered as politely as I could, forcing my cheeks back.

'Not Mistress Cowan, is it?' she asked, concerned, then pulled her stick back.

'Yes, that's her. I'm her new maid.'

The shopkeepers exchanged knowing looks, but said nothing. The old woman bent down and disappeared behind her small wall of crates; only her bum waging in the air as she searched for something. Re-emerging, she hobbled over to me and placed a flask of white powder in my hands. She forced me to meet her gaze.

'Use this when their backs are turned. Put a little in their drinks.'

I was confused, but they both only nodded with assuring eyes and pitiful faces. They continued to watch me as I left.

There wasn't time to think about the odd conversation—a shot fired nearby. My body jumped, and I searched for the origin.

A voice thundered over the panicked crowd, 'Get your filthy hands off my food, rat!'

It was a bald man of thick build clasping the wrist of a small girl that looked about my age, if not younger, with the same petite build DeeDee had, revealing her own fist clutching an apple. His grip was so strong that it seemed as though he'd snap her arm like a twig.

Without realizing what I was doing, my body once again took charge; walking me into the commotion.

'I believe this belongs to you, miss… I saw you drop it earlier,' I said to the girl who was clearly in pain, wincing and grinding her teeth. In my hand was a gold coin, which was more than enough for an apple.

'This has nothing to do with you! Piss off!' the man growled, spit spraying towards me in a fit of aggression.

'I wasn't speaking to you,' I responded, unfazed.

This seemed to make the man even more furious; he even turned red, veins bulging on his neck and forehead as if he were about to explode.

'Let her go. This is more than enough for a piece of fruit.'

That didn't seem to sway him; in fact, his grip tightened. The girl winced and attempted to pry his sausage fingers off.

Having had enough, I dropped my bag of goods and lunged forward, head-butting him as hard as I could. He released his victim as he stumbled back, blood spurting out of his potato-shaped nose, which seemed to have already been punched on multiple occasions—clearly not a favored man.

That was the final straw. Like a bear, he reared back, puffed up his chest and raised his arms high. He growled and swung his fists clumsily, as if he were a drunk—left swing, right swing. Both of which I was quickly able to avoid. The ruckus we'd caused seemed to bring a large crowd, and not soon after, bets were being placed.

He bent over and kicked his leg back, much like a bull about to charge. The move was predictable, even for a big dumb oaf. As he clambered towards me, shouting with ferocity, I calmly stepped out of the way, watching as he smacked his head clear into a stone wall. He collapsed, unconscious, into a pile of old human waste. The fight was over before it even started, and the people who placed the bets mainly seemed to cry in dismay and annoyance.

Before any of us could move, two soldiers marched through the crowd. Everyone quickly dispersed in fear.

'What's going on here?' one of them asked, stumbling as he walked. The smell of alcohol wafted off the both of them in waves, making me feel overcome with the need to vomit just by smelling them.

No one stepped forward, the stall owners all looking at them like wide-eyed fish.

'If someone doesn't answer in five seconds, then all of you will be going into jail for the night!' he proclaimed, threatening the onlookers.

'It was her! She started it!' Mino shouted in terror, pointing at me with a shaky finger.

The soldier's attention turned towards me and the street rat who started the whole thing, both coming closer. The taller of the two stopped at an uncomfortably short distance. The other soldier was shorter, chubbier, and waltzed right past me, grabbing at the cowering girl who attempted to break free but unfortunately to no avail.

The taller soldier of darker skin and equally dark eyes—almost black and close together—began to speak, clearly groggy and having trouble standing still. 'You must be new here. What's your name, girl?'

'Um, Farrah?' I staggered my reply, unsure if I should tell them.

'You seem unsure about that answer. Is that your real name? Or don't you know?' he ended with a chuckle, causing the other to laugh.

'It's Farrah,' I answered again, louder, making them stop.

'Well then, Farrah, you do know that street brawls are frowned upon, unless there's a legitimate cause for it, don't you?'

'That man was hurting this girl over an apple. She was hungry, and I tried to help and pay for it.' I pointed to the cowering girl behind me, who I thought would back me up.

'What man?' one soldier asked.

Without answering, I nodded in the direction of the unconscious man.

The soldiers' eyelines followed my gesture.

'Him? You took him down? All by yourself?'

They looked at each other, clearly skeptical.

'You do know that lying to a soldier is against the law,' the shorter of the two added.

They soon began to scowl and loom over me in offensive positions.

'She did it; Mino saw her! We all did!' Mino spoke again, his wide eyes looking at me as if to apologise.

'Very well… Come with us, Miss Farrah, and we'll take you to your new room for the night. You'll love it, lots of friends to play with.'

A smirk grew on both of their drunken faces as they escorted me to what I suspected was a jail cell.

Looking back, I noticed the chubby soldier manhandling the poor girl, a repulsive grin consuming his cheeks as his eyes ran over her.

'Are you sure you guys don't want to drop by a bar first? You know—to make sure you're really drunk?' As soon as those words left my lips, I knew it was a stupid thing to say. The tallest soldier gripped tightly onto my forearm and shot me a dirty glare.

Just as we were about to be escorted away, I noticed in the crowd something suspicious, two men talking and whispering secretly as they watched on with eagle eyes and evil wry smiles. One of them signaled to the other with a shake of his head to go away as if he were planning something.

What a great way to start in a new city.

***

We were escorted through a maze of sludgy, bland-coloured pathways to an area that seemed more empty than the rest of the city. We came towards a brick wall with a large double-gated entryway guarding what seemed to be a great pit of consuming darkness.

'We hope you enjoy your stay here,' the short stumpy soldier whispered to me. After he moved away, the intense smell of alcohol still lingered behind, causing my nose to crinkle.

They pushed me closer to the gradually opening iron-barred gates. Echoes of pleading and shouts of agony crept out of the hole, making it even more ominous and terrifying.

Further and further down we went, our footsteps mingling with the torturous echoes and screams from below that amplified as we grew ever closer. Finally making it to the dark, dank bottom where the sinister noises emitted from, we reached a dim hallway. Whispers and chatters loomed before me as the both of us were dragged by an aggressive soldier itching to get rid of us.

I expected to see single cells as I passed each barred room, but no, the rooms they used as cells were large, bricked ones with a curve that arched from one end to the other. They must be what the ancestors used for storing wine barrels.

Different groups of people were locked in each; looking closer, I noticed some were lifeless clumps covered in blood. Arriving at our assigned cell, my eyes surveyed the other few prisoners and began judging them. Then, just as I was about to stop scoping out my surroundings, they were quickly alerted to the largest person in the room, sitting on their own with their back turned, covered by a large beige coat with different-coloured stains on it.

'Get in there, you rats!' the soldier growled, brutally shoving me inside. I stumbled to the dirt floor in a heap.

'Hey! No wonder you don't have a girlfriend, Goff, you asshole!' The girl ran to my side and helped me up.

The door screamed shut, and after a sharp click of the keys, the soldier by the name of Goff left us with a huff and grumble. My partner in crime helped me up and lent me a shoulder to lean on.

We searched for a place to sit for the night. Finding one that wasn't either bloody or smelling of piss was going to be a struggle, and I scrunched my nose at my limited options.

'Hey! Let's sit here!' the girl said, waving me over. As I approached, she patted a somewhat clean place between her and what looked like a puddle of dirt-soaked vomit.

Something was familiar about this girl—I mean, more than having only met an hour ago—it felt like I'd always known her. I eased myself down, careful not to touch the gross patch of smelly mud next to me. Having to sit cheek-to-cheek with a stranger wasn't an ideal night for me, but it'd have to do.

'Thanks for ruining my day, by the way,' was all I could think to say.

'Ahh… yeah, sorry about that,' she responded uncomfortably.

An awkward silence settled between us.

'My name is Tiery,' she said, breaking it, and offered her hand with a smile; an expression I definitely did not expect to see in here.

'Farrah,' I answered, accepting her hand. 'So, are you a regular here?' I asked, trying to kill time.

'Haha...um, yeah, you could say that!' she replied, rubbing the back of her neck. Her eyes trailed up to the damp brick roof. There was something about this girl, something behind her eyes and the way she looked at me reminded me so much of DeeDee. Her petite figure and the fact that they looked to be around the same age. Those eyes of hers were so bright and pure, like carved emeralds with flecks of silver in them that twinkled in the light. Her hair was more of a rusty ginger than strawberry blonde, and as she untied her ponytail from her piece of rope, the curls tumbled down gracefully and bounced into a full double curl at the bottom.

'How long have you been living on the streets?' I continued.

'As long as I can remember,' she replied with a more solemn look. She turned to me. 'Why did you stand up to that man?'

'I don't know… I guess I just had enough seeing people be treated as lesser,' I said, honestly. It was a comfortable feeling to have someone to open up to.

As Tiery and I talked away, I couldn't help but feel that someone was watching us—more specifically, me—but every time I turned to look, the feeling disappeared. Analyzing and glaring at my other inmates, I found they were either asleep or were so drunk they couldn't care less about a pretty girl in their cell, let alone two of them.

'What's wrong?' Tiery asked.

'Nothing, I just thought—' the familiar sound of a screeching iron door interrupted me, drawing the attention of every sad soul in it. Four men of varying builds wandered in with grimacing faces and threatening glances.

'Play nice, boys… I don't want to have to put you in the pits again,' Goff warned as he locked the screechy barred door. He flashed me a quick glance as he walked off, as if to say 'Have fun'.

The men's arrival seemed to change the mood of the group cell from bored to terrified, as everyone scattered from the new arrivals. Tiery's eyes also widened in fear, as if she knew who or what they were.

Watching her, and the way she was looking at these men, was causing paranoia to set in and my heart to race with anxiety.

However, due to the fact that it was almost midnight and I hadn't been able to rest ever since I came here, thanks to the unforgiving mattress I was bestowed, exhaustion seemed to outweigh my anxieties, and I found myself overpowered by sleep. Not the best place to fall asleep, but definitely not the worst. Too paranoid to fully allow my mind to rest, I just laid my head on Tiery's bony shoulder and closed my eyes.

***

A terrifying screech of pure horror filled the air, forcing my heavy lids open. A sudden and jarring pain punched into my gut. I heaved, and a puff of excess air forced its way out of my mouth. Feet and fists filled my vision as blow after painful blow bombarded my body. I had no idea what was happening or why, but I was frightened and could hear poor Tiery screaming at the top of her lungs. I could barely see her being held back by one of the large men, kicking and squirming in his grasp. All I could think to do was curl up, close my eyes, and wait for the nightmare to end as the other three bulky strangers pummeled me over and over.

One of them stopped abruptly, and without opening my eyes, I could hear muffled sounds of violent force and screams of pain. I warily opened one swollen eye, as much as it hurt, to see what was going on.

A hulking, dark-skinned man stood in front of me like a wall, his thick arms outstretched in defence. His back was covered in countless scars of different sizes and textures. One of his arms, I quickly noticed, was different. It shone, reflecting the bleak light lines that ran down it in a neat pattern. At the end, where a fist should be, was the form of a large sledgehammer.

Echobriome?

The men that'd been beating me stood back, unsure of what to do. They all squirmed in place, adrenaline coursing through their black hearts.

Tiery was still being held by the neck by one of them. He thrust her forward, using her as a shield like the coward he was, and egged the others on to kill the man in front of me.

Both launched themselves towards the great man twice their size, and he did the same, meeting them in the middle and taking a great swing of his hammer-shaped metal fist. It slammed straight into the side of one of the men's skulls, completely crushing half of it and making teeth and blood fly out of his broken jaw. His lifeless body slammed to the floor, blood and brain quickly pooling around it.

Meanwhile, the other man also raced towards him, but before he could even touch the fierce warrior that protected me, my guardian's bloodied echobriome arm swiftly morphed into a beautiful sword and violently crossed paths with the desperate thug, cleaving him right in half, spraying the walls and arched roof in a horrific yet spectacular crimson colour.

I couldn't see from my point of view, but whatever look my saviour had made, the man that held Tiery pissed himself and let her go. Tiery's face was painted with fear and she quickly scurried her way to me, both of us protected behind the great wall of a man. We held each other in comfort, closing our eyes, too terrified to watch. The final man's wails of pain and fear forced us to imagine what was happening only a few short steps away.

It finally went silent.

Both of us peered up at the man, our eyes nervously wandering over to his echobriome arm as it morphed back into a normal human hand covered in blood.

'Thank you,' was all I could say as he slumped down next to me.

'You're welcome… Farrah,' he replied with a weary sigh.

'How do you know her name? Oh, wait, you probably heard her say it before,' Tiery smiled, the split on her bottom lip stretching.

'I did… but I already knew her name. Your name. From before,' he casually said, closing his eyes.

'Okay, you know my name, but I have no idea who you are,' I blatantly replied.

'You know me, you just don't remember, and I don't blame you…You knew me as Lucius.' His eyes looked back, dark and almost sad.

Tiery, apparently bored, scurried off to take a closer look at the dead bodies for some sick reason.

'You worked for my family…' I said, slowly, 'with Agnes.'

'That's right. We saved you. I loved your parents, Farrah. We both did.' His eyes grew more solemn.

'Look at this,' Tiery said, waddling over like a crab. In her cupped hands were three small leather pouches filled with rough, round pieces of old metal with an emblem on them.

'Lord Cowan's, looks like,' he answered, unsurprised.

'What?' Tiery huffed, baffled.

'His spies must have told him you were in here and paid them to kill you,' Lucius speculated.

'Why would Lord Cowan pay these men to hurt me?' I asked in disbelief.

'Your father knew lots of secrets about the company and the only way they could make sure that none of it would get out was to kill all three of you… But when they found out that Agnes and I took you away they hunted us down like dogs. We had no choice but to hide you right under their noses.' Lucius's eyes closed as he began to rest again.

'The Drake family,' I added, seeing it all come together.

'That's right.'

'But how did Lord Cowan know where to find me?'

'We suspect that someone told him,' he answered, seeming to be holding more back than what was being said.

'We?' Tiery once again interjects.

'Your parents were double-agents… spies for the group of people against everything the Company stands for.' Tiery and I intently listened in, our mouths both ajar.

'What or who is the Company?' Tiery asked the same question I was wondering myself.

'The Company is a group of powerful people whose ancestors are said to be the ones who ignited the Great War and brought on the Apocalypse. Their goal, among others, is to have control over everything and control the rest of humanity with an "iron fist", as the ancestors used to say.'

Tiery and I looked at each other, then back at Lucius. My mind started to hurt and a headache started to grow. Rubbing my temple out of exhaustion, I needed a minute to let all of this information to set in.

'So—wait, Lord Cowan had known where I was this whole time?' I almost yelled, and it slightly echoed through the room. The others shushed me as they tried to sleep uncomfortably, looking back at Lucius with equally annoyed eyes.

'It seems so,' he continued. 'The Company will not stop until all potential threats are taken care of… Lord Cowan is relentless, and bloodthirsty.'

'Ha, you think!' Tiery chuckled sarcastically.

'I'm sorry, Farrah… we tried to protect you. Instead, we failed.'

'It's all right, Lucius. You did your best and I'm grateful for that.' I couldn't blame them, I didn't even know I was being protected, let alone that my life was being threatened by powerful people.

'Time to go, sweetheart!' A familiar jangling of keys alerted everyone itching to get out. Goff stood by the blood-soaked door, undisturbed by the carnage the room contained, as if this kind of thing happened every day.

'Come on,' the guard pulled me up, not caring about my pain or the sight of my bruises or possibly cracked bones. He dragged me into the hallway before I could stop him. I grabbed the bloody barred doorframe as we passed, pressing my face between the slits.

'Wait, Lucius! How do I find you again?' I was desperate to see a friendly face once more.

'Don't worry, Farrah! I'll find you!' he shouted back as I was tugged away from my saviour and new friend.

Once again, I found myself at the entrance of the jail. I embraced the feeling of cold winds brushing past my hot, bruised body. I stood there with Goff beside me, watching. I met his expectant gaze.

'What are you waiting for? Go home,' he said, answering why he was staring at me.

'Aren't you going to escort me?' I asked, expecting to be dragged by the arm once again.

'You're not a child. Go!' He replied, agitated.

And so I left. Wandering back, haggard and sore, I tried to remember as best I could how to get back to my other pen, where I pretended to be a 'good doggy' and do what I was told.

Agnes told me that there was a spare key under the stone by the first step in case we returned sunset. I opened the door to a house so dark, one would think it was abandoned. I made my way as quietly as I could to mine and Agnes's shared room. Passing the reception room, a whisper caught my attention. It wasn't from a person, but from the same book that I saw earlier. Drawing it out of its place, I realised that it's almost identical to the book my father left me. I took it as payment for the beating I got earlier, thanks to Lord Cowan's generous goons.

When I reached the servants' quarters, Agnes was still awake.

'Farrah, where have you been? Oh my god, what happened to you? Your face!'

Agnes rushed to me, tears welling and brows turning upwards. Her hands lightly grasped my face.

'It's nothing… I'll tell you in the morning. I'm tired now.' I declined her soft touch and care and slowly took off my clothes, my limbs aching with every movement. Afterwards, I fell into my unforgiving bed.

I waited for Agnes to fall back asleep so that I could hide my book with the other. It didn't take long, since she'd already been half-asleep when she saw me. Once I heard her snores, I gingerly rolled off my bed and quietly tore open the mattress. I reached into my clothes for my new treasure. I pulled out more than expected, having completely forgotten that I still had the leather pouches Tiery showed me—and not to mention the strange white powder that old woman gave me. I could use it later, maybe. Another bonus—leverage against the enemy.

Chapter 12

I could barely open my swollen eye. My skin felt stretched, like I bought it a size too small. I got up slowly, frowning like an old man. My aching body was a reminder of last night's unfortunate events.

Wandering over to the pitifully sized square mirror with the crack through it, I looked at my face, which I hadn't done for a long time. I could hardly recognise myself. Half of it was purple and blotchy, with large lumps protruded from my split lip and eye. Feeling around my head, at least three more protrusions throbbed under my hair—once brown and wavy, now black and covered in filth.

'Farrah!' Agnes barged in, already dressed and out of breath. Her brows were furrowed and her eyes were large. 'The master would like to speak with you.'

My thoughts jolted to the memory of where I left my stash, the book being number one on my mind. Checking inside my mattress, I desperately scrambled around, my heart pounding louder and louder. The hiding place was empty—no vial, no bag of coins, and more frighteningly, no books.

Shit. Those Bastards must have come in here and taken it when I was out.

Making our way down the halls to my fate, I came to realise that I might have more leverage over them than they did me. Whatever they threatened me with, I would double it—triple it—for my father, my friends, and my family.

Lord Cowan sat proudly before a feast of fruit and assorted pastries, all displayed on gold-trimmed plates upon an ivory silk tablecloth. Mistress Cowan sat beside him, sipping on a tiny teacup, pinky held high, giggling at one of her erotic novels she loved so much.

'You wished to see me, Master,' I said, interrupting his breakfast.

'Good lord!' Lady Cowan said, dropping her book to her lap. 'What on earth happened to you? You look like you've been trampled by a pack of wild alderans.' A smile of delight spread across the Mistress's face. Her amber eyes were brighter than ever, as if she knew what really happened. 'Are you all right, dear? It doesn't hurt that much, I hope.'

'Was there something you wanted, Master?' I said, ignoring her comments.

'Yes, I wanted to talk to you about something. Come here.' He waved two fingers towards himself, beckoning me.

I inched forward..

His hand struck like a viper, grasping at my throat. A nasty grimace fell on his face, his eyes red with fury. As he pulled me viciously towards him, the other two watched; Agnes, shocked and frightened, and the Mistress, smiling, obviously aroused by the spectacle.

'If you ever steal from me again, I will make sure that next time you and your poor innocent Agnes die a horrible death by my hand. And let me assure you,' his voice faded into a whisper, 'I will enjoy it.' His tongue ran along the edge of my ear. Strands of his gell-slicked back, blonde hair tickled my cheek and nose. Horrified, I tried to recoil, but his grip on my throat was so strong that I had trouble breathing.

He finally shoved me back, and I immediately began coughing and huffing in relief, rubbing the newly traumatised area. Agnes clung onto me in worry, rubbing me softly with her delicate little hands.

'As punishment for your thievery, you will be spending the day chained in the boiler room cleaning your outdoor wear over and over until every last spot of blood and filth is gone. Understood?'

'Yes, sir,' I spat through my gritted teeth.

'Agnes, get the chains and cuffs and take her there,' he said, waving us away like flies, then returned his attention back to his slice of orange.

'Yes, sir.' Agnes bowed and led me to the boiler room without a single thought of rebellion.

The opening of the door introduced me to the suffocatingly hot room that had a sad dim light barely in a low ember glow. A small old stool and dented old tin bucket waited for me in the middle of the stained room and as expected, a pair of chains bolted to the floor beside them.

'I'm sorry about this.' Agnes said, her head hung low and eyes as dark as the situation

'It's alright. It's not your fault. You're just doing your job. Protecting yourself.' I replied half-heartedly, giving her space to walk past me.

Patiently she waited for me to take a seat on the swollen wooden seat, her hands shook as she attempted to place the rusted steel cuffs on me. Accidently dropping one in the process only for me to catch it before it clanged onto the concrete floor. She met my gaze and without the need to speak I cupped her shaking hands and placed the cuffs on myself. With a sharp clink of the locks.

Agnes ever so slightly closed the door, always making sure I could see a friendly face before it was closed, and I was alone. The last thing I saw was a sorrowful gaze that glistened like jewels from the tears she was holding back, a squirrely maid that was terrified of her masters, just like all the others.

What else was I to do but sit and scrub and stew in my festering rage towards all the uptight, pompous jackasses like the Drakes or the Cowans? I let myself become consumed by my hunger for revenge against everyone who thought of themselves as mighty gods. Allowing every memory I had of my life to flash past me, I realised they were mainly filled with horror and terrible sadness.

Miles and DeeDee, Mum and Dad, Ms. Turner… everyone.

As each minute passed, as my fingers bled from scrubbing away, and the feeling of steel shackles rubbing once again against my wrists which were bolted to the floor by my feet, I promised not only to myself, but to everyone like me.

I, nor anyone else, will have to be treated like shit—worse than shit—ever again!

This is the last day I will be serving these wolves. I vowed to make a stand and see them suffer.

***

Finished with the repetitive scrubbing, I laid out my now-spotless outdoor wear. My fingers were cut and the skin had lifted from the splintered handle of the scrubbing brush. I sat, formulating a plan of escape, intending to return and rescue Agnes when I could.

I waited, fidgeting, waiting for the dodgy door to open. My outdoor clothes were fully dry by the time it did, Agnes entering with a disheartened expression. She hobbled towards me, a pathetic metal dish of sourdough bread, mandarins, and iffy-looking cheese centered on it.

Her hand brushed mine as she handed the sad portion of food to me; a non-verbal form of apology. Her big eyes looked at me.

I watched her leave, anxiety rising the closer she got to the door. I reached for the knife that she had left behind—a useful lock-picking tool—and hid it in one of my apron pockets before she turned around. When she reached the doorway, the moment seemed to slow down; I could hear my heart beating in anxious anticipation and hopefulness.

The door closed.

I jumped into action—picking the locks of my shackles with my knife and setting my raw wrists free. I removed the stupid apron, checkered dress, and dress shoes that pinched with every step. And in less than a minute, rushed to get my newly clean outdoor uniform back on, without caring how damp it still was. I hurriedly slipped into my outdoor wear, then shoved the lumps of bread, mandarins, and wedge of cheese in my pockets because I might be hungry later if I get out.

Almost throwing the stool at the wall below the vent, I was frantic, anxiety ridden about the brutal retribution I and most likely Agnes would get if I was to be caught. Throwing those undesirable thoughts away and swiftly swivelling my knife to unscrew the screws that held the vent in place. Finally, onto the last screw using one hand and the other one to hold the vent steady so I could catch it before it fell and softly leaning it against the wall next to the stool before I hoisted myself up into the tightly confined steel tunnel, wiggling my way through the maze of corners and dips being as quiet as I could so as not to alert the devils below. I'd completely forgotten that Lord Cowan was usually in his office working whatever devious, sketchy plans he was cooking up during this time. The Mistress Cowan was probably sleeping or lazing on her favourite chaise lounge, drinking and reading one of her beloved erotica novels.

My only issue was that Agnes might tell on me in fear of her own life; but on the other hand, if I did leave, then she would be the only one to be punished. I was torn between my selfishness and my desire to protect her from the evil monsters that owned this house. Although I was fully aware that I stood in the open, conflict ravaged my mind like a storm, as I slowly wandered down the hall, not watching out for any dangers.

'Farrah! What are you doing out!' Mistress Cowan alerted the house and almost caused me to jump out of my skin. A nasty scowl scrunched her perfectly painted-face as she stormed toward me. 'Get back in there until we say you are free to go!'

The discord in my mind deadened and the only voice left told me to run. My body once again took charge and leapt into action, running at the speed of a bullet out the door with my sore arms pumping as fast as they could. I ignored the crushing pain in my chest as I breathed in and out, sounding like a steam train puffing away.

When I left the mansion, I didn't let myself even think about looking back—just running and running—ignoring everything; the screaming Mistress, the soldiers chasing me, the bystanders watching on as I sped past, a frigid wind quickly following suit.

I'm sorry, Agnes, I'm so sorry... I promise I'll come back for you.

Before I knew it, I had lost the soldiers and ended up in a place that I didn't recognise. I looked around my surroundings as I waited for my heart to calm down. The whole area seemed cold and dark, and something felt off. Shadows moved amongst the dark corners and crevices of each disheveled building, which looked more torn apart and abandoned than usual. A shiver crawled up my spine, feeling eyes watching on in the shadows with hunger. It seemed as though with every step I took, a lifeless body lay not far from me— some more decayed and smelly than the others. Few men strolled at varying distances past me, drunkenly swaying and wailing happily as they slapped each other on the back. Suddenly two sober men passed by, obviously walking with a particular destination in mind.

'Who are you betting against tonight?' one of the men's voices passing by caught my attention, as he talked louder than normal.

'The Litherian,' his friend answered, 'there is no way he can beat a Kraznian.'

'You haven't seen this Litherian, though. He's different... He's like the size of a mountain.'

The two men passed by me, clearly not noticing a panting, injured, strange girl in the middle of the path. As they walked by, strategizing on their bets and plans, something inside me told me to follow. I did, but at a cautious distance.

The new area we entered was desolate and gloomy, and seemed more depressing than the rest of the districts I'd passed in my blazing speed. Windows were boarded up and buildings seemed to be falling apart in the mud they lay on. No one was on the streets—this seemed to be more of a reclusive community, possibly because of the lack of soldiers. In fact, this place seemed to be the only area the soldiers didn't visit. After scoping my surroundings, I would have had to say that it was possibly the most sad, rundown area I'd seen since I'd come here.

It must be the slums of Buson.

I followed the two men from a distance when they suddenly turned a corner into a back alley. I did the same, watching as they slipped behind an old wooden door. When I peeked inside, I found a boisterous bar full of drunken, smelly people, all cheering, fighting, and (obviously) drinking. The two men made their way down a flight of hidden stairs that disappeared into an odd-looking hole in the ground. Below, there was a warm light and various echoes that gave me an upsetting flashback to the jail cell. Shaking it off, I noticed them disappearing into the light and noise.

Swallowing my fear and nerves, I inched my way slowly down the unknown—and potentially dangerous—hole of chaos.

Sweaty, drunken bodies thrashed together in a mass of angry flesh.

'Come on, get in there!'

'Don't be a pussy!'

'Get up! Jackass!'

These were just a few of the comments being flung around from one side of the underground basement to the other. All of them were being directed toward the centre, but I couldn't see what was there. Forcing my way through the wall of drunken, angry men and half-naked women, I was unsure of what I was about to find.

I finally had shoved my way to the front, and saw the reason for all the commotion, and it finally clicked: this was a fighting ring. Well, not exactly a ring per say, more like an invisible barrier had been marked off, warning the drunken bystanders to watch their step.

And what was even more disturbing was I recognised one of the shirtless men flailing about in the middle.

Lucius!

The monster he was fighting was almost twice his size and as pale as a sheet. He had scars that looked like they formed some sort of pattern on his arms and chest of tribal designs I'd never seen before. The two of them were locked in a fierce battle, swiping and jabbing each other without remorse; like two beasts in a battle to the death. They paid no attention to the bystanders watching and cheering on.

'Lucius!' I screamed as loud as I could. I did, but only for a second. When his eyes met mine, his whole demeanour seemed to change. His echobriome arm morphed and shifted into a large hammer just as the hulking white mountain of a man charged at him from behind with clenched fists and overpowering ferocity in his eyes. Even with Lucius's back turned, he seemed to sense that his enemy was close enough, and in the blink of the eye swung his morphed arm as hard as he could. It smashed up into the great beast's chin, causing him to fly back through the air. When he landed, he was knocked out cold, making his fans boo and hiss.

And with that, the fight was over.

Lucius turned and looked directly at me, then brushed past me in a slump as he reached the wooden bench where an old blood-stained towel lay waiting. He patted the blood out of his wounds, giving them a quick clean as I watched, waiting for him to say something.

'What are you doing here, Farrah? Actually, how did you even find me?' he asked with a tone of slight annoyance, weary from his battle. He had slight worry in his eyes as he poked at my wounded face and let out a gasp of shock.

'I actually didn't know you were here. I just followed some guys and stumbled onto this place.' I started to regret doing it. Judging by the look on Lucius's face, he wasn't pleased I found out his little secret. A person behind the bench handed him his feeble amount of winnings, which looked barely enough to even get a drink.

'And if you followed someone to a sketchy brothel, what would you do?' he asked, placing his arm around me and leaning on me for support. The sheer amount of man hefted upon my shoulders almost made my knees buckle and give way, but I didn't want to embarrass him about his weight.

'Point taken. I ran away from the Cowans,' I admitted, slightly pleased with myself.

'Wow. Okay then, but what about Agnes? You know what will happen to her, right?' he asked, both impressed and concerned for his old friend.

'Don't worry, I have a plan to get her and the book back under the cover of darkness tonight, when they least expect it,' I said, projecting a confidence in my half-baked plan I didn't entirely feel.

'Well, I guess you'll need somewhere to stay until then. My place isn't far from here, you're welcome to stay with us.'

'Us?' I asked.

'I'm married,' he revealed, nodding forward toward the exit. We waded through all the angry bystanders walking out, feeling cheated out of their money and pissed off at the winner.

***

I crashed into a humble cottage, a man the size of a bear half-unconscious on top of me. Stumbling in, I dropped him down onto a small wooden stool, unable to carry him much further.

'What the hell is…'

A beautiful slender woman of amber-coloured skin vibrant

green eyes, and full bow-shaped lips hurried over, startled by the commotion. Her long braided raven hair swished from side to side as she rushed into the small, dimly lit room that was both a dining room and kitchen.

'What is this—Lucius!' She rushed to her wounded husband's side. After she realised he would survive, her frightened eyes darted to me. 'Who are you?'

'This is Farrah… Farrah... this is my wife... Keela,' Lucius tried to stay awake enough to explain. He winced at the pain in his side with each breath.

'Farrah… *The* Farrah? Oh my goodness, I never thought I would meet you in person.' Her attitude almost instantly changed from defensive to elated.

'Uh, hello?' Lucius interrupted. 'Injured person over here!'

'Oh, yes! Sorry, babe,' she laughed it off and returned to tend to her husband. 'How much did we get?'

'You knew he was fighting like that?' I asked, shocked.

'Yes. It's the only way we can make money and keep a low profile from the Company. It's either this or I sell my body. But Lucius would never allow that to happen,' Keela curtly answered my disagreeable tone and judgmental face.

'I see.' I reply, sinking my head, looking away out of embarrassment.

'So…what can I help you with, Farrah?' Lucius, more lucid, lifted the drink placed in his hand.

'What makes you think I need something from you?' I crossed my arms.

His response was a look that needed nothing else.

'All right, fine. I need your help. I know about my past and I want the Company to pay for what they did and what they are doing to all of us. I want to change things for the better, but also so that I can see them suffer.' This brought a smile to both their faces.

'They stole from me. They killed my father and took my mother away.' Before I knew it, everything I had bottled up burst out of me like a volcano of hatred and bile, everything I was feeling. All the darkness that had grown from the years of torment and violence. Every last painful memory flashing in my mind.

'Okay,' Lucius said, interrupting my hateful rant.

'What?' A grin broke out on my face—an odd feeling since I rarely ever smile. It felt good.

'I said, okay. I'll help you... Your parents saved me and treated me like family. I'll help you, Farrah.' He smiled back, opening his arms for me to embrace him.

'You two must be hungry after all that excitement. Let me fix you something.' Keela smiled, finishing the bandages and preparing the cuts for stitching later. Caringly rubbing her husband's arm, they shared a loving look.

'By the way, what is a Litherian?' I asked. I already knew that the pale beast he was fighting was a Kraznian; when I was at the Drakes' mansion, I used to sneak a peek at books and found one about the different races. An image of a Kraznian is something you can never forget.

Keela and Lucius both looked at each other for a minute, considering their answer.

'A Litherian is a human of any race or colour with mutation in their blood, this mutation allows Litherians to have an extreme threshold of pain they—*we* are the only humans who have the ability to use echobriome if we lose a limb in battle. We also have the ability to heal faster, but the scars from the wounds are left behind,' Lucius explained.

'So you are a Litherian?' I asked, already positive of the answer he would give.

He nodded with a shamed look.

'How did you lose your arm, may I ask?' I continued, though I knew it to be a sensitive area of discussion.

This led to Lucius rubbing his shoulder, where his body ended and the metal began. Keela put her arms around him, leaning into him with a worried brow.

'It was my punishment. After Lord Cowan discovered what had happened, his men captured us on the run and took us back to Buson. Upon learning of what happened to you he decided to make me suffer by killing my wife and making me watch. I didn't want her to die so I offered him something else—me. Instead of killing me, he decided to take something else away from me and find any way he could to throw me into jail. If I was walking down the street, I would go to jail. If I was in the wrong district, I was to be thrown in jail. And if we attempted to escape from Buson, then he was to kill my wife, Keela, and throw me into the mines to suffer.' He ended with his head slunk down, shielding eyes that were misted with tears.

I didn't know what to do. 'I'm sorry, Lucius,' was all I could bring myself to say.

'What? It's not your fault, Farrah. I promised your parents I would protect you, as did Agnes. I am a warrior. It has always been in my destiny to protect you and defend you.' He paused and took Keela's hand. 'The both of us have chosen this path because, like you, we understand and dream of a day where no one is slaughtered for stealing or kept as a slave. This is our mission in life.' His strong eyes clasped onto mine, showing me that what he spoke was really what he felt.

'Enough sadness—dinner is almost ready,' Keela said, breaking the depressing silence in the room.

We chatted under the warm glow of the candles and a small fireplace, a mug of frothy warm beer in hand and a plate full of tough meat and stale bread. We talked and talked without a care in the world, about the past and plans to change the future. I laughed and smiled so much, far more than I ever had, and this was one of the best nights I could remember. At the end of the meal, only one thing was left on my mind.

'My father left a red leather-bound book behind for me. Do you know what it is?' I asked, finishing my tankard of beer and rapidly pouring another.

'Yes…There is also supposed to be a twin book. Do you have that as well?' Lucius asked, now fully rejuvenated as he munched on a chicken leg.

'I did…I took it from Lord Cowan's bookshelf. Ms. Turner gave me the other one before I left the Drake manor,' I explained without remorse.

'Ha! That's good, they stole them first,' he laughed so hard he almost choked on a brittle chicken bone.

'Do you know what they do? Why are there two of the same book?'

'They are kind of like a way of communication. They are magical, Farrah. If you have one of the books and one of your confidants has the other—someone you can trust, mind you—you can write your message on a page, it will disappear and reappear on the twin book. Your father and mother used it as a means of telling our allies the Company's plans and secrets before they found out.' He paused, chugging a jug of beer. 'However, Lord Cowan stole one of the books from your parents after they killed your father in order to trick and trap his enemies.'

Intrigued by this new information, I nudged my chair in closer to him as he continued.

'You have to go back, Farrah. I know you don't want to, but you have to. If Lord Cowan has both of them, then he can plant one of them anywhere and learn all about the plans we have for overcoming the Company—there is more than one book scattered among the cities and outposts. And if that happens, they will be in grave danger. We all will be.'

His hands cupped mine, almost consuming them as he looked deep into my eyes—into my shaking soul—terrified by knowing that what I had to do could lead to my death.

***

Under the cover of darkness, and with Frey-like precision and stealth, I made my way all the way back to the last place I wanted to be.

I let out a sigh of relief when I found the spare key placed right where it had been the day before. I unlocked the door, and the only thing that greeted me was the darkness. As I went to gingerly close the door, thick arms grappled me and strapped my arms to my side. I tried to scream and escape, but a firm hand had already glued itself to my mouth.

'Welcome home, Farrah. It's so good to see you again.' That horrid voice slithered its way through my ear as Lord Cowan twisted me around sharply. His golden hair was no longer slicked back, but hung in limp strands across his forehead. He wore a sadistic smile on his lips as he dragged me, kicking and screaming, into a room where Mistress Cowan and a beaten and crying Agnes waited.

It was a small, dark red room I didn't remember, filled with vile disgusting things—whips and chains and canes and spears. This truly was the darkness that lived in this house. Lord Cowan slammed my body against one of the wooden pillars along the blood-coloured wall, forcing me to face him, and smiled an evil smile as his large hands pinned my bruised body down. His tongue slithered from the bottom of my neck to my eye, and before I knew it, I was cuffed behind my back.

Terror swept through me, imagining that what had happened to my poor DeeDee was about to happen to me and I couldn't do anything to stop it. His hand moved to my throat, actually choking me this time as he forced his disgusting tongue into my mouth. His teeth clashed against mine as he kissed me harder and more vicious as the others watched on.

He tore my shirt open with obvious desire for my shaking body, then grabbed me by the throat again and threw me on the bench behind him like a rag doll. The mistress gave him a thick, black leather dog collar with a silver ring in the middle to make it easier for him to handle me. Tears began to form and spill down my cheeks as I sobbed for my life.

'That's just making me harder,' he said as he hastily unbuckled his pants.

A loud thud of something slammed next to me. It was Agnes. The Mistress was licking her lips, and while Lord Cowan began maliciously thrusting away at me, she began beating and hitting poor Agnes as hard as she could. A nasty pain rapidly set in, throbbing inside of me as his cock shoved itself in further and further.

I felt small amounts of warm liquid trickled down my legs and the strong metallic smell began to set in. I began gasping in pain, and even pleaded. This didn't stop them.

'It's been ages since I had a virgin,' Cowan exclaimed, as they both began to laugh hysterically.

'Light this for me, baby,' Cowan commanded his mistress as he reached for the drawer and pulled out an old cigar. As commanded, Mistress Cowan lit it her lips curving in pleasure. He only had two puffs before he began stubbing it out on my collarbone, making me scream. The pain was so much—too much for me to bear. I looked over at a crying, beaten Agnes who also looked at me, broken. The way DeeDee looked at me when I caught her and Lord Drake in his office, then before my eyes there she was again in Agnes's place, whispering to me with a sad smile. My mind began thinking of anything else to dream of to make the pain and sadness go away. But she was still there, smiling at me as she always did, comforting me as I did her.

'Don't be afraid. It's going to be okay.' Her voice flowed in the wind like a gentle whisper.

Before I could stop myself, my voice tore free from my lungs, 'Oh DeeDee! I'm so sorry! I'm so sorry, DeeDee! Please forgive me!'

The pain was too much for me to stay awake, and my eyes fluttered shut. I never wanted to open them again. Turning my feelings and emotions off, I blacked out from the pain.

Chapter 13

Feeling like a former shell of myself, there were very few things on my mind as I walked towards the market square for Mistress Cowan's supplies. One; that I had the overwhelming desire to no longer live, and two; the only thing keeping me alive was the thought of seeing DeeDee again. Although the second one was impossible, I knew that there was the next best thing. The closest connection I had to her—her twin brother. He was here, somewhere, but the only image I had of him was a photo DeeDee had taken twelve years ago. It was my best shot.

The powerful sensation of unabashed invisible eyes staring at me from every direction made my skin crawl, in the intense fear of last night's unforgettable events had been spread around like idle gossip. Paranoia consumed me, they could see what they had done, they could read it on my face, Maybe they wouldn't be able to find me if I just hid in a deep dark hole.

I'd reached the marketplace where I'd met Tiery, and it looked more or less the same. Mino caught my attention as he watched me with squirrely eyes, tapping and fidgeting away; he knew I was here to see him for supplies, but he looked anxious. I didn't hold it against him for ratting me out; no, he was merely protecting himself. He'd been afraid of those soldiers, and he had every right to be. I would have done the same thing if I were in his position.

'Ah… Farrah, dear! Mino is so happy to see you again!' he said, clearly faking it, signalling my location like a fog horn. His forced smile bared all his yellow teeth. 'No hard feelings about the other day, right?'

'I need a few things today, Mino,' I said, ignoring his awkward attempt at an apology.

'Of… of course. What will it be?' Mino said, dialing down the false pleasantries.

'I need jojo fruit, jackfruit, wild paikar berries, some cactus apples, and… ghost berries,' I whispered the last item on the list, knowing that it wasn't exactly legal.

Mino's eyes widened. I must not have said it soft enough, as the nosey woman from before wandered over. Mino didn't deny my request and got to packing straight away, discreetly putting the ghost berries in a separate parcel, one that didn't bring attention and I could fit in the inside pocket of my jacket.

'You wouldn't happen to have another flask of that white powder lying around anywhere, would you, miss?' I asked, turning to the old woman. Her face brightened with excitement over one of her few customers. She scrambled to her stall with glee, frantically rummaging through her supplies. Finally, she straightened, flask in hand.

'Be careful, dear,' she said, pushing it forward with her cold, bony fingers.

I almost jumped back, *she's too close.*

'Are you alright dear?' She asked sincerely, brows risen.

'Yes, sorry I'm fine.' I forced a smile, shaking off the nerves.

I graciously accept repaying her kindness with a soft smile.

'Before I forget… have you seen this boy? He'd be older, and his name would be Francis,' I asked, scrambling to search for the picture I took with me of DeeDee and her brother.

'That's an old photo…' Mino observed, squinting and leaning in.

'He would be about twelve years older than this.'

'I know a Francis that looks like him,' the woman said, tapping her chin as she glared at the image.

'So you recognise him!' I asked, optimism raising my voice.

'Yes, he and his sister used to run errands for their father before the father died. Poor Francis fell sick after that, so his sister had to become a maid for the Drake family to keep up with the medical payments. Poor girl. Try the wellness center… It's about half an hour away from here. I'll draw you a map.'

With the map in hand and a spark of hope in my cold empty heart, I followed the dirty piece of rag with the chalk line on it to the letter, trekking through empty alleyways and poo-smeared walkways, turning this way and that. My friend (the guard) who wasn't far behind, kept a war distance, pretending to look at clothes and fine ribbons, thinking I wouldn't notice, but thanks to Cowan's attention I notice everything know. But I knew the only way I would rid myself of this annoying brute would be to lose him in the streets. I found myself at yet another marketplace. This time clothing and other non-perishable supplies were being sold. Two long lines of market stalls ran along the sides of the street I stood in, and I was met with a dead end of a sheer rock cliff face. Casually making my way to the small crowd and passing the first two people naturally so as not to seem suspicious, then dramatically making my move, zigzagging from left to right, turning and spinning around the quizzical faces. Eventually losing him and tightly turning down a skinny alley way. Looking behind me to make sure I had truly lost him and giggling out of slight confidence, double-checking the map to make sure I had made the right turn in the unknown streets that surrounded me, I back-tracked a few paces and found the correct path that led further into the city and finally made it.

The wellness centre was a concrete mass of pillars and thick, cracked walls. I passed through the splintering doorframe to find a space filled with cots, blankets, rags, and whatever else the sick and elderly could manage to sleep on. I was shocked that people actually sought help and medicine here, considering the sad crumbling state of it. Old plastic sheets were used as dividers in between the pillars and were scattered throughout the sad, smelly, tan complex the same colour as the surrounding stone and rock.

Cringing at the sight of it, I made my way to an old worn-out office desk near the front. There, sat an indifferent looking young woman doing her own thing, letting people by without so much as a glance.

She wore broken glasses that looked to missing a lens, which didn't seem to faze her, and despite the grey nest of straw-like hair that sat precariously on top of her small head, she had soft-looking fair skin, small brown eyes, and almost non-existent lips.

I felt invisible as I stood in front of her, waiting to ask her my question as she worked hard biting away at her hangnail. When it was clear I was getting no recognition, I cleared my sore throat.

'What?' she said, not looking at me.

'I was just wondering if you had seen this boy in here? He would be about twelve years older by now... a young man,' I answered politely, expecting the same back.

She sleepily stared over her crooked frames, staring right through me.

'We got a lot of boys here.'

I held the image close to her, with clear eagerness written on my hopeful face.

She sighed, and glanced again at it and looked back up at me.

Rolling her eyes, she dramatically exhaled and yanked the photo out of my fingers. Her small eyes glared at it.

'I don't know—try the terminal ward upstairs. I think he might be there,' she answered, returning to her pesky hangnail.

'Thanks.' I nodded, giving the best smile I could. She waved it away as if it were nothing.

As I made my way toward the concrete steps at the far back wall, I felt my senses devoured by the stench of rotting flesh and disgusting noises of dying bodies. I couldn't help but bump into people that, in turn, bumped into others as they visited their loved ones or got treated. I wasn't sure what I was stepping in, but I knew it wasn't good because of the decaying smell and random rubbish and gauzes that were strewn around. Not watching where I was going, I stumbled over a wooden crate being used as a chair and fell into the hooded figure in front of me.

'Hey! Watch it!' he yelled, turning around with a tired frown.

I recognised him, and I could tell from the change of his face that he recognised me too, and we both stared at each other, shocked.

It was a badly injured James Drake, most of his face puffy and bruised, his right eye swollen shut and oozing a gross yellow fluid. He was hunched over and leaning on a battered old stick that he was using as a crutch. A brace was held tightly against his knee for his clearly broken leg that didn't touch the ground.

'James?' I whispered. My jaw dropped open and my eyes widened. I never thought I would see any of the Drakes again.

'Who? I think you have me confused with someone else.' His face turned pale, as if he'd seen a ghost.

'You're kidding, right? It's Farrah, from your family home? I used to be your maid?'

'I'm sorry, I think you have the wrong guy,' he answered, expelling air with a forced smile. He averted eye contact and forced his way past, practically running from me.

He paused and glared at me until his eyes landed on my fresh burns. His eye's widened.

He knew.

Pulling my collar up to cover it, I simply replied 'I'm sorry. I thought you looked familiar.' I apologised, forcing my way away from him as fast as the thick crowd allowed me. Shaking the interaction off and eventually slowing down as my beating heart calmed down.

Unsurprisingly, another mass of sickly bodies awaited me. This time most of them lay in the cots, coughing and sneezing and creating gross, colourful fluids with their bodies.

I scanned the area for any distinguishing marks and there—just as I was about to zoom past it—a big bright spray-painted 'T' on one of the old cement posts. Feeling a little more confident, I strode along the rows, my eyes working quickly. There weren't too many in this section, and—

And there he was. Lying in a cot, pale as a ghost, with dark bags under his eyes, strawberry-blonde hair with a slight whisper of curl, and orange freckles splattered across his white cheeks, just like his sister.

I stood, staring like a stupid naked and damaged statue, as I looked at an identical image of my dead best friend. The world seemed to slow, floating by. I couldn't believe that I actually found him.

Shaking the dumb look off my face, I slowly and nervously walked closer. Butterflies swirled in my stomach and cold sweat formed on my forehead as my mouth went dry. I loomed above him like a grim reaper—still stumped as to what to say.

He flinched at my shadow and covered his eyes to identify the creep staring at him.

'Can I help you?' he said.

He had the same eyes as his twin sister.

I sat down beside him, my mouth ajar.

'Um… Hi, sorry… My name is Farrah,' I said, offering my hand timidly.

He pulled his weak body up with his bony arms, rubbing his tired eyes as he slumped over. 'Farrah…? Farrah… I've heard of that name… Do I know you from somewhere?'

DeeDee must have told him about me in her letters.

'Um… I worked with your sister, DeeDee. She was my friend,' I answered quietly, still nervous. My mouth was as dry as the desert.

'Farrah! That's right, she told me about you in her letters! She loves you so much.' His whole demeanour changed as soon as he heard his sister's name; he even began smiling.

'Yes… um… She told me about you, too. In fact, she showed me this photo of you two when you were kids.' I replied, rustling around in my pockets for the picture I smuggled out of the house.

'Here.' I handed it to him and he gasped with glee.

'Where is she? Is DeeDee with you?' he asked, bouncing in his cot with excitement.

I was speechless; I didn't know what to tell him. If I revealed the truth, would he literally die right there?

'She couldn't make it today. I came in her place.' I lied through my teeth to a dying man.

'Oh… so why did you come to see me?' he asked, his positivity dissolving as he sunk back into his thin mattress, making it squeak softly.

'I came… I came because I wanted to see you. And meet you in person. The famous brother, Francis!' I lied again, unable to look him in the eye.

'I see… Well, here I am! Impressed?' he asked, striking a pose with his hand behind his head as he wiggled his eyebrows at me seductively.

I laughed, just a little.

'So why else are you here in the lovely golden city of Buson?' he asked dryly.

I didn't answer at first, focusing on pulling a stray thread out of my grocery pouch and twisting it tightly around my fingers.

'I got transferred to Lord Cowan's home about a month ago,' I confessed; it was the first piece of truth I'd said so far.

His eyes widened and he slightly leaned back. Apparently everyone knew what the Cowans did to their servants.

'Oh… I'm sorry,' he consoled, resting one of his cold, scrawny hands on my fiddling ones.

'I just wanted to see a familiar, friendly face,' I finally admitted with a slightly guilty face.

'I see… you wanted DeeDee and came for the next best thing.' His assumption was correct, and I nodded in slight shame.

'It's okay! Really, I get it. I would probably do the same in your position if I wanted to see my sister too. Which I do, but that's never going to happen… Just… I mean, if you need someone to talk to, or just want to come and bask in my general beauty and handsomeness, that's okay,' he said.

He wasn't like anything I'd expected. I'd thought I'd see a frail young man on his deathbed, coughing his lungs out, and instead I found another version of my DeeDee. Their personalities and appearances almost identical—apart from the whole gender difference thing. Other than that, I would have sworn I was sitting face to face with my friend again, talking as we usually did.

'Anyway, I should be getting back to my masters; they're expecting me' I tried ending casually with an eye roll, though I had the full intention to come back for more visits.

'You should get those looked at,' he said, nodding at the small circular scorch marks on my chest. I pulled the collar of my jacket over them, casting my gaze away from his.

'It was good to finally meet the infamous Farrah,' he said, smiling a friendly goodbye.

'You too… I'll see you again soon, Francis.' I nodded and gave a gentle side smile back.

As I got up and turned away, I felt his hand on my wrist.

'Wait! DeeDee would never give this to anyone else, not even a good friend. Why do you have my sister's photo of us?' he asked, concern in his now croaking voice.

I didn't know how to respond. The memories of what happened came flooding back to me again, haunting me, forming a hard lump in my throat. I just looked in his general direction, showing him the sadness in my eyes.

'You said she 'was' your friend… People only say that when…' I could see in his weary eyes that he was connecting the dots, and he let go of me. Tears welled in his eyes and rolled down like waterfalls on a mountain.

'Oh god, no! N-Noo!' His screams of grief and sadness made the rest of the building and surrounding area stop and fall silent with shock and alarm. He screamed like a wounded animal; he lost his family, his sister, the light of his life, the only connection he had to this mortal, mundane world, his only reason left to live.

Everyone around us stood in silence, watching on, and then one by one they bowed their heads as they realised that something or someone was gone. They knew what it was like to lose someone close to them, or felt the dread that one day it would happen.

I didn't know what else to do. I didn't want to tell him what happened. I didn't want him to find out he had other things to worry about—his own life, for example. I just turned and left the poor, grieving boy, who kicked and squirmed and raised his voice to an almighty roar of nonverbal vengeance towards the clouded sky.

I walked past the numerous statues of sorrowful men, women, and children, whose dark auras swept off of their bodies in waves and seeped into mine. Making my way out of that place, their sadness felt all too real and was suffocating and emotionally depressing. Stumbling and bumbling away from the dark concrete building, I could still hear poor Francis's voice squeal and holler at the pain. I felt like I couldn't breathe; the sadness that enveloped me deprived me of air.

I honestly don't remember how I ended up back at the house. My walk back from the wellness centre was just a blur.

Emotionally worn out from the day, I wandered into the kitchen by the front door, dead-eyed and drained, where a tired Agnes greeted me with as much energy as she could muster.

I didn't respond. I didn't even look at her. I just plonked the groceries on the kitchen island and gazed into the emptiness before me.

'Did that woman have another vial?' Agnes asked as she rushed around, preparing her tools and heating the stove in preparation for tonight. It reminded me of Ms. T, which brought a smile to my face.

'Are you all right?' Agnes's hand rested on my fist and shocked me back into reality.

'What happened? What's wrong?' she asked again, her brows rising in a high arch of worry above her cracked round glasses. I didn't want to concern her with my depressing visit, so I just nodded silently.

'I had a strange encounter with one of my old master's children, James Drake,' I answered with one of my quandaries that I was definitely confused about.

This comment made her jump as she took her hand away and began unpackaging the grocery pouch, clearly disturbed.

'Oh yes, what happened?' She continued unpacking, then started lining up all the ingredients, including the alcaline root she already had hidden away in one of the darker cupboards of the kitchen, accompanying it with the ghost berries (apart from the cactus apples and grapefruits) in front of the wooden chopping board that sat in front of the small window looking out to the courtyard.

'He acted as if I were a complete stranger, and said that I was mistaken,' I continued, suspicious of her behaviour.

Her back turned to me as she began cutting and grinding away. After a moment, her muscles relaxed, and she stopped to look out the window.

'Farrah, I don't want to keep anything from you. You're my friend, and I loved your parents… I overheard something… the night before you were arrested,' she began, slowly turning around with her head down. 'The Master and two other captains of the guard were talking away in the Master's office. They were planning a hit on you. Those men who hurt you… they were ex-soldiers dishonorably discharged for murderous intent and an attempt of robbery of the Master's safe.

'The Master told the men about the plan and to tell the ex-soldiers that if they completed the job that they could be soldiers again. James somehow learnt about it and didn't entirely agree and tried to stop it and was beaten for it. He was told to forget about you and to pretend that you were a complete stranger. That is the only way he can be safe and stay alive,' she finished with a sigh of relief, her puppy eyes looking up at me sorrowfully.

'I see… Thank you for telling me. I really appreciate it. You're a true friend.' I smiled at her reassuringly.

'But when we arrived at Buson, James was terribly injured—he had a freaking pipe in his chest! How is it he's able to walk or stand—or breathe for that matter—after such an injury?' I flailed my arms about. Just thinking about it was incomprehensible, not to mention impossible.

'Well, as one of 'pure blood', James Drake has certain privileges that the common folk or servants like us do not,' she said, not really answering my question. Agitated, I waved my hand for her to continue.

'There is a place under the wellness centre. A lab. Only a few people are allowed down there. They say they keep people and creatures down there for…"harvesting".' She paused, looking at my wide eyes as I listened. I couldn't hide my shock and curiosity.

'They keep the strongest of any creature, even humans, and "harvest" their blood, bone marrow, and whatever else, to use on themselves. Litherians are humans with a mutated gene that have the ability to withstand any pain or punishment you can throw at them. And Kraznians, as you may know, have the ability to become stronger with every strike you give them. Their bones can become as strong as steel, their skin as tough as diamonds, and their strength is like no other. Some also have the ability to grow into giants five times their regular size. They're rare and difficult to catch, so they keep them for a long time until they have another. There are many labs just like that one, and they harvest from other creatures. They steal their powers and abilities for experiments and greed. This is but one of the darkest secrets we know about the Company, Farrah. They are more evil and disgusting than any of us know. Since James is a 'pure blood', he was given such a treatment and now has Kraznian blood flowing through his veins.'

My skin crawled. Just the thought that I was above that place today, oblivious to what was going on, was sickening. A sad silence fell over us as Agnes went back to the ingredients I had bought. I just stood there, taking in everything she'd told me. I was feeling faint after everything that had gone on—it was one horrible thing after another, and it felt like it'd never end. My leg bumped a stool as my legs became jelly, and I slumped down onto the tiny stool. Resting my head in my hands, I closed my eyes and just let all of this bizarre information sink in.

I needed a break from all the darkness and disturbing thoughts that ran in my mind. Something fresh and mundane to lighten my view on this miserable world we lived in.

'So what are we doing here?' I said, changing the discussion to the ingredients along the board.

'This is my plan,' she said, proudly grinning from ear to ear.

'What plan?' I asked hesitantly.

Just as I thought I was going to talk about boring everyday things, Agnes just had to throw something else at me.

'I don't want you to go through what happened last night ever again. It is a regularity, but I never thought that they would do that to you,' she said, sadness in her voice.

'What plan, Agnes?' I asked again, more sternly.

'For payback, and so we can escape once and for all. I promised your parents that I would protect you. That no harm would come to you so long as I was your protector and your shield. When the Cowans drink this tonight, their greatest fears will come to life.

They will be filled with horror and torment, and won't have any time to stop us from running,' she said, excited. Everything in her demeanour told me she was positive her plan was foolproof.

'Why don't we just poison them and get it all over with?' I asked a little too loudly, causing Agnes to give me a stern look to shut me up.

'Because if we did that and ran away than it would be clear to the soldiers, we killed them. Besides, with the entrance to Buson closed we won't have any place to run to and it will only be a matter of time before they find us and skin us.' She returns, clearly having thought it all through.

'Okay… so what do all these ingredients do?' I asked, trying not to seem skeptical.

'The vial the woman gave you, that induces the visions. The ghost berries enhance the fear receptors to make them think that their greatest fears are really there in the room. And finally, the alcaline root masks the taste and pauses the colour change the berries produce, so that they think they are only drinking the pleasure drug the jojo fruit and wild paikar berries give,' she answered, pointing at each in turn.

I still wasn't as optimistic as Agnes. Chemical experimentation and drug use is very intricate and dangerous work that can't be played around with. Too much and they'd think that we were their enemies and try to kill us, but too little and they would only be paranoid and take it out on those closest to them. But either way, once they recovered, they would find us and kill us for what we'd done.

Chapter 14

The intercom system began buzzing at an infernal hour in the morning, causing both Agnes and myself to shoot up from our sleep, praying that the world was ending. Realizing we weren't that lucky, Agnes sauntered out of bed, half-asleep, and rubbed her sore, red eyes to answer the little yellow box. There could only be one possible reason why the Master and mistress called for us at such a late hour, fear pounded through my body as fresh memories poured back into my wounded soul and tormented mind. Not wanting Agnes to see, I shoved my burning salty eyes in my sad pillow, begging to be allowed to go back to sleep.

'Yes, Master? How can we help you?' she asked, fighting back a yawn.

Muffled voices answered. I couldn't make out anything, as I had shoved my head under my thin pillow, trying as hard as I could to go back to sleep.

A familiar hand gently rocked me and coaxed me to alertness. I reluctantly uncovered my head, revealing a messy nest of frizzy caramel hair. My dry mouth gaped and I fought the urge to go back to sleep.

Agnes simply said, 'They request our presence.'

'So does my pillow… Fine, let me get changed,' I replied, sour faced, unable to fight back the sarcasm.

'No. There isn't any time for that,' she replied, stone-cold and unamused.

Once we arrived in the meeting hall, we discovered something rather unexpected. Mistress Cowan was lounging in a bergère armchair—a delicately carved rosewood frame ending with feline paws as its feet. Beside her stood a small oak table with only two items; a carafe of vibrant purple liquid—the one that Agnes had prepared earlier—and a spare stemless glass.

She sat casually, her legs crossed and arms thrown over the armrests, wearing the most bizarre and outrageous black leather outfit I'd ever seen. Long shiny boots rose above her knees and thick straps ran across her torso. Much smaller pieces of leather covered her crotch and breasts, and she wore long black gloves that also ran above her elbows. On her face was an odd-looking mask with cat ears. In one hand was clenched a brown whip with five large nails sticking out. In the other, a stemless glass of the violet concoction. Hopefully the hallucinations would kick in soon.

Looming in the shadows of the small alcove behind her, the Master watched on with lustful eyes while he puffed on one of his favoured cigars. He was entirely engaged in the disturbing scene he'd designed.

'Ready to have some more fun, ladies?' Mistress Cowan asked, baring all her teeth in a sinister grimace.

Intense fear struck me again, and my whole body vibrated as a fierce coldness enveloped me.

'Agnes, you will be assisting me for this part,' the Mistress instructed as she lifted herself up and placed the glass of liquid on the flat armrest of her chair. She cat-walked a few steps towards us, the deadly nail-spiked whip dragging behind her.

'You have been a very naughty girl, Farrah,' she cooed. 'Your master demands you be punished.' The Lady continued flicking her deadly weapon in an attempt to scare me. A lump formed in my throat so large it almost choked me.

'Agnes… tie her up,' she said, nodding to the ropes that were pinned to the walls on either side of us.

Now, standing almost an inch from me, her amber-coloured eyes seemed to grow darker, almost into the shade of blood. Without taking her eyes off me, she ripped off my nightgown, revealing my chest and fresh wounds from the night before.

'Lift your arms up,' she whispered, smiling.

Without looking at me, Agnes tied my wrists so that I could not put them down.

As the Mistress slowly circled around to face me, she lifted her whip up to my chin and simply said one word:

'Kneel.'

I refused, looking the she-devil straight in the eye, showing her my strength; this seemed to shock her slightly, as her eyes widened. But it passed, and she raised her free hand and smacked me in the ear so hard I collapsed to my knees. I heard her boots settle behind me as poor Agnes and Lord Cowan watched on.

'Farrah…' Everything in me clenched when Cowan's deep voice flooded the room. 'You have been accused of the following accounts: theft, fleeing from your duties, and murder on four counts. And I, as your master, have found you…*guilty.*' He emphasised the final word with confidence and a hint of pleasure. I watched as he poured himself a glass of the potion in preparation, thirsty for blood and eager for the erotic pleasure of witnessing such a horrid sight.

'Your punishment is five lashes of the spiked whip. If you scream or shout in any way then the punishment will be doubled,' he finished. Walking out from the darkness, he settled into the Mistress's chair for a closer viewing spot and leaned in, covering his malicious smile with anticipating praying hands.

'Begin,' he commanded. And with the swish of the whip, a violent, fiery sting struck across my back. The first strike already drew blood, and I could feel it stream down my back.

The second strike made me wince, and I bit my lip as hard as I could to not scream. I could hear Agnes sobbing as she watched, horrified. The third caused my whole body to start shaking as the cold began to set in from the rapid blood loss. The whip slashed back as the Mistress prepared for the fourth one and, in doing so, she sprayed Agnes and the Master with my blood. The fourth struck and I began to curl forward in pain, tugging at the ropes binding my arms, summoning all my strength to not cry or scream. I knew I would not survive a second round. In her excitement, as she whipped her weapon back more harshly than needed, one of the nails became lodged in the wooden floorboards, irking her as she grunted and pulled with all her might, tearing it free with one less nail to impale me with. The final lash was by far the hardest. I could feel the nails digging deep into my back and flesh, tearing me open. I couldn't stand it any longer—I screamed, but I fell forward as hard as I could to knock myself out.

The next part was a blur of mixed images and muffled sounds. I saw Agnes screaming for my help—pleading for me to save her with her arms stretched out as they took her away. I closed my eyes, pretending not to see.

The next time I opened them, the master walked over to my limp body, and knelt down to look straight at me. He leaned forward to whisper something, but I couldn't make out the words.

I finally completely blacked-out from the pain and blood loss.

Did the drink work? Or is this just a dream?

***

I lay there in a pool of my own sticky blood, half naked and pretending to be knocked out, motionless and frightened. Lord Cowan and his Mistress continued to drink, dance and fuck violently. Often using poor Agnes as a patsy for their sick desires and games. As the hours went by and the night grew darker, the jug of wine emptied, just as they thought their fun couldn't be ruined hallucinations and thoughts began running wild.

Mistress Cowan began to scratch and itch at her arms concerned as to why she holds them up and there seemingly as plain as the nose on her face hundreds of bugs and tiny creatures running and burrowing into her skin, slowly eating away at her. Her clawed fingers weren't enough she had to find something fast a knife anything to dig them out. As she frantically scratched and dug small holes into her arms Cowan himself walked around thinking that his superiors were in the room threatening him because of his knowledge of Farrah and him keeping her a secret for himself. As he tried desperately to talk his way free from his punishment, he imagined them telling him something he could do. The only thing that would free him. To slaughter every one of their enemies, who conveniently stood behind the red door. As he grabbed a Ka-bar Knife that hid tapped under the nearest table he stalked towards the door swallowing his fear and all the emotions that came with it. Unfortunately, in the real world, the only person in that room was Agnes asleep, worn out from the pain and sexual violence they had put her through. In his eyes it wasn't her, but there was no one there to tell him otherwise.

***

I slowly opened my eyes, and the blinding pain of light ignited a powerful headache. I felt queasy and the need to vomit was overwhelming. Blinking a few more times, I realised I was in my bed in the servant's quarters. I felt myself clutching a sticky old Ka-Bar tactical knife—it was almost glued to my palm by all the blood caked on both my hand and the scary-ass knife, but whose blood was this?

Then, lying there facing me, pale as a sheet, eyes blank and cold, was Agnes. Her glasses, bent in half, sat between us, and a large pool of blood had dried around us. I sat up to look at her, then myself, and the knife I was holding. *No, no, no*—I felt panic pressing in on me, but forced myself to calm down. Think. *It couldn't have been me. No, this didn't make any sense. Where would I have even gotten this weapon?*

Before I could do anything, the wooden door slammed open and two soldiers with guns walked in.

'Farrah, maid of Master Cowan, you are under arrest for the murder of Agnes Miller,' he said while standing over me, a great tower of a man with wrinkled yellow skin, a cap desperately trying to hide a receding hairline, and dark brown eyes filled with judgment and disgust. He and another younger man with curly blonde hair and small eyes man-handled me up and out to the reception room. This was a sign from the Cowans that they were finished with me. There was no way to explain myself out of this, and no one would believe my truth over their lies. Waiting in the reception room was Master Cowan, a sobbing Mistress Cowan in his arms, her face covered with a handkerchief, and six other soldiers waiting with arms at the ready.

'I just don't understand why poor Agnes had to die!' Mistress Cowan wailed stiffly, attempting to use acting skills she only wished she possessed. 'S-She was o-our best s-servant. Why w-would you do such a thing? W-Weren't we good masters to you?' She continued sobbing loudly with dry eyes.

'Farrah, I am ashamed that I let you into my home, that I let you sleep under my roof,' Master Cowan interrupted, pulling his wife close in a pathetic addition to her terrible performance. 'For your crime against humanity and other races alike, you are sentenced to the mines to serve out the rest of your life with the other murderers and barbarians. Take her away.' Lord Cowan waved the guards toward me, turning his face aside in mock disappointment.

The two guardsmen from before lifted me up and guided me away.

My body and soul were void of feeling. After seeing one of my protectors, one of my friends, dead, and being named as her murderer on top of everything else that had happened—DeeDee's death, and then the death of poor Miles, whose only crime was loving DeeDee. My parents, who only wanted to do what was right and suffered for it. And now Agnes, who wanted only to protect me, and that was her crime—It was the final straw. Fury, the likes of which I've never felt before, bubbled up inside me, and I let it fill every crack and crevice of my being.

As we walked from the room, I noticed out of the corner of my eye one of the nails still stuck in the floor from last night. Like a bolt of lightning, I ran for it and yanked it out of the floorboard. Everyone, now shocked and threatened, began to fire upon me.

A searing hot white fire of energy and confidence flowed through me and in an instant a series of images flashed in front of me. It was as if I could see the future seconds before anything happened—and with a snap they disappeared. A wall of bullets came flying towards me, and as if instinct had finally kicked in, time seemed to stop, and the bullets slowed considerably to the point where I could actually see them and dodge them with ease and poise. I raced to the closest victim, grabbing the tall, snarling soldier's gun barrel and smacking him one, two, three times in the temple until he blacked out. The soldier next to him turned as quickly as he could, pointing the barrel towards the shadow-like fighter only to have his barrel snatched as well and twisted upwards until the exit point faced him. I yanked at the gun strapped around his neck, forcing him down, which allowed me to step on his head for leverage, jump off, and air-kick the oblivious soldier behind him straight in the cheek, knocking him out instantaneously. One of the younger soldiers tried to get the drop on me as he lunged to my back with a dagger in hand, but my surprising strength and speed was too much for him, and with one swift move I twirled around grabbed his wrist and sliced up through his neck with his help.

With the desire for a bloody vengeance, the wrinkled soldier with blonde hair charged at me, snarling. I tried to dart and distract his line of sight, but he was able to follow and I only managed to slash at his eye with the rusted nail, which burst like a pimple on impact. Another soldier managed to grab me from behind, but I slammed him against the adjacent wall, winding him, causing him to flop on the floor like a fish. Finally, there was a stumpy soldier, his face so red it looked like I stole his pot of gold. Without any defence, it was easy for me to jab him as deep as I could, right into the side of his fat, flabby neck.

I looked back at a disgruntled Lord Cowan and shocked Mistress Cowan that were being protected by the final two soldiers. I glared at the both of them, assuring them that their time would come, and that it would be slow and painful, and I would enjoy every bit of it. Noticing the Lord's jacket hanging on the coat hook by the door, I swiped it and swung it over my back. If anything good were to come out of this unfortunate experience, that would be it. With that, I bolted as fast as I could out the door and into the unknown.

***

Lucius was the first thing that popped into my mind whilst I ran for my life. However, trying to remember how to get back to Lucius's place, which I'd only been to once, was one thing, but doing it whilst being chased by blood-thirsty soldiers was another thing entirely. I knew that I needed to stick to the shadows—a place where only the dark, dangerous creatures hid.

As I ran along the mouldy wooden buildings, I began to recall the direction I headed last time towards the fighting ring. I darted through the alleys, flinching at every unfamiliar noise. I had to hurry, but it felt like danger was lurking all around me.

Finally arriving at the bar, I could see the welcoming light pouring from the windows that held the drunken men that sang and hollered from their second home. Last time I came to this place, I didn't take into account the structure's subtle exterior beauty— the second-story balcony protruding from the front, relying on steady pillars of wood to keep it from sliding off. A steeply pitched roof with a large front-facing gable crossing the second story of the building and twin narrow and tall oriental windows on either side. And a decorative crossbar using thick timber wood that also framed every other edge of the building. Cables and wires ran towards it as they did many of the other buildings that lined this extremely humble district. Charming, yes, but seemingly a little rundown from the past years. A decent sized sign swung above the door named the favourable place: The Drunken Willow.

Navigating through the building was slightly difficult, since none of the intoxicated bodies seemed to care for anybody else. Passing through, I excused myself in a softened, timid voice so as not to trigger any sort of fight if I shoved too hard or knocked anyone over. I weaved in and out of the drunk, happy groups of men clinging to each other as they sang along to the music being played poorly, each instrument playing with different ways— either too harshly, or too softly—and one musician didn't seem to even care about what song they were playing. Eventually I made my way to the bar, where I figured I could ask the bartender if he knew Lucius.

'Excuse me, sir!' I called as loud as I dared without grabbing anyone else's attention.

No answer; it seemed that the spirited noises around us drowned my soft voice out.

'Hello? Excuse me!' I shouted above the ruckus and boisterous laughter.

Again, nothing. I went closer towards him so that we were face to face and he could see me trying to get his attention.

'Bartender!' I yelled.

Finally, I got him to notice me.

He was a large man with tan skin and tiny silver scars that ran in different directions up and down his arms. A ring of stubble surrounded his slim, almost non-existent lips, and a thin veil of black hair fell on top of his head that showed his scalp clearly. His dark emerald eyes caught sight of me, almost lying on top of the beer-soaked bench he worked behind.

'What can I do for you, miss?' he asked, as he wiped clean a beer mug with a dirty towel.

'I was just wondering if you knew where Lucius lived,' I inquired, still in a high voice so that he could hear me over the noise.

'Lucius, Lucius… Sorry, I don't recall anyone by that name. Could you describe him?' he asked with a booming voice, naturally loud enough to hear over everything else.

'Um… Let's see… He's about this tall, muscular, caramel skin— oh, and he has an echobriome arm!' I answered hopefully.

'I'm sorry, love, I don't recall someone like that,' he answered, shrugging his shoulders.

'Oh, come on, dad! He comes in almost every second day and buys at least a keg of beer before his fight!'

I turned to see a young woman with flaming red hair slip in and out of the slumped-over bodies, holding up two trays of empty mugs as she made her way to the bar. She wore a dirty pale-blue dress and brown apron. Her unruly hair was barely contained by a knotted string, allowing you to see her dark green eyes—the same as her father's, but her pale skin and brilliant red hair must have come from her mother.

Resting the trays down and putting the mugs behind her to be washed, she continued.

'That's Keela's husband; she helps around here sometimes when it's not too full. These drunk arms try to feel her up because of her appeal. Hell, I would too, if I were a lesbian.'

Her strong, confident demeanour impressed me and even started to give me energy.

'Why do you want to know where they live? If you don't mind me asking?' Her curiosity piqued, as well as her quizzical brow.

'We're friends from way back. I just got here, and they said if ever I'm in town to visit. Only thing is, they didn't give me a map or even an address.' I joked, hiding the truth behind my smile.

'Oh, why didn't you say so?' She smiled back and slapped me

on the back with one of her strong beer-carrying arms, right onto my wounds. It took everything within me not to scream out in pain. I bit my tongue and dug my nails into my palms as the stinging died down.

'They don't live too far from here. Give me a minute and I'll draw you a map. I'm Sylvie, by the way, and this is my dad, Frank.' She continued speaking as she zoomed around like a bullet, waving her hands up to show her customers she could see them holding their empty jugs.

'I'm Farrah—it's nice to meet you,' I said as quickly as I could, trying not to impose on their business.

'Nice to meet you too, Farrah. You know you shouldn't be walking around this area at night,' she continued, and was still, to my amazement, working at lightning speed. By the third interruption of our conversation, she let out an annoyed huff, 'Dad? Has Tiery arrived yet?'

'No, she was supposed to be here four hours ago before the night rush. I bet you anything she's back in those bloody cells again,' he answered, matching her annoyed tone, rubbing the dirty towel around a drenched mug harsher than before.

'You guys know Tiery?' I joined in, honestly amazed by them even saying her name.

'Yeah. She lives here from time to time in exchange for working. That is, when she's not getting herself in trouble and thrown into prison. We tried taking her under our wing after her aunt passed away. Her mother had left her and she had no place left to go like many of these kids you see on the street. She wasn't born to be a street rat, if you know what I mean.' Sylvie explained, lowering her tone solemnly.

'Wait, you're not an orphan like Tiery, are you? A theif?' Frank asked, lowering his voice so as not to alert the drunken patrons. His brows furrowed in agitation as his dark green eyes intensely looked at me, almost boring a hole in my head, waiting for my response.

'No! No! I'm no thief! I swear! I am just being wrongly accused of something and Lucius said if I needed protection then he would be there for me! That's all, I swear!' I frantically responded, waving my hands as I did so until his fearsome scowl slowly softened, leaving behind a slightly skeptical look.

'Soldiers aren't after you, are they?' he continued; a singular brow raised as he gave me the side look.

If only he knew.

'It's all right if they are, we won't rat you out. We take pride in taking care of those who stand up to the Man,' Sylvie said proudly, showing off her perfect white teeth with her grin.

I smiled awkwardly, unsure of how much I should reveal.

'Let us know if you need work or a place to stay. You're welcome here anytime, Farrah,' Sylvie offered with a serious face as she handed plates of bread and bowls of stew to the customers next to me.

'As long as you pay rent,' Frank added on, his serious look remaining.

'You hungry?' Sylvie asked.

'I don't have any money,' I replied honestly as my stomach growled as loud as it could.

'You'll have to owe us. Besides, you don't want to miss out on my split pea and ham stew,' she added. Her father grumbled away, disagreeing on the offer.

She elbowed him to stop and pushed past him, giving him a stern look as she got a plate ready.

Sitting there in the crowded room of beefy strangers, I felt vulnerable open to attack. Hate-filled eyes surrounded me, as if news had already spread. The fake news that had painted a target on my back so that the soldiers could run from house to house, building to building, raiding every crack and crevice to capture me. Anxiety and nerves rose higher and higher, and my leg began to shake, and in turn my fingers drummed the table in the same panicked rhythm. Sylvie plonked down the bowl of soup and a plate of bread, knocking me back into reality.

'You all right, love?' she asked, concern in her eyes.

'Yes, I'm fine. Sorry, I'm just a bit tired,' I lied.

'Well, don't worry. Once you've finished with your meal, I'll have the map ready for you to take and you can be on your way,' she said with a warm smile as she scrubbed a dirty mug.

Slurping away at the thick stew, I could feel the warmth of its heat spread throughout my body, making me more calm and full. The bread, although stale and crunchy, filled me even more, and dipping it into the stew made it all come together in a magnificent symphony of taste.

Scraping away the very last of the stew, I noticed a piece of paper slide into view with lines and names.

The map.

Looking up, I meet Sylvie's friendly gaze.

'I told you it was good, didn't I!' she said as she commented on her own cooking.

I couldn't answer as my mouth was still full with the last bite I could scrape out, so I only nodded in response, making her giggle.

'Here's the map I promised you. It will get you where you need to go. Just turn left as you get outside and follow the directions and you'll be fine.'

As she picked up the empty bowl and plate, I stood, taking the map with me.

'Thank you so much for the dinner and the directions. And, well, everything,' I said with deep gratitude, reaching to shake her hand. She swatted it away and pulled me in for a big hug.

'Don't be silly, I should be the one thanking you. Every night is the same old thing; drunk men trying to get at me, or some idiots starting a fight and me and dad having to chuck them out. You made tonight more bearable. I hope I get to see you again,' she said, giving me another toothy smile and a final hug.

Now, with a full belly and more confidence in which direction to take, I left the bar—still sticking to the shadows for safety. My eyes were glued to the map and I was second-guessing myself with every turn I took, but I eventually arrived at a familiar door.

After three sharp knocks, the wooden door creaked open, and I was pleased to see a friendly face; Keela.

'What are you doing here at this hour? What happened?' her eyes widened in surprise but her mouth was smiling in delight.

'Who is it, Keela?' Lucius's voice came from upstairs, and his footsteps quickly followed suit as he stomped down the carved wooden staircase. When he reached the doorway, he looked genuinely surprised. Resting his arm on his wife's shoulder, he asked, 'Farrah, what are you doing here?'

'I'm sorry. I didn't know where else to go,' I answered, exasperated.

'Where's Agnes?' Lucius asked, his voice holding a hint of concern.

'She's dead. They killed her. I woke with her next to me, the both of us covered in blood. I was holding a knife,' I answered, whilst forcing my way into the warm fire-lit room. 'I didn't do it, Lucius. You have to believe me. They're framing me for her murder. Soldiers are out looking for me. I didn't have anywhere else to go.' All of this emotion started bubbling up—anxiety, sadness, rage, everything—until I couldn't hold it in any longer. My chest seized and the thought of breathing escaped me, my mind raced a mile a minute, making my hands flutter like trapped birds. Keela was right behind me.

'It's all right, dear, just calm down; here, sit. Lucius, get a cup of water.' She grabbed me before I collapsed, aiming me at one of the stools.

'Just breathe… in and out.' She rubbed my arms comfortingly, keeping her eye contact with me.

All I could do was focus on her large, green eyes. They seemed to glow from the fire. Nothing else mattered, apart from breathing rhythmically—in and out, slowly—to calm my heart and relax my chest. She smiled.

Noticing the alarmingly large patch of dark reds that covered the back of my shirt as she carefully took my jacket off, her body stiffened in shock as she stared at the enormous amount of fresh blood that absorbed the dry patches that were left behind.

'Keela...? What is it?' Lucius looked disturbed by her silence.

Not a sound from the both of them could be heard as they caught sight of the amount of fresh blood that seeped from my wounds.

'Farrah… Why didn't you say anything?' Lucius growled. 'Keela… prepare the poultice. I'll grab some bandages and a clean shirt.' Lucius ordered, as his wife snapped herself out of it and became more alert. The both of them rushed around like headless chooks, Lucius pulling the table away for more space and laid a hessian blanket down, then a large bowl of warm water with an old cloth draped over the edge. Grabbing my arm, Lucius forcefully laid me down as if I were unconscious and tore the back of my bloodied shirt open. The large dried patches of blood caked cloth that stuck, tore away at the fresh raw wounds that were carved into my back. In doing so, a sharp pain began causing my back to burn and twinge badly enough for my eyes to well up. Folding my arms, I stuck my head in, ashamed of the tears and readied myself for them to cleanse the nasty oozing gouges that ranged in size and depth across my back.

As Keela gently wiped and dabbed away at the dried blood, Lucius sat close by me anxiously, hunched over with his hand on my shoulder for comfort. It was an odd feeling to experience, support and kindness from others was a new thing, a strange yet warm feeling of true joy in knowing that there were people who truly cared for me. Not because it was their mission or duty, but because they needed to for the sake of someone they deeply loved. Without realizing it, I began to moan and weep aloud, causing

Lucius to firmly grip onto my shoulder and Keela to stop what she was doing.

'What's wrong Farrah? I'm not hurting you too much, am I?' she asked worriedly.

'No… It's not that… I just don't remember feeling like this before… Feeling safe and protected… I like it.' I answered through the sniffling and tears that blurred my vision.

They both smiled back with love in their eyes.

'I'm almost done. I just have to put the bandages on and you can put a new clean shirt on,' she soothed.

'Thank you,' I whispered.

'There you go. Have a drink of my freshly brewed tea. Drink all of it. It will help numb the pain.' She kept rubbing my arms as she handed me the mug. 'That's it. You're staying with us, Farrah. There is no need to be afraid. You're safe now.' She added on in a motherly tone.

Lucius made a sound like he was clearing his throat, to which Keela responded with a death glare.

'What is it?' I asked.

'Nothing… Let's just hope that Cowan has forgotten about our connection. If not, we're all fucked,' he said, sharing his concern. Keela stood, walked over to him and slapped him on the arm.

'Don't mind him, Farrah. He worries about nothing. You're tired. I'll make the spare room up and you can sleep here for the night. We'll figure out what to do tomorrow,' she said, ending the conversation.

That night sleep eluded me; every time I closed my eyes, memories—terrible memories—crept out of the darkness. DeeDee, lifeless and bloody; Miles heartbroken and stiff on the cross beside me; Agnes slaughtered like a lamb; and Francis screaming in pain for the loss of his only family. As I tossed and turned, thrashing my head to shake the dark thoughts out, I could hear arguing voices beyond the wall. Recognizing the voices of Keela and Lucius, I could barely distinguish what they were arguing about, but instinct told me that I didn't need to, I knew exactly what they were saying.

***

Morning, and no noise could be heard from outside, not even footsteps or children's laughter. Something was wrong.

I found Lucius standing by the door, armed and ready, thinking just as I had that something bad was about to happen. Armed with an axe in one hand and an arm shaped like a large hammer in the other, he was prepared for anything.

Utter silence lay outside. Within it, the feeling of a dangerous presence lurked, ready to strike at the most opportune moment.

I tried to step ever so lightly to get to the knife that lay on the kitchen table, but Lucius struck a warning glare as if to say 'don't move'. I waved him off and kept going. Just as I reached the knife, a floorboard let out a sharp creak. Within seconds, men were smashing through the windows and doors both upstairs and down, pouring in from outside. The warriors surrounded us with their weapons.

'Surrender, Farrah. Or we'll kill your friend,' the leader spoke. He was a captain; I knew this because instead of green, he wore an ash-grey uniform. There was a black leather strip around his arm with a Medal of Honor pinned to it and a cap of grey trimmed with black. His grey-blue eyes narrowed at me and Lucius, forming daggers, and he scowled.

Before I could do anything, Lucius began to fight against them, quickly darting right and left, aiming his terrifying weapons at their targets with deadly accuracy.

'Lucius, stop!' Keela shouted as she raced to the top of the stairs from the room she was hiding in. All the guns pointed at her. Three accurate shots fired, and she dropped, tumbling down the stairs into a heap at the foot of the staircase.

All of us stood in silence, shocked.

'No…' Lucius ran forward, his echobriome arm automatically morphing back into its normal state, scooping her up to check if she was still alive. He cuddled her close, trying to shake her awake. His hands covered the wounds that spurted out fountains of blood that quickly pooled at his feet. As he muttered away, rocking her, the soldiers stepped in.

'Arrest them,' the captain commanded.

Two soldiers took my arms as I watched on, tears rolling down my face and mouth slightly ajar.

Not another one.

Instead of risking tearing them apart, the soldiers prepared something and jabbed it into Lucius's neck, knocking him out almost immediately.

***

I was once again sitting in a smelly, dank, dim cell, crowded with other miserable folk like me. I didn't know what my future held or what plans Lord Cowan had for me, but I knew it would be something despicable.

'Farrah?' a muffled voice called out from behind the depressed crowd in front of me; it was almost lost beneath the murmurings that echoed off the wet walls.

I heard something shuffling closer, moving the other dying bodies out of the way. It was my old cell mate from last time, Tiery.

She was somehow dirtier than before, as if she'd been sleeping in the mud and shit outside.

'It's so good to see you again!' she yelled, causing every other person to cover their ears and face us with disgruntled looks.

'Yes, you too,' I replied, holding my breath as she went in for a hug—one I hoped would be brief.

'Although I didn't expect to see you in a place like this again. How did you end up here, anyway?' she asked, slumping down beside me.

'I could ask you the same thing,' I retorted, with a slight jerk of the chin and side look.

'You know, same old, same old. This time they decided they had enough of me. So the took me here. Like everyone else they get sick of.' She answers vaguely, with a snap at each word and arch of her nostrils.

'It's a long story,' I answered, and she gave me a disappointed look.

'What about our friend over there?' she asked, nodding to the large lump of unconscious Lucius in the corner with his back turned.

'That's a long story, too… What is this place, anyway? I noticed it took us longer to get here than it did the prison,' I said, not wanting to get into the depressing details.

'It's because this is the cell for transportation. To the mines,' she answered more softly this time, looking down with a fading smile.

'The mines?' I prodded.

'The mines of Buson. It's the place where they put the criminals they are fed up with and don't know what to do with; the dark heart of Buson,' she said, gravely. 'That is where we are going tomorrow. And that is where we will be until we die.'

Chapter 15

In the early hours of the morning, the iron door that kept us locked up in the dank, smelly hole screeched open. A soldier holding a folded pile of grey clothing stood by, casting a silhouette in front of the golden rays of the sun. His shadow dominated the back of the rock wall.

'Get these on. You got five minutes. If you're not dressed, we'll drag you out naked,' his voice warned as we all covered our sensitive eyes to glance in his general direction. He tossed the nicely folded clothes into the middle of the room and slammed the door again. Everyone scrambled to the pile, desperate not to be humiliated in public. Even Tiery charged forward, pushing her way into the crowd and diving head-first into the swarm. After a lot of bear-hugging and biting, she scrambled out, a bundle tucked under her arm.

'Here, I managed to get you a pair of clothes too,' she panted, handing me a pair of grey pants and a shirt.

'Looks like you also managed to get yourself a cut lip,' I answered sarcastically whilst taking the offer she generously snatched for me.

'Ha, yeah. You get a lot of those when you're fighting for survival,' she answered, then laughed at my concerned expression.

'Do we have to get dressed here? In front of everyone? I asked. Really not wanting to.

'Yeah but don't worry, I know a trick, so that no one see's anything.' Good, my breathing smoothed.

'What about Lucius?' I asked, looking over at the large body who hadn't moved the whole time.

'I didn't see any in his size. Besides, he doesn't seem to care, anyway,' she answered, concentrating on taking her smelly, stained clothing off. It was at that point something strange caught my eye—at the base of her spine, there was a stump with a scorch mark. I distantly recalled something that Ms. T said when she spoke about her tail.

'Only people in my family have tails. That is the way our genes have been written ever since the Great War. I had to take that away from my daughter when she was born, to save her.'

'Huh,' slipped out of my mouth.

'What?' Tiery asked as she rushed to get dressed. She gave me a cheeky wink. 'You finally figured out you're into girls?' I laughed. 'No, not that. I was just thinking.'

'Well, you'll have to do that later. Time is almost up and you haven't put your shirt on yet,' she reminded me, giving me a warning look.

Fast as a bullet, I shot my hands through the sleeves and slipped my head quickly through the correct hole.

Just as I had finished, the door sprang open once again, welcoming a bolt of brilliant golden light into the ill-lit room.

'Time's up!' he declared loudly, whilst pointing his gun toward all of us.

One by one we lined up without argument, waiting patiently whilst four other soldiers came in. Two held a set of chains linked together and the other pair, as a show of extra strength, walked in with guns.

Lucius still laid on the floor, which was noticed by one of the armed soldiers. He got his partner's attention and nodded in Lucius's general direction, for which his partner just shrugged. One strolled over to the lump of unconscious man, and began to poke at him with the butt of his weapon.

'I think the captain shot him up with too much of that stuff,' he answered as he warily continued to prod at the poor man.

The man still standing at the foot of the door rolled his eyes and gave out a sigh, clearly annoyed.

'All right, we'll have to carry him in last. Leave him there till the others are in,' he commanded, waving his hand to step away and leave Lucius be.

We were paired off in four groups of six and chained together at the ankles and wrists for transportation. They forcefully guided us with their weapons raised, pushing us to move out the door in unison. The cold shackles and chilling, depressing echoes of chains clashing together sounded like ringing bells, signaling the disappearance of what little freedom we once had.

We walked down the hall, of which a long windowless wall of bars ran across, until we were faced with an open cage perched atop a transport vehicle. Three of the same green rusted trucks exactly like the one that transported me to Buson sat alongside it, each mounted with tall, barred cages on their backs. All of them were large enough to nicely fit six exiled prisoners to their destination.

We filed in two by two; myself and Tiery were beside each other at the front of the first truck. We were forced to stand in a certain position so that a thick silver loop sat by our feet between us.

One of the younger soldiers, the smallest of them all, managed to squeeze and weave himself in and out of the neat lines of smelly, dirty prisoners. He locked us onto the base of the cage for safe measure.

As the trucks switched positions to load the rest of the prisoners, I noticed the two soldiers from before talking off to the side. One was rubbing the back of his neck, as if he were unsure of a plan the other was explaining to him. Perhaps about their final unconscious prisoner—the most dangerous and volatile of us all—Lucius.

The trucks were now full and ready for delivery, everyone trapped and waiting. All of us were standing, confused, murmurs floating in and out of each of the trucks until the sound of a fifth truck came out. It reversed into the same position as the others, facing the open gates to the prison. Two large soldiers emerged, hauling my friend out with gritted teeth and pulsing arm veins as they struggled to do so, shuffling as fast as they could to the cage. Once inside, they slammed his body down with great relief and satisfaction. This time, they used large chains to entrap him further, wrapping them over his body and locking them onto the steel loops on the floor.

With all slaves on board for transit, we set off. A convoy of hulking trucks slowly made their way out of the city of Buson. The dawn sun made the wooden houses and steel roofs shine in a bevy of yellows, oranges, and golden browns. It was almost beautiful. Lining the streets were a parade of commoners forming a standing processional, each wearing grey as though they were in uniform. All watched on, hands to their front, with solemn looks in the knowledge of where their people were going. They say if you are condemned to the mines, then you are condemned to a fate worse than death. None of us even deserved to be thrown in jail. Many of the slaves that were convicted were mere thieves stealing for their families, or 'male prostitutes, who had no choice but to do what they needed to survive.

'How far is this place?' I asked Tiery, mostly to distract myself.

'Dunno,' she answered with a shrug.

She seemed to be less sad and hopeless than the others. Perhaps she actually wanted to leave the city, or maybe she had a plan in mind of escape.

We spoke no further as we made our way out of the gates and turned down a neighbouring valley, slimmer and more direct than the others. It looked as if it had more of a purpose as it led us to the mines and our inevitable future.

Just above the roaring sounds of the truck convoy's engines, I could hear the leading one-manned motorcycle, and I knew we were being tailed by one just like it—meaning even if we were able to escape the cages, there was no way we would all escape the motorbike in the narrow pathway.

Subsumed by the haunting noises that bounced off the chasm walls, a scream couldn't be heard, even if it came from your own lips.

Further and further into the densely walled unknown we went— it seemed as if we were travelling forever and going nowhere at the same time. At one point I feared I would never be able to hear anything again, aside from the overpowering metallic noises that permeated my ears and rattled my brain. Up ahead, a blue light could be seen; a new opening to the maze of rock and stone. We'd finally arrived. Slight elation rose within me, only to be crushed by the knowledge of why the noise had stopped. The convoy of trucks fanned out, allowing all the new workers to see their new home. The ground sunk, and up ahead were five large holes of blackness that sat proudly in the walls. They were different sizes and heights, with workers of different species pouring in and out under the lash of a whip. Tunnels bore into the supposedly impenetrable white and yellow stone, lined with massive metal halves welded together into giant circles once inside the dark terrain, clearly developed by a genius who thought of magnification and electronic transportation could be combined for efficiency. Freshly dug trenches on the base of the quarry led straight to large buildings running along part of the edge. The control centre for the cylindrical capsules used to help haul large boulders too big for the slaves to carry themselves emerging from deep within the tunnels the brave miners carved out.

Campsites were scattered all around. An odd rotting stench stung my nostrils, causing me to cringe. It was like rotting roast meat with a hint of a sickeningly sweet smell, sort of like a cheap perfume a 'woman of the streets' would wear, but worse. I was barely keeping myself from gagging outright. That was until I heard the horrific gurgling sound from two slaves away as they began hurling up as much as he could, inducing everyone's gag reflexes—even some of the guards couldn't control it. When I was able to settle my gut again, I scoped around, and my eye caught sight of a pit set away from everything else, which everyone seemed to avoid. That was where the smell was coming from.

'Welcome to paradise!' a pot-bellied, ape-like man yelled, his sarcasm eliciting laughs from the guards. His arms opened as he swung wide the door to our cage, pushing in a scrawny boy who scrambled for the keys as he stumbled between us.

We were all released from the cages, but most of us were still shocked at the view, gawking and speechless at the inhuman environment. In my whole life, I never could have imagined such a place as this.

Surrounded by guards and armed men prepared for an escape attempt, we stood ready and waiting for whatever came next.

Looking out at the sad surroundings before us, I couldn't help but notice great beasts of two classes were also enslaved here. One I knew wasn't native to this land, a fantastic looking creature called an Icelandic malbrole. It was a large creature with rough dry skin, large robust body, with a large flat bone plate in place of a horn, tiny eyes and ears atop a large oversized head, a sloped back with stumpy back legs and slightly larger front ones. They're harmless if unprovoked and mostly deaf due to the fact that they headbutt rocks and large boulders to get to their food. Five of them were chained to pikes with only six feet of iron chain. Placed before them were flat carts with boulders chained down to keep them in place.

The other creature I knew all too well. The leviathan helminth, a gigantic worm-like creature that has the ability to burrow deep into mountains. From my vantage point, I could only see one, its swollen body moving slowly up the ridge opposite us and towards a newly formed cave entrance. Atop him sat his enforcer, a guardsman holding a large, sharpened stick used to encourage the poor creature to keep working even when it was tired or sick. Impressive scars covered the poor thing's body, giving me the sense that it had been here a very long time.

The pot-bellied ape-man stood before us on a small crate that screeched under his weight.

'You were brought here because you are the scum of the city. The inbred shit no one wants. When they don't know what to do with vermin like you, they send you to me,' he said, rubbing his hands together proudly. His beady little eyes glared at his new victims.

'You can call me King Gunnar. This is my kingdom and I am the ruler!' He gestured proudly to his domain as his soldiers cheered and waved their weapons above their heads.

Whilst looking around, he noticed Lucius still unconscious in his cage.

'Why is he still in his cage?' Gunnar asked, pointing with one of his sausage fingers.

The soldiers that came with us just looked at each other, waiting for anyone else but themselves to respond.

'He's still asleep. We didn't know what to do,' one of them answered nervously.

The "king" growled and waved his hand at two of his own men, both holding scary-looking metal rods with prongs on the end.

Taking their places, both of them quickly stuck their weapons in and jabbed Lucius, giving him an electric shock to wake him— and wake him they did. Startled and angry as ever, he snapped the chains tying him down like twigs. He then rose, growling and drooling like an animal prepared to strike.

'Wow! This one's a keeper! He'll be handy, won't he boys!' Another rowdy roar of applause followed. Everyone watched in mixed emotion as Lucius was tied and dragged out of the cage like an angry beast, frothing at the mouth.

'Now that everyone is with us, you're going to make your way towards the mine. My right-hand man will assign jobs to the correct people. From there, your captains will take you to your assignments. We are so happy to have you,' Gunnar finished, rubbing his meaty hands together. He met my gaze with a menacing, evil smile; one I was all too familiar with.

Slowly and cautiously making our way down the ridge, Tiery grabbed my hand, perhaps for comfort or support; either way, it felt nice to know I wasn't the only one that felt uneasy in this environment.

Large crosses were scattered to the right of us—the same crosses that Miles and I were on. An elderly man hung from one of them, his body stripped of clothing and blood-stained skin baking in the hot rays of the morning sun. He hung limp and frail, unmoving; one would think him dead if his chest weren't rising up and down. The shadows of the wooden structures loomed over us almost hauntingly, letting us know that that was the only way out of here. Whips cracked and screams of pain echoed as the leather and steel slashed at the poor worker's backs, overseers barking orders at the weak and wounded.

There weren't only humans here; there were some Garudans too. Their tails were chopped off and their skin was paler than the usual vibrant crimson, as if they'd been drained of hope. There were also a few Ravagers, which were humans who had reverted into their more animalistic, savage side—similar to a Griever, yet still having a soul, cracked and cooked skin as hard as rock formed as their armour, and barely a piece of clothing to be found, with dog collars to keep them tamed and in check.

Three long wooden tables lined the entranceway of each of the mines. A line of workers, mainly women, worked away, passing a rock down the line. I couldn't guess why, but I was sure I'd find out.

Before us stood a tall, muscular man, his torn shirt revealing his large boulder-shaped arms covered in a coating of his own black hair, all the way down to his sausage fingertips. A soggy cigar hung outside his non-visible lips that were concealed by his well-maintained blonde mustache that combined with his naturally black beard—an odd combination, but who's to judge. If anyone laughed or said anything the wrong way, they would surely be disposed of quickly.

'My name is Captain Kovak… If you have any questions or complaints about our lovely facilities my men have generously made for you, you can come to me. I am sure we can find something else to your liking… Isn't that right, Tommy my boy!' He shouted in the direction of the man barely hanging onto dear life on the cross, causing the guards and soldiers to guffaw and cackle with an almighty roar, some of them holding their sides as they did so.

'Now put your hand up when you hear your name and you'll find out which area you will be working in,' Kovak said as he opened a paper, placing old reading glasses just on the top of his lump of a nose.

As he read aloud, one by one, the people I traveled with slowly put their hands up and were taken away in different directions.

Lucius was taken to the largest mine and had a large basket strapped to his back. The last thing I saw was him looking back with an empty stare and turning his back to me. There I was, tears welling in my eyes, not falling, just resting at the ridge of my lids, thinking I would never see my friend again. And I knew that it was my fault that he was here with me, my fault that his wife was dead.

Next, Tiery. Once her name was called, her grip on my hand tightened with fear and she looked at me with big, worried eyes.

'Tiery!' Kovak repeated in anger, holding a hand on one of his muffin tops.

She didn't respond, but continued to look at me as if she were asking me to do something. All I could do was look back at her and squeeze her hand to reassure her everything would be okay. Wrenching myself out of her tight grasp, all I could do was comfort her and try to assure her everything would be okay.

She understood. Then, slowly, she raised her hand.

'Here. Sorry, I wasn't listening,' she lied and made her way to her captain, who took her up a path to one of the smaller mines.

Finally, it was my turn.

'Farrah—rock sorting and eratice handling,' he called out, more agitated now thanks to Tiery's fear.

Making my way past the remaining slaves, I was met with a woman as pale as a Kraznian, with snow-white hair tied back with a piece of dark grey cloth. Her figure was stick-like, further exaggerated by the homemade dress she wore with torn holes for her arms and head. It dropped to the floor, erasing her figure, giving the illusion of a body wasting away.

Her pale blue eyes looked straight through me as if I weren't there.

'Gilfy,' she said, introducing herself coldly.

She turned and walked away, not allowing me to introduce myself, expecting me to follow. I did, but kept my distance.

We walked until we reached the tables lined out in front of the mine. She stopped and pointed to the empty spot between her and an elderly woman with weathered skin and a hunched back that made her half the size of me. Her skeleton-like fingers felt around through the many rocks in front of her, her eyes distant.

She must be blind.

'This is the rock-sorting station,' Gilfy said nonchalantly.

'Your job is to sort out the regular rocks from the gems and achrolite. If you don't know how, just remember achrolite is hotter than regular rocks because it's a natural explosive. Once you have distinguished one from the other, place the achrolite rock in the bowl next to you and the gems in the basket by your feet. Place the regular ones in the mine cart in front of you,' she instructed, pointing this way and that, not really showing any sort of eye contact.

A small iron-barred cage sat by her on the table studded with iron bolts, and a spine-chilling noise of clicking and low, lispy trills came from inside.

'What's in there?' I asked nervously, not entirely sure if I really wanted to know.

Without answering, Gilfy opened the small, latched door with a squeeze. Thick black legs slowly and hesitantly came out. Gilfy offered her hand and the creepy-looking creature accepted it. The giant insect was a thing of nightmares; eight legs, large pinchers like a scorpion and two smaller ones atop its mouth, beady little red eyes, and a chunky scorpion-like tail. The creature sat calmly on her palm as if it were a statue.

'What is that thing?' I politely asked, trying to keep my face straight and not cringe.

'It's called an eratice bug. It's what we use to clean the sediment off of the achrolite. It's too dangerous to do it by hand, so we have these creatures to do it for us. In turn, they get the nutrients in the sediment and the crust encasing the achrolite. They turn some of it into a sort of milk and use it in defence if they feel threatened,' she explained, smiling away like a proud mother at the disgusting little creature sitting in her palm.

'Only more experienced people are allowed to handle these creatures, though. They are still wild and unpredictable. You must treat them with care and respect, and they will do the same.' She gingerly placed the little beast back into its tiny cage. 'Do you understand your tasks?' she asked as she began working away.

I simply nodded and began sorting.

I can't believe this is my life now.

***

As the sun slowly sank into the sandy ridges that bordered our cage, the guards and overseer, Gunnar, retired to their common tent to let off steam and drink, taking away whoever they desired to keep them company.

The rest of us were herded back into the mines like sheep by the unlucky, ill-tempered guards who drew the short straw of night watchmen. My hands were blistered and burned from the heat of the achrolite rocks and soothing them in a bucket of dirty water was just what I needed to end the dull, painful day.

'Hey,' a drained, yet familiar, voice whispered as its owner slumped down on me.

Tiery was grey, covered in dirt and dust. Her once-beautiful blonde hair was now dirty and speckled with black gunk, and bags hung under her tired eyes. She was practically falling asleep on top of me.

'How was your day?' I asked, trying to keep her awake.

This was answered with silence, followed by a sad sigh.

'I have to dig the mine… Can I get in on that?' she asked, pointing to the water, a glint of hope sparkled in her puppy eyes. Not waiting for a response, she waded her hands in. I couldn't help but notice the hundreds of bruises and cuts that riddled her hands and arms. They reached all the way up to her shoulders, both of which shook from exhaustion.

'I almost got magnetised and flattened by those damn tracks.' She took a giant gulp of my water, almost draining the entire thing.

The cool evening breeze gusted into the open pit and swirled around as if it were a living entity trapped by the same thing we were, giving our burnt and beaten bodies a delightful sense of relief as it raced around us until it gradually dissipated.

The line for the lovely smorgasbord of slop, gruel, and gunk had begun to form hesitantly. No one knew what that disgusting crap was made of, but there were some disturbing theories floating around. We had found ourselves one of the most favourable seats away from the cold evening breeze just under the lip of the cave, one that gave us a vantage point to see all the pathetic wonders of the bleak world we now lived in. The sad wandering slaves, the bored roaming guards who liked to pick which of the lovely women they would bed each and every night. The Malbroles stayed where they were forced to stay out in the cold, out of convenience to their masters, curled up as tight as they could to fend off the frigid night air against their newly opened wounds.

Lucius slumped over and, just as exhausted, had plonked his boulder basket down for the day. His eyes caught my line of sight. He didn't seem to care that I was watching him, nor did he want to come over and see me; he just slumped down and let his body go from the intense pressure it endured.

It was up to me to speak to him. I felt guilty about what happened and how he became trapped here with me.

Swallowing my nerves and putting one foot in front of the other, I casually walked over and sat right next to him—almost touching my arm to his. He didn't seem to care about what I had to say; he kept his eyes closed and head tilted up. He just sat in silence; as did I, waiting for the right time.

'I'm sorry about Keela,' I finally broke.

Nothing.

'I didn't mean to get you two into this mess,' I continued. A slight sigh crept out of him. 'I didn't know where else to go. I didn't know what else to do.' I kept making excuses, pressing him to respond. 'I swear I didn't know they knew our connection.' It was my final plea for forgiveness. He sighed.

'How could you? It had been so long since we last met. It was a slim chance of him remembering our connection and where I lived. It's… not your fault.' His last sentence seemed forced as he pushed it out. I knew he didn't fully believe it.

'Look, Farrah. I just need time to accept what has happened. I know my duty is to protect you. But… just give me time,' he replied again. This time, he lifted himself up and walked away from me, leaving me to sulk in his absence. A lump of sorrow formed in my throat, telling me I needed to cry instead forcing it back down.

'Don't worry, he'll come around,' Tiery said, having clearly listened in.

'Yeah, I know,' I politely responded, showing a glimpse of my true feelings about the whole situation.

'Wow! Are those Garudans?!' she asked with a soft, yet excited voice.

Following her line of sight, I noticed what she was gawking at. They were the same creatures from before; the ones with their tails cut off to a stump, long limbs, and sunburnt-coloured skin. They didn't seem to notice they were being watched, either. That, or they didn't care. We observed as they slinked away into the darkness of the mine, discreetly carrying sticks for light as they went.

'Let's follow them,' Tiery said, nudging me as she got up to follow suit, her eyes glued to where they disappeared into.

'No, wait! I don't think we should.' I tried to stop her, keeping my voice low so as not to attract the attention of the guards who were too far away to even care. She went anyway, and I let out a disagreeable growl of annoyance and followed her, hunched over, and walked almost like an animal. The both of us followed the light down the dark paths of the mine shafts, turning this way and that, squeezing through tight crevasses and sticking to the shadows until the light stopped and indistinct whispers began to emit from it. The Garudans were quietly speaking in their native tongue.

'I can't understand what they're saying,' Tiery whispered as soft as she could.

Leaning in further, I could just about make out a few words. And for some bizarre reason, I understood.

'I think they are speaking of rebellion,' I said, a little unsure.

'Wait, you can understand them?! How?!' Tiery shouted, alerting the Garudans to the spies nearby.

Before we could escape, one of the largest ones leapt out of the shadows and grabbed us with its large hands, forcefully escorting us towards the others, all gritting their teeth and growling at the interlopers.

It was clear who the leader was in this group of natives. He had braided black hair with trinkets weaved throughout, more scars along his body than the rest, and was showing a disgruntled dominative stance. A slash stretched across one of his eyes.

'What are you doing here?' he asked in English with a hint of a native accent that sharpened each word used.

Tiery was too afraid to speak, looking at the tall creatures with scared puppy eyes and shaking out of fear.

'I want to help you,' I answered, unable to stop the words coming out of my mouth. It was something I never thought I would be able to say; I'd always kept those thoughts locked up inside me, but rebellion had always been my dream. I never thought of actually doing it, not until now, which had not only shocked the Garudans, but also Tiery, who didn't really know what I was talking about.

I was second guessing myself until memories started flashing by. I tried to think of one thing that happened that I loved whilst being a slave and a maid. I couldn't think of anything, nothing at all; the only good things were the people I met in the same position as me. But then I watched them all taken away from me, and it was always violent.

'You can understand us?' one of the female Garudans spoke, asking me the same question everyone was probably thinking.

'I guess so?' I answered, just as shocked. I never knew I could understand different languages, especially Garudan. Barely any human can speak it. Only those trusted most by the Garudan tribes have the privilege to drink the sacred water of health and knowledge.

The leader stepped forward and sniffed me with intense curiosity.

'You have it in your blood,' he determined. 'One of your ancestors must have had some of the sacred water. Once one person of your line has drunk it, the powers the water gives you stay within your bloodline.' He concluded with a quizzical look and a raise of the brow ridge where an eyebrow would have been on a human.

'Not many have it in their blood, only a few were ever trusted outside of the tribes to be given the water. Are you sure, Marta?' one of the younger-looking Garudans asked.

'Marta? Isn't that an old family name?' I asked in an attempt to break the ice.

'Don't think you can speak to us as if familiars. Filthy Meatbag!' The female Garudan spoke. Her eyes were fierce and her nose wrinkled in disgust as she spat out the insult which was common for them to use against humans. She was smaller than the others, but her aggression seemed to compensate for it. A large black tattoo stretched along the left side of her rib cage. Slashes from a whip riddled her body, as did the others, but one of her cat-like ears seemed to be missing; only a jagged remnant remained, as if it had been torn off.

'Don't mind Firth. She has never had the best history when it comes to trusting humans,' Marta explained, placing his arm in front of her and creating a wall between us.

'Our names are handed down every generation. We are named after our fathers and mothers. It is the only tradition we have been able to keep,' a seemingly younger one answered, uncomfortable with our presence but trying his best anyway.

'My ancestor was named Marta,' the leader answered by severing his companion's electrifying glare, stepping forward.

'I see,' I responded in kind.

'You said you wanted to help earlier… I am denying your offer,' he said bluntly. I stared at him, confused. He then turned his back to face the stone wall of the illuminated cave.

'What are you talking about?' Tiery asked, panicked. She was beginning to hyperventilate as she asked, 'Farrah, what is he talking about? Help with what?'

'Why not? I want to help!' I yelled, not accepting the answer.

'You are a human,' the female Garudan replied in Marta's place. 'We cannot trust humans. Your kind are greedy and violent. You only want to help for your own benefit.'

My blood boiled as it had many times before when I felt the desire to fight.

'I have seen death! I have watched my family be torn apart. My friends were brutally tortured and killed. I have seen the darkness of which you speak in humans and, believe me, I am not one of those people! They are corrupt, dark beings that smile and laugh at others' pain and death. They are the real monsters, not us!' My emotions burst out as everything bubbled to the top. Tears of sadness and anger flooded down my face as I gritted and ground my teeth in rage. My speech seemed to shock everybody in the room as they witnessed my true feelings become unveiled; even Tiery stood in awe. I had to take a breath, trying to calm myself in order to speak again.

'We are not like them, Marta. We are like you. Downtrodden and treated like filth on the bottom of a boot. We want to join your rebellion. That is, if you'll have us?' I looked at Tiery. I didn't even think to ask if she would consider joining, I just assumed, considering her living conditions before.

'Right?' I asked her, waiting, hoping, for the correct response.

She simply smiled, her teeth shining in the dim light of the torches.

'Hell yeah,' she replied.

I smiled back at her, then turned to an intrigued Marta. Eventually he nodded, albeit sceptically, without thinking of his disagreeable companions.

'Now, tell me your plan,' I said, smiling a wide smile of complete and utter joy and happiness.

Chapter 16

It'd been about two months since Tiery and I spoke to the Garudans and been accepted into the fold, as it were. The plan was difficult and risky, but if timed correctly, had potential to succeed.

Convincing the other workers and slaves would be simple, but considering I wasn't really much of a 'people person', and the art of persuasion was more in Tiery's wheelhouse, I let her take the lead on that particular task. Eventually everyone, even the Kraznians, agreed to fight with us to free their people; although it was going to be difficult to keep the Kraznians and Garudans from fighting each other, considering their sordid past.

The riskier part came from ensuring everyone knew their roles, as well as successfully stashing potential weapons throughout the abandoned caves to take to the city. Gilfy was more than happy to milk the eratice bugs, then storing it for later use.

Tunneling our way back to the city was another matter entirely. If we dug by hand, by the time we reached the city everyone would have possibly died of old age. So while some of the achrolite miners toiled away, workers from other stations would slip in and transport rocks out in whatever they could carry. At the end of the day, we managed to fool our handlers into thinking the amount left over was the only amount the miners could find; when in fact we'd all been sneaking small portions in the abandoned tunnels.

When the miners set off explosions to go further into the mountain, a small team heading towards the city simultaneously set off their own explosions, the sound from the workers effectively masking our progress. At night, we would set up structural beams that prevented our tunnel from collapsing, as well as clear excess rubble. We had to take shifts, working all hours of the day, to free ourselves and our families. Freedom—once and for all.

'Gilfy, are you almost ready?' I whispered into her ear, calmly as if we were having a normal conversation.

'I think so. I just need a little bit more,' she replied softly, her eyes darting about nervous.

'Good.' I nodded, taking a sip of dirt-riddled water out of my waterskin. I casually strolled over to Tiery and Lucius, the latter of which hadn't spoken much to me since we got here. In fact, he hadn't really spoken at all, and acted as if he were avoiding me.

'Is everything on track?' I asked, sitting down beside Tiery. Lucius's demeanour noticeably changed and he slightly shifted away.

'Yes, Kole estimates that we are less than half a kilometre from the city's underground sewage system. Tomorrow night, we strike,' she confirmed, slightly uncomfortable with the weird tension between Lucius and I.

'Kole?' I asked, furrowing my brows, annoyed; both because she spoke to someone without telling me and also because I didn't even know who the hell she was talking about.

'Yeah, Kole. The tall dude that used to be the financier for the city. He was the one that stole money from the city's nobles and spread it to the city's people,' she said, expecting the dots to align for me. When she saw my lack of recognition, she went on.

'He's the skinny dude with the golden skin and the raven-coloured hair and the big burn mark on the side of his face—the reason why he's half blind. That was his punishment before he got thrown in here.' Her eye began twitching as she impatiently watched the cogs turn half-heartedly in my head. Finally, I got it.

'Oh! That guy. Yes, good choice. But next time talk to me or

Marta about it. We don't know if we can trust all of these workers; they could be spying for the others,' I reminded her.

'Why don't you trust my instincts?' she crossed her arms tightly, insulted.

'I do trust you. It's just, when you think a guy is cute or hot, you think he can be trustworthy. Remember Sid?' I replied calmly, attempting to get her to see reason.

Sid was a worker a little older than Tiery. They'd became close within the first week she was there. He was one of the most handsome of all the men and knew it. His thick bleach-blonde hair and charming smile and charisma had all the women falling over each other. Even a bashful Tiery, who caught the handsome prince charming's eye. When she wasn't with me, she was with him, and she told him everything—from her life, her dreams, and, unfortunately, our plans. Not long after, we were brought outside and whipped until our backs were numb, told to forget any hope of escape; all while Sid watched, as the overseer handed him a small bag of money, an unsurprised and stiff look upon his face as he looked a tearful Tiery straight in the eye.

'That's not cool, Farrah. You know I feel bad about that,' she retorted, then pouted, upset.

I felt bad almost instantly. I shouldn't have brought it up. She didn't know he was a spy, and hadn't thought he would rat us out. That day they'd ran out of crosses, so they had to lash some of us until they thought our plan had been erased from our minds. But it only made our desires for escape and vengeance even more powerful. And all of the workers who didn't want anything to do with it turned to our side, after they witnessed our will and strength and the power of belief in a brighter tomorrow for us all.

'You're right, I'm sorry,' I apologised honestly, timidly placing a hand on her shoulder. After a second, she placed her hand on mine, patting it softly.

'It's okay. I forgive you, always,' she smiled, pressing my stiffened hand against her cheek. My breathing shortened as she did. 'What else do we need?'

'We need someone to spike the guardsmen and their masters' drinks,' I explained.

'I'll do it,' Tiery volunteered, confidence and excitement flickering in her eyes.

'No,' I said, a little too quickly. 'We, uh, need someone smaller and lighter on their feet.'

'I'm the best you've got! I was raised on the streets—I stole for a living!' Her voice began to raise with her agitation.

I gave her a firm stare that left no room for argument.

'Fine.' She folded her arms and stuck out her bottom lip.

When the silence settled between the three of us, I found I didn't have the words for Lucius. I bit my lips and stared at him awkwardly, rocking back and forth on my heels. Anxiety was building to the point where I was losing focus, so I decided to come back later. As I turned, I was shoved in the shoulder, hard, by Tiery. When I looked down, she nodded toward Lucius, her eyes encouraging.

I swallowed my annoyed growl, but I knew in my heart she was right. Enough silence.

'You gonna join us?' I asked, not really knowing what to do or say.

'I swore to protect you, didn't I? It's my duty to be by your side... no matter what,' he answered begrudgingly, avoiding eye contact.

After a moment of silence so awkward that it even snapped Tiery out of her sulk, Lucius got up and walked away.

'He just needs time,' Tiery tried to comfort.

'Yeah, I know,' I replied, slightly depressed from my fifteenth attempt at talking to the wall.

'Now say I'm the best,' she demanded, still agitated by my earlier answer.

'Tiery, the first time we met you were caught stealing and I had to bail you out,' I scoffed.

Her face fell, shoulders drooping. I cleared my throat.

'But you can be one of the ones to throw the achrolite at the tents and guarding stations if you like,' I offered in an attempt to cheer her up.

'I'll have to think about it,' he replied, obviously still upset.

Having had enough of her childishness, I left her muttering to herself.

I didn't want her to be the one that poisoned the guards out of fear for her safety. I needed someone I had less of a connection to, someone with more skill at being quick and light-footed, someone they wouldn't suspect.

And that's when the idea struck—a kid! Those little miscreants were the best at not being noticed and could easily hide behind barrels and other things.

Pip would be perfect!

Pip was the smallest of all the kids; even in daylight, people would bump into her constantly. Even though she was older than most of the other kids, they still picked on her because of her size. The poor kid was a loner in her own generation.

The problem was finding her; since she was more of a recluse, once finished with her tasks she tended to slink off into the caves for the night.

'Adam!' I yelled across the quarry, unintentionally bringing a great deal of focus on us both, spiking my anxiety.

Luckily, I grabbed his attention as well, albeit a tad embarrassingly. His cheeks flushed as everyone's eyes turned to him, and he rubbed the nape of his neck as he skulked over.

Adam was an ex-soldier that was thrown away by Cowan because of his ideas of the laws; he believed they should be changed to benefit the people. This, as you may have guessed, irked the Lord, and Adam's family were stripped of their titles for raising a child with ideals. He was a young man with defined muscles and a strong core, taller than most and stronger thanks to his willpower. His skin was tanned from working in the brilliant rays of the beating sun—whose radiance paled in comparison to his golden hair; and his blue eyes were the colour of the sea just before a storm hit.

'Farrah, do you think you could have yelled a bit louder? I don't think the Lord heard you all the way in Buson,' he commented, sarcasm dripping off his tongue.

'Sarcasm doesn't become you. And I didn't think it would be so loud,' I admitted, blushing slightly.

'What is it?' he asked, barely moving his lips. He stepped closer, effectively blocking anyone from being able to make out what we were saying.

'You know Pip?' I enquired.

'Yeah, the little one. What about her?'

'We need her if the plan is to work. Keep tabs on her. Find out where she goes at night, but don't let her see you,' I instructed.

'Consider it done.' He nodded before setting out to find the final key to our freedom.

***

It was time. As the blanket of night fell, the stars shone down on us, wishing us luck. The guardsman and soldiers had slunk into their massive tent and began drinking their weight in beer as they always did, singing and laughing as loud as they could—giving us the perfect cover. A few envious night watchmen stood guard over their untrustworthy sneaky workers, muttering amongst themselves. The only other sound came from the Ravagers locked away in their cages, mauling their dinner as viciously and messily as they could.

Our scouts stood by, watching as our pawns mingled below to make the guardsmen think that everything was as it should be. The rest of us snuck by, waiting for the perfect time to strike.

Pip, the key component to our operation, was nervous but eager to show her bullies who was the bravest.

'Kole, how much further?' I asked in a hushed tone, eagerness and agitation coursing through my veins.

As much as I believed in us, I couldn't stop myself from thinking: If this doesn't go down well, then we're all dead.

'Just two and a half feet by my calculations. We are here,' he said, pointing at the stolen map of the city and mines. 'The city's sewage system should be right below us, which leads straight to the slums. If we hit the entrance point with the leftover achrolite, the mountain will connect to the sewage river and then we should have more than enough space for everyone to file out. But I think we should send a message to the houses close by and warn them what's coming. After all, they aren't our enemy.' His eyes met mine, steadfast, and I doubted I had much of a say in the matter.

'I agree,' I said with a nod. 'We'll have to use some of the kids to go into the river and enter the city to warn the people and then let us know that it's safe.'

He smiled, seeming relieved. 'Sounds like a plan.'

'Good, then it's time. Pip! Take this and splash a little drop into their mugs. Wait until Adam gives you the signal,' I instructed, confident in our plan. I crouched down to the pint-sized girl that was casually leaning against the cave wall, her arms crossed as she picked at a hangnail. Once she took the milk, I turned back to Adam.

'Adam, you and the others take care of the guards. Take Pip with you. Once they're out, let me know, and a group of us will come and finish the job,' I said, then dropped my voice so only he could hear, 'but make sure she doesn't see anything.' He glanced back at Pip before nodding.

'Why can't we just use the helminth or maybe a couple of those malbroles? Either one would make quick work of it and we don't have to worry about the guards or the caretakers of the mines,' Tiery whined, clearly anxious.

'Because if we use either one of those things then we'd alert not only the guardsmen on this side, but all the soldiers in Buson, and before we know it, we'll be captured and finally hanged because they'll have nowhere else to put us. Besides, don't you want to get your own slice of revenge on those scumbags?' I explained for the umpteenth time, giving her a cheeky smile as I handed her a small, very warm bag of deadly explosive achrolite rocks. She seemed slightly calmed by this, so I turned on my heel towards the others.

'Right. Do we all remember the next step?' I asked the mixed kinsman surrounding me. Amongst the many humans were the few Garudans who originally began this whole thing; only, they'd planned to kill everyone and escape to freedom. One of the reasons why I was begrudgingly elected to take over—the other reason was because they may have also wanted to kill the only Kraznians who stood on the opposite side of the tunnel, so this was for everyone else's safety. After all, we wouldn't want a bloody riot between each other before we even began.

'A small group of volunteers with pistol-accurate aim and strong arms will be given a bag of achrolite each. Those people will have the honor of getting back at those wretched lowlife bastards out there, and it will mark the day that we took back what we deserved!' I unintentionally raised my voice out of excitement and pumped my fist up into the air. It triggered a round of equally ecstatic applause and whoops.

'Kole, Tiery, Lucius, and I, as well as a small squadron of men and women, will make our way to the wellness centre to rescue the Kraznians and Garudans and whatever else they are keeping below. The Garudans will go with Adam and another squadron to free the slaves on sale—every last one of them. Pip will go with the Kraznians to find out where the Lord will likely be hiding out and relay the information back to us. Finally, the rest of you will create a distraction to throw them off everyone else's tasks. Cause chaos.'

I finished, confident that our plan would work.

'Before we begin, are you all sure you want to do this?' I asked, concerned for the volunteers' welfare.

'Yes, we're sure.' The man who spoke up was the spokesperson of the human group, a bloated fellow with white hair, wrinkled skin, and eyes that held the wisdom of an older generation. 'It's time that we take our lives back. I've been here for thirty years, many of us have been, but we were only petty thieves stealing food or what little we could to feed our families. It's time that this world changed for the better. And if this fails, then we'll at least be remembered in this moment that will echo throughout time.' He ended with a nod, assuring me by the confident looks on all the young and old faces behind him that they all thought the same.

I smiled, empowered by their conviction and determination. They all looked towards me for a chance of freedom and a better life. Not only was I honoured, but I also felt the burden most leaders do, or at least should, of keeping my word. It made my nerves all the more twisted at the terrible thought that this all could fail.

Adam and Pip raced back to us, exhausted. Adam was covered in light sprays of blood, as were the two men that went with them. One, however, seemed less fortunate, with a nasty slash across his arm.

'Is he all right?' Tiery asked before anyone else could, helping him down with the assistance of a more elderly woman.

'It's done. Whatever we're going to do, we need to do it now!' Adam confirmed between exasperated breaths.

'All right.' I nodded, assuring an anxious Adam that I already knew. 'Now the group of volunteers with achrolite bags get their turn. Those that were chosen, come with me, and we'll give those bastards a real show!' This brought forth cheerful applause, followed by eager hands fighting over pouches. I watched the desperation, the hunger, the need for vengeance in each of their eyes, and I felt something in me stir. 'Tiery, give me your bag,' I commanded, holding out my hand without a thought.

She returned it, adding a confused and slightly upset frown.

'I said that only a few people could come with me to do this task,' I continued, opening the bag and fingering the very warm, almost hot raw achrolite. Everyone watched, confused and anxious. 'All of you have suffered at your captors' hands, slaving away for nothing. Punished for being weak and tired, or even dying. Many of you have suffered for almost a lifetime. I've changed my mind.' I looked up at the mixed species that came together as one whole. 'You all deserve your revenge. To end this terrible time and bury this unforgiving place. We all began this journey together and many of us will not survive it. But let's start it all together with a satisfying bang!' I held up a rock as a signal that was immediately received.

Everyone, every single slave, got handed a piece of rock. It didn't matter if many of them missed. There were so many of us that it was a sure thing that we would destroy the camp of horrors together as a new society of thieves, killers, and vagabonds.

Lining the pathways and ridges of the mine's floor, we stood, encompassing the oddly silent campsite of our drugged captures and their 'king'. A calm stillness fell over us as we stood, watching in the knowledge of what this momentous event would mark, and how it would most likely echo out through the passages of time.

'Ready!' I screamed, raising my glowing rock as a signal for everyone else to do the same. 'Aim!' Taking a stance and a breath, I prepared my muscles to throw as far as I could. 'Fire!'

Brilliant flashes of colour streaked across the night sky as all of the volatile achrolite rocks sang through the air like red fiery comets. All at once, they touched down violently on different locations of the campsite. They tore and ripped apart every inanimate object and drugged victim it could find. Unfortunately, even the poor innocent creatures… the Malbroles who had been forced to labour under their masters' cruel fists, just like us. There was just no way we could set them free. This was the only place they knew, the only place that smelled familiar. If we had freed them they would have been hunted and trapped again, never able to be truly free as they once were so long ago.

Every single now-freed soul was speechless; many were smiling from ear to ear, while others just gaped in awe at the magnificent spectral of raw energy. The aftermath was even more spectacular, and at the same time darkly hilarious, as the flames and explosions spewed forth a rain of blood, intestines, legs, arms, heads, and flesh of our enemies that treated us as lesser. Hopefully this would be the first of many massacres by my hand. Marta could be heard laughing hysterically as the blood and flesh rained upon him. Even the Kraznians were slightly smirking at the sight of it. The humans, however, were mostly frightened and disgusted. Some ran inside the mines for cover, others even vomiting from the burnt flesh smell.

But not me, nor Tiery; who just stood by me, staring and smiling away, tears of complete and utter happiness falling down her blood-stained cheeks. The feeling of her life shackles finally being lifted off of her, finally allowing her to breathe the first breath of freedom.

'All right, time to go! Let's finish what we started!' I called as loud as I could over the remaining explosions and roaring flames. Those that heard began to let the others know, which triggered a virus-like spread of command until everybody was with me. We staggered slowly, one step in front of the other, but from this moment on, every step we took we took for ourselves.

Less than a foot of dirt was in our way; on the other side was freedom and sovereignty as well as a whole army of blood-thirsty soldiers ruled by a tyrannical Lord. The weapons we had stored and hid throughout the cave systems were brought along and handed out, every man, woman, and child, young and old, human and other, held their ground gripping onto their weapons tightly, eager to free their friends and family. Between us and him, though, were thousands of innocents who were bound to be caught in the crossfire.

***

The earth shook and vibrated as the wall from the sewers cracked. Within moments, it burst, and from the smoldering remains sprung the liberated slaves. The roar of battle echoed throughout the city, alerting the Lord and everyone else that slept peacefully to the sounds of freedom.

The cries of liberation became infectious as the word spread, causing the rest of the city to awaken and raise weapons against their tyrants.

Fires ignited and danced along the lower city towards the nobles and the houses of the soldiers. A horn blasted from atop the city gate's spire, officially declaring war between the city's people and the nobility.

Lord Cowan sent word to fetch the captains of the soldiers, and within minutes they had arrived. The torches ran faster and spread onto each other as the city's people pillaged and roared for justice and sovereignty.

Clothed in his nicest attire—a black and gold-trimmed silk dressing gown—Lord Cowan awaited his poorly dressed men; all out of breath due to the urgency of their meeting. Their shirts and coats were out of place from rushing through the door; but they stood, awaiting orders.

'The mine has been taken over and the men are most likely dead,' Cowan said flatly. 'The culprits run rampant in the streets. They must have a leader. The soldier who brings them to me in chains will get anything they desire and perhaps be promoted to the first general of Buson. Take down this stupid uprising and kill anyone who defies you.' Cowan gave each man a stern look before dismissing them with the flick of a wrist. *And a strong suspicion of who it might be.*

His mistress held the door as the captains passed, but none noticed her, each too focused on their prize for the leader in chains.

She glided across the floor to her husband's side, holding his arm and resting her head on his tense shoulder.

'Didn't Karn say he wanted her alive? Why didn't you hand her over in the first place?'

She was always a smart one, always knew what questions to ask and what the answers to many of them were. But by God, he swore that she, nor anyone, would find out the answer to the reason he kept Farrah—why he wanted her so much and thought the mines would break her. She was his god-daughter, his late best friend's child, no matter how much he tried to fight it, deny his connection to her, the overwhelming knowledge that anyone connected to her be it by blood or friendship would also be put to death no matter how weak that connection was. 'Why don't you go to the meeting room, dear?' he replied in a calming tone, disguising his true feelings. He held her cheek in his free palm. 'I'll have my two best soldiers come and protect you.' It was a lie, and he covered it with a smile of love.

Which she could see straight through, but did as she was told just the same. Her arms unwound from him, and she walked out of the room, escaping the swirling darkness that consumed it.

Chapter 17

Ear-piercing cries of dying men rang throughout the so-called 'Great city of Buson'. Explosions and carnage, the clashing of steel and fists, shots of firearms spattering all around; pure chaos had erupted, and the war between the impoverished common folk and Lord Cowan's power-crazed soldiers had begun.

Blood spilled on both sides as no one held back, the fierce battle waging throughout the streets.

The objectives I'd given my team were clear: secure the wellness centre and capture the evil Lord.

As anarchy reigned around us, safely making it to the hospital was our first priority. Lucius and a frightened but willing Tiery were by my side, with a terrified Kole cowering behind me. Our wall of warriors forged a path through the chaos, leaving behind a trail of bloody corpses.

I wasn't really taking notice as to whether we were going the right way, but luckily Lucius was as he carved our way through the soldiers. Tiery was gripping my hand so fiercely that my fingertips turned purple. Fear had consumed her, as it did with many of the others who attempted to appear brave as they ran in, headfirst and unprotected, towards the enemy soldiers adorned in armour and helmets. They might as well have been naked, but they still forced their fear back and continued fighting for what was right and just.

A pair of the miners volunteered to protect Kole while Tiery and I stayed alongside Lucius who, as the rebels got to know him, became more respected than anyone else. Alfie, the taller and most agile of the two volunteers, formed the left side of the shield of chivalrous warriors, and Sonny-Boy formed the right side.

I don't really know what Sonny-Boy's real name was, but ever since I met him, everyone just called him 'Sonny-Boy', or 'Sonny' for short. The name stemmed from his childish features and boyish charm; which made his age impossible to determine. He never corrected us, however, as he rarely ever spoke, and when he did, his voice was very soft and gentle, like a young boy's.

This, of course, made him the perfect target for the noble cougars whenever their husbands were away on business, allowing him to steal some from the wealthiest houses in all of Buson without any suspicion. That was until he got caught and taken to the mines.

We closed in on our main objective and were greeted with spreading fires, as well as discarded pieces of debris and shrapnel from small pocket explosions; but there it was. Sandbags and large pieces of furniture were stacked on top of each other, protecting the precious insides filled with the weak and defenseless.

'Stop right there, or we *will* shoot you!' a voice called out. It sounded young, and when I saw the speaker, I knew he couldn't have been more than fourteen. The barrel of his gun peered over the wall, as did the top of his scruffy light brown hair dusted with ash. The barrel shook in his hands, and he looked at us with wide eyes.

'We mean you no harm! We are here to help you!' Lucius called out, raising his empty hands in a sign of trust—albeit not while being entirely honest.

No response was given, yet frightened murmurs could be heard from behind the barricade.

'How do we know you're not lying?' the boy shouted back.

'Because if we were here to harm you, you'd know by now,' I replied, shouting over the nearby gunfire. There was another pause while the guards murmured behind the wall, deciding what to do.

'All right, you can come in—but you have to hand over your weapons,' he agreed.

Lucius was about to argue, but I stopped him by putting my hand on his tensed arm.

The barricade opened, giving way to a fresh surge of occupants. We shuffled in as fast as we could, crouched over warily and hugging onto each other as we moved.

We spilled into the decrepit building, and were immediately greeted by elderly men and women, wives and children, and the expected sick and injured. The boy who held us at gunpoint seemed to have been pulled off the streets and was as frightened as the rest of them. Others like him lined the barricade, although some seemed to be elderly men far too old for fighting, or even moving about, for that matter.

Looking around, all I saw were the scared faces of the innocent people that were unfortunately caught up in the middle of a war they didn't know was for their futures.

'Farrah? Farrah?! Farrah, it's your friend, Mino!' a dirty, bleeding, yet familiar face shouted through the crowd. The shopkeeper's expression was happy, clearly grateful to see his friend alive; and I was surprised to find I felt the same relief.

'Margo, come see! Come see, it's our friend!' he waved over yet another familiar face—the woman with the unruly bird's nest for hair that always tried to coax me into buying her strange exotic spices.

'Hello, dear, it's so nice to see you safe and sound,' she said with a weakened voice. Her demeanour was different from the last time I saw her. It seemed to be fading, as if the war was draining her; which was to be expected, honestly. But as I looked closer, I noticed a large patch of blood had soaked her clothes on the side of her stomach. There were bandages hidden underneath to stop the haemorrhaging, but I feared not enough was being done.

'Oh, Margo! Are you all right? What happened?' fear choked me.

I made my way to her with open arms, hands hovering over her stomach. I could feel others watching me, and caught a few looks of sympathy, but my focus returned to her wound.

'I'm fine. It's okay, honestly, dear. I'll be okay, you'll see. Nothing can kill me that easily.' She smiled, but it was weak.

I was consumed by my friend's well-being, but a coughing sound from Lucius reminded me of why we were there.

'Right. Mino, is there anyone still here that's worked here before? Perhaps as a nurse or doctor?' I ask softly and calmly, the nicest possible way I could.

'Mino thinks so? Why?' he asked, matching my soft voice.

'My friends and I are here because we need to speak to someone who's worked here and who might have information we need,' I replied honestly, but kept it as vague as I could.

'You could speak to Doc Juine, but Mino thinks he doesn't have that much time left. He said he got hurt in an explosion,' he replied.

'That's great, Mino! Where is he?' I asked, so ecstatic at his response that I grasped onto his arms tightly and shook him.

'Uh, on the second floor,' Mino replied again, confused and a little bit frightened by my happiness.

'Come on,' I mouthed to my comrades behind me.

We waded through the bodies of dead or dying men, as well as terrified women and children who all strangely seemed to be staring in our direction. But it wasn't out of curiosity that they were staring at us and whispering away. No, it was because of fear of one of us in particular—Kole. The marking on his face frightened them because only the most deserving were branded in such a way; it was seen as a bad omen, a curse; whoever bore a mark such as this would be forever seen as a cursed being.

Kole lowered his head, and his feet scuffed as we walked further in. A surge of defensiveness overtook me. Grabbing onto his hand, I walked beside my friend whose eyes glistened with gratefulness as we walked hand in hand towards the stairwell. My head held high, showing every single shocked and surprised face surrounding us that I didn't give a damn what they thought; he was my friend.

We headed towards the crowded staircase, where grieving family members and loved ones mourned their dead, one of the few places left that wasn't swamped with strangers. I knew when beginning this battle that there would be unfortunate casualties, but it didn't make it any easier to hear the wails and sobs of sorrow bounce around us as we passed through, heads down, eyes straight. Finally arriving at the top of the stairway of perpetual sorrow, we found ourselves at yet another area, bursting to the brim with the sick and injured.

'Holy crap, we're never going to find him at this rate,' Kole muttered, as we all stood gawking like fish.

'Dr. Juine! Has anyone seen Dr Juine!?' I yelled, forcing my voice to spread as far as it would go.

And as expected, the whole room paused and turned to look our way. No one seemed to answer for some time, their wide eyes simply staring at me. It got to the point that even the rest of the team looked at me with red-faced embarrassment.

'What?' I shrugged, unashamed of my outburst.

'He's over here!' A hand thankfully flapped not far from where we stood. We made a beeline toward the frail-looking middle-aged woman who sat beside a man lying in a cot. He seemed unappreciative of her clearly unwanted help; his eyes scowled at the sight of her as he cursed under his breath.

The woman's light brown hair was styled in a short pixie-cut, and a brown cardigan was draped over her flat, stick-like figure. A floral button-up shirt peeked through, and it seemed as drained of colour and starved for life as its wearer was. There was an unusually clean chain resting on her chest, a small silver cross at its centre. It was so well-maintained it looked brand new, as if she had polished it every day. Regardless of the fact that we were indoors, it glinted brightly, almost as much as her pale green eyes did while she looked at a group of strangers with misplaced hope.

'My name is Blanche. I'm a nun for the church of the people. It's so nice to see more of god's children… Even the marked ones,' she introduced herself, holding her hand out warmly, directing her last remark to Kole, who forced a quick smile. Thankfully, Tiery took her greeting on behalf of the rest of us.

'Mr. Juine?' I began, breaking through the silence and mixed emotions that swirled around us.

'*Doctor*… It's *Doctor* Juine, not Mister,' he responded gruffly.

It was hard to judge from the way he was lying, but by the look of it, he wasn't a very tall man—in fact, his feet were roughly an inch away from the foot of the cot. He wore a long, patchy coat riddled with stains and torn holes. The ends of his sleeves were mangled, showcasing stumpy fingers poking through, and what must have once been a nice uniform but was now shredded. If he had a neck, it had disappeared behind the fat rolls of his potato-like face, which held a collection of small features; beady little eyes, a bulb of a nose, as well as a virtually non-existent mouth, which were all twisted in a sour expression. There was almost nothing nice to say about him. However, I could admit that he did have very luxurious black hair, albeit disheveled from the tossing and turning.

'So. What do you want?' he grumbled, not attempting to get up, or even move, for that matter.

'Forgive us, sir, but we have reason to believe that there is a secret facility below this complex… containing certain assets we wish to release,' I spoke in a hushed tone, aware of the woman watching intently.

This question gave him a start, and his eyes shone in recognition.

'I don't know what you're talking about,' he answered, turning his head away.

It was clear that it was going to be difficult to convince him to let the poor creatures go, which to him were just experiments. I forced myself to muster as much patience and calmness as I could.

'I think you do, sir. We only want what's best for them. Just point us to a secret passage or door and we'll be on our way.' I looked at him, trying to make my eyes big and watery, attempting to provoke some humanity from him. His stern expression did not change.

'Those things are monsters,' he spat. 'They shouldn't be on the surface to begin with. They shouldn't even exist. Who cares if a few of them go missing? We all have to die someday.' He didn't make eye-contact, though I could feel that this was his honest belief.

The woman sitting on the other side of him looked both confused and shocked at his reply.

'What are you talking about, if I may ask?' she spoke, her voice so soft it was barely audible.

We all looked at each other, not knowing if we should tell her the truth in case it caused panic amongst the already frightened people. Tiery, deciding not to join the rest of us in our telepathic conversation, just started talking.

'There is a secret building under this one that the nobles are using to steal powers from innocent creatures. We have reason to believe that Dr. Juine here is one of those people who've been conducting the experiments that steal abilities from the prisoners. We want to free them.' Tiery turned back to us, likely having felt the daggers we were glaring into her back.

'What?' she asked, blank-eyed and confused. Kole nudged her, a nonverbal way of saying 'idiot'.

The poor woman's eyes were the size of saucers, and her skin was paler than a few minutes ago.

'Dr. Juine, is this true?' she asked in a squeaky tone.

He looked back at her apathetically, as if to say 'so what', then finished with an eye roll.

'The Lord sayeth, 'A righteous man cares for the needs of his animal, and yet the kindest acts of the wicked are still cruel'',' Blanche said, holding her necklace. 'Abusing and killing those who are innocent is a sinful thing to do, Dr. Juine, even if it's because someone else told you to. God created every creature big and small, even those who came from beneath. It is him who hears their cries of pain and anguish, it is he who feels all their suffering. Why would you do such a thing, knowing your soul will be judged?'

'Because he doesn't have one. Who needs a soul when you have money? Right, Dr. Juine?' I answered for him, feeling anger rise towards this man; one of the many who feed the nobles' hunger for power and wealth.

Resentment clouded his eyes as he was bombarded with judgmental stares and looks of disgust.

'God doesn't exist, you stupid woman. If he did, don't you think our ancestors would have been saved all those years ago? Those stories that we were told to remember are just that. Stories, fables to invoke hope and create fundamental beliefs in each other. The ideas of hope and salvation died long ago when the war began, so don't spout that nonsensical dribble at an already-dying man.' He ended with a growl, baring his teeth and snarling like a wounded animal that was being backed into a corner.

Although, frankly, it didn't really seem that he was dying. The wound he had wasn't nearly as bad as half of the others surrounding him, so why was he being so overly dramatic?

'Let me try to talk to him,' Tiery whispered, as she softly patted my shoulder. I reluctantly stepped aside, allowing her to squat in front of him. She took a breath.

'Dr. Juine… Stop and listen… Do you hear that outside? The war? It's the sound of change, of a new era. It is the sound of hopeful men, women, and even children fighting for a brighter future. They've had enough of living in silence, being squashed down to nothing, suffering as the powerful look down upon them. Upon us… Upon you.

'We all have a decision to make; either defend the side that doesn't care if you live or die, or fight for a better life. One like the ancestors had, but even better and more beautiful than ever before. You must decide what you want out of the rest of your life. If not for you, then do what you've been taught to do, and help save our lives.'

Tiery's words rang true, leaving us all to reflect on if this was the path we truly wanted, and if it was, then what did we want out of it? What kind of future were we fighting for?

Dr. Juine seemed to be thinking about the situation as he looked around at everyone's hopeful faces—apart from mine, which showed nothing but slight annoyance.

What is there to think about? The answer is simple!

'There's a hatch under the receptionist's table,' he said with a sigh. 'It's an entryway to the tunnel that'll lead you to where you need to go.' Tiery must've spoken to something deep inside him; which was fortunate for him, because I'd started debating torture as a means to hurry things along.

'Farrah?' a familiar voice called out from amongst the others, a voice I never thought I'd ever have the pleasure of hearing again.

Through the gaps of moving bodies, a pale, sweet face peeked through, trying its hardest to see its target.

Francis was still alive. My heart skipped a beat as I was overwhelmed with relief and thankfulness for his safety. He was still in the same bed, which I didn't realise was only ten cots away from where we were; but there he was, smiling with that precious face that reminded me of my dear friend, his sister. I hurried to his side.

'What are you doing here?' He still seemed drained from the last time we met, when he found out he would never see his sister again.

'We're here to rescue some creatures from captivity under this facility,' I replied truthfully, forcing my grin to show all of my teeth.

'What?' he asked, clearly shocked and a bit frightened at the thought of it.

Lucius gave me a look of stress as he shook his head towards the stairway.

'I have to go, but I promise I'll explain more later. Tiery will stay with you. Right, Tiery?' I looked behind me at Tiery's blank stare. She likely saw this as me thrusting her upon a stranger.

'Ah… yeah, sure. I can stay,' she answered, a bit taken aback.

It was a win-win situation for me; not only did I want to keep him safe, but it also kept her out of harm's way. If there was something or someone guarding the secret lab, I didn't want her to get hurt—but she didn't need to know that.

***

The passageway was dim, narrow, and dripping with dark intentions. The wood structure used to hold up the failing dirt roof was old, splintered, and moulding; and from it came a disgusting musty smell that made the humid air even more unbearable. Torches burned, though they were dim as embers, and we found ourselves having to squint and trace our hands along the walls.

We travelled further and further down into the pit of darkness that sucked any light it could find into itself. Nothing could be seen or heard, apart from each other's frightened breathing and muffled steps, and it felt as if we were gradually losing our senses. Finally, an ominous green light appeared from under an old heavy steel door. Lucius nudged me out of the way as he clenched his fists, morphing his echobriome one into an axe ready for anything that was beyond. He kicked it open, eliciting a loud screech from its hinges.

A frigid air exploded forth, committing us to the sickening, strong waft of unknown chemicals. Green lights caged with rusty wirings hung from the ceiling and swung ever so slightly, flickering in the breeze. A maze of bookcases blocked our path, some covered in dust and cobwebs, others cleaner and filled with an array of jars of liquids. Within the containers floated things such as eyes, hands, scales and fetuses of unknown creatures. Behind the cases were six long stainless-steel tables, three on either side of us, and all proudly showing off their contents; beakers, test tubes, scattered papers with scientific dribble scrolled across them, as well as a myriad of other scientific tools and equipment that seemed to be well worn from the years of service. Upon the walls beside the tables were pictographs, anatomically correct images of various creatures, notes, and clipboards with charts on them.

I was becoming more creeped out by the minute as we took it all in, and felt the hairs on my arms rise as we slowly made our way past the shelves of grotesque displays. There was yet another door, one that had already been unlocked; and by the sounds of it, the culprit was still inside. Heavy thuds, ruffled papers, shattered glass—all while someone mumbled away. Inching the door open to peek through the crack, Kole, Lucius, and I squashed in as close as we could to see just what they were doing to these creatures. Alfie and Sonny were forced to wait by the side, itching to see for themselves what horrific experimentations and tools lay beyond.

The ceiling launched itself even higher until I couldn't even see where it ended. It seemed to be an old underground experimental facility the ancestors had managed to build shortly after the war, and they began discovering the creatures. They believed that using the new species' DNA would help them survive the radiation from the bombs, so they built places like these to launch experiments in desperation to survive in the once toxic atmosphere. Generations had passed and the facilities were thought to be long forgotten, only to find that the higher born members of society had been hiding them for their own selfish desires. Now and then when I had felt the urge for rebellion, I would sneak into the Drakes' library and steal books to read—I'd always had a hunger for knowledge I could never quite satisfy—and he had countless volumes on this subject in particular. *Now I see why.*

Enormous clear capsules were locked into even larger machines that lined the walls, all with tubes and cables of every size protruding from them. Encased inside were Kraznians, Garudans, humans, as well as other monstrous things I had never even seen before. All of which were suspended in the liquid within the capsules. Some were missing limbs or pieces of flesh, others looked to be humans mutating into something else entirely.

'Oh my God... What are they doing to them?' Kole voiced what we were all thinking.

'I don't know, but we need to end this. Now,' Lucius answered confidently, anger colouring his voice.

He forced his way past me and Kole, seeming intent on hunting down whoever it was that chose the worst time to return to this place.

As Lucius stormed off, his arms stiffened and swelled until his echobriome arm formed into a beautiful yet deadly curved sword, ready to kill the scientific weasel nearby. The rodent in question was scurrying around, preoccupied with his frantic ramblings, unable to focus on the danger that stood only meters away. When we approached, I saw what a weasel he was; or at least, that's what he resembled. He was a tiny little man, with a patchy snow-white five o'clock shadow, great big ears, and whispers of bleached hair barely clinging to his scalp. He grasped onto a stack of research papers for dear life, as if they were more important than him, and he continued to mumble away frantically. That was until Lucius held the tip of his very sharp morphed sword a whisker away from his neck. His beady eyes slowly looked up towards the fearsome gaze of his killer.

Instinctively and without a second thought, our weasel's little fingers dropped his jumbled papers, raising his shaky, misshaped hands above his head.

Kole bent over and picked up a few pages that slid towards his feet, curious as to what exactly they were doing to their helpless captives. Polaroid images paper clipped to a few of them along with medical notes of the progress and things they planned to do to the subjects followed by question marks scrolled in every which way. No matter how many years he studied them, he wouldn't even be able to scratch the surface of what it was all for.

'Take whatever you want… I won't stop you,' he offered with an old man's quaking voice.

'I want your life,' Lucius snarled, baring his teeth as the sword slid ever closer to the quivering man's neck. My body took over as my arm swung forward and grasped onto his weaponized one, forcing him to lower it.

'How did you discover this place? It's supposed to be a secret,' he asked, seeming genuinely surprised by our appearance.

'It seems as though your co-worker has a weak sense of loyalty. He squealed like a little pig,' Alfie scoffed, smugly smiling away.

His beady little eyes darted towards me, his entire body shaking in fear as a cold sweat emitted from every pore.

'Please, I'll tell you whatever you want. J-just spare me, p-please,' he stammered, clasping his hands together as he literally begged for his pitiful life.

'How do you release these poor creatures of yours?' I demanded as I looked down upon him, fighting back the urge to kill him myself.

'What?' A wobbly, nervous smile appeared, as if he thought the question was a joke. When he read the seriousness in our expressions, he blurted out, 'You can't.'

Lucius moved his sword back like a lightning bolt, nearly causing the small man to wet his pants.

'We've come here to free these poor things you've trapped and tortured. Tell us how to open the capsules,' Kole spoke up, standing at a distance, squinting at the scared sweaty scientist using his one good eye.

'You can't!' the weasel repeated, frantic. 'If you open their pods they'll die; the capsules are the only things sustaining their lives. There is no way of freeing them without subjecting them to horrendous deaths.' The small man began to sob, sweat pearling and rolling down from his receding hairline as he kept a shaking eye on the sharp weapon against his skin.

'Then why are you here alone?' I asked, folding my arms tightly so as not to strangle him.

This one question was met with silence, as he quickly thought about his response. I could literally see the cogs spinning around in his balding head.

'I am a scientist. It is my duty to look after these creatures and make sure they are all right and keep our data from bandits and looters,' he answered, looking as genuine as he could.

None of us believed him.

'Where are the others?' Alfie asked with a sharp tongue.

'I-I don't know what you're talking about…' the man sniffled. 'These are the only specimens we have.'

'No, that's wrong; it has to be,' Alfie snapped. 'When I helped clean the slaves before they were sold, the city always made us save at least two of the best for something secret. The boss never told me why they were worth so much, and I got curious, so one night I followed the soldiers. They took them here, to the wellness centre. I swear there must be more.' He sounded like he was trying to convince us as much as himself, his eyes darting along the walls.

'Are you sure, Alfie?' Kole asked, concerned.

'Yes. I'm sure. I wouldn't be making things like that up!' he yelled, defensive, though his eyes showed a bit of his uncertainty.

'Okay, okay, I believe you…' I answered with a smile. My peaceful expression hardened the moment I looked back at the pathetic scientist, whose face now told of slight agitation.

'You heard the man. Where are they?' I stalked closer, appearing as intimidating as I could, a threatening gleam shining through my eyes as I stiffened my entire body.

'These are the only ones here, I swear! Your friend doesn't know what he's talking about—' he stopped short as Lucius began to prick his face, forcing blood to trickle out.

He wasn't backing down, wasn't changing his answer, but he didn't need to. A muffled mumble came from a double door behind a row of capsules. The small man became even more agitated and gritted his teeth.

'Alfie, Sonny—you two stay here with our friend. The others and I will go check it out,' I commanded, not keeping my eye off of the vile little weasel quivering in front of me.

An ice-blue light emitted from the cracked door that the noise had crept out of. We all exchanged anxious glances. Kole quickly searched the area, picked up a pipe, and stood by one side of the door whilst Lucius stood on the other side, holding his morphed arm in front of him. I took centre, my hand twisting the knob and swinging the door inward.

We were stunned by the horrors that greeted us. My eyes were so wide they started to hurt, and I felt as though all the blood had drained from my body. It resembled a giant freezer; cold, white, and misty. The old vents rattled away, miraculously still pumping in the freezing air. Before us stood rows and columns of at least sixty cages of semi-conscious and half-frozen creatures squashed into the barred boxes half their size. Tables of blood and hooks hung from above, displaying limbs and corpses split in half. Translucent tubes of red liquid ran themselves into every different cage. The three of us were frozen in place, taking it all in, mortified. After a minute, I tore my eyes away, and, forcing myself out of the horrific thoughts that consumed my mind, reminded myself of why we were here.

'Kole! Quickly find a valve and stop whatever's being given to them,' I demanded, feeling my heart pumping a mile a minute. I turned to my other side. 'Lucius, try to find something to unlock the cages. We need to hurry!'

Once I finished with orders, I scurried around, trying to find something myself.

Lucius didn't need to find anything; the moment he touched one of the locks with his echobriome sword, it seemed to cut away like butter.

I found a pair of stained pliers on one of their operating tables. Rushing over, I began prying free the locks and helping the drugged residents out carefully.

The more lucid ones stood and helped the others walk out. One by one, all of them became free, although none looked very good after the strange drug that'd been pumped through them.

'Are they all right? Will they be okay?' Kole whined.

'I think so. Many of them seem too drugged, though. Perhaps we should lead them out in groups,' Lucius suggested, looking at a drained, semi-lucid girl that looked a bit like his late wife.

'You're right. We'll each take one out, including Alfie and Sonny,' I directed, pulling one of the youngest in my arms. A Garudan boy, by the looks of it. The once ruby-red skin was drained to a pale salmon hue and he shivered against my skin.

'What about the scientist they're guarding?' Kole enquired, heaving the arm of a large Kraznian man over him and taking in most of his weight.

I paused in the doorway, thinking of the only viable option so that he wouldn't be able to hurt any of them whilst unguarded.

'Kill him.' I looked back at Kole's disturbed face as he swallowed hard at my answer. Lucius pushed past with four unconscious, fully grown adults in his arms. He walked out with ease, striding past an eagle-eyed Alfie and Sonny; both still keeping their sights glued to one of the main perpetrators of this atrocity.

'Alfie, Sonny. One of you will go and get a rescued victim and take them out of this place; the other has to stay behind, though, and dispose of this one as quick as you can. The choice is yours who does what,' I tasked, waiting for a response as the Garudan boy cuddled up to the warmth of my body.

'I'll do it.' Alfie nodded, accepting the gruesome deed with a devilish grin. He then loomed over the terrified scientist and soon-to-be victim.

'All right, don't take too long,' I instructed before making my way out of the cold cement room of horrors, carefully cradling the child in my arms.

One after the other, we traveled back and forth, walking the victims from the dark and up to the light. Before long, every one of the tortured souls had been rescued. The final task was to find out how to shut the pods off; the creatures that where being kept inside were not themselves anymore, and keeping them alive was only torture. The weasel man was right, rescuing them would just bring them more pain. Kole—the smartest of us all—was sent down, along with Alfie and Sonny to investigate and take care of the saddening situation.

The first floor of the wellness centre was now flooded with frightened and confused innocents. Those injured from the ongoing war were amazed and disturbed by the existence of a secret passage leading to a sinister experimental laboratory from which their new fellow enslaved and brutalised compatriots had emerged. Many of whom were still drowsy from the medication and could barely speak.

'Farrah! What is this?! Who are all these people?!' Mino asked, his brows raised and eyes darting from person to person.

'It's a long story. And you deserve to hear it, but now is not the time,' I answered, blood pumping with adrenaline.

Murmurs erupted from upfront amongst those behind the barricades as they looked onwards through the mist and smoke. I joined them, and we all saw something we never expected.

Chapter 18

An exhausted yet exhilarated Pip bounced forth atop one of her fellow Kraznian guards, giggling and smiling away with every bump, an odd sight to see in the middle of a war. Behind them, the other Kraznian closely followed suit, determination in his eyes as he struggled to keep up with the others. The pair were darting towards the centre; they knew we would be waiting for their news with eager anticipation.

The little warrior leaned over the head of her Kraznian, smirking away with absolute joy in her eyes.

'We found him! He's being protected heavily, though,' she said with a raised voice, pleased with the fact that for a moment she isn't the shortest out of everyone.

'That's amazing Pip! Great work!' I said, smiling at the state of my brave little friend.

Kole, Lucius, and Tiery all step in closer, eager to learn the whereabouts of the bastard Lord they, like most, desired to see suffer for his crimes.

'He's being protected by a legion of guards not far from hereat a tavern in the slums,' she said. As she did, my mind fixated on 'tavern', and terrible ideas began to arise.

If the Lord had his spies and goons following me every time I was out in town, then surely they would tell him about the tavern I visited before going to Lucius's home. And if they followed me inside, then they would've seen who I talked to...

'We need to go now. No time to lose!' I commanded, anxious and terrified that, if my suspicions were correct, another friend of mine, another innocent, was in grave danger.

'Wait, what about them?' Tiery asked, turning her head to the frightened stares of the people trapped in the wellness centre.

'Alfie and Sonny can stay behind and protect the people inside until the war is finished. I know you won't want to hear this, but I need you to stay behind as well. Look after the survivors from the lab.' I told her, and as expected she responded with an ungrateful scowl, which gracefully softened as she thought about it. I rested a hand on her limp foot and gave her a smile, genuinely grateful that she agreed.

I then turned my attention to the two men behind me. Both Alfie and Sonny were posed like strong soldiers, ready for anything. I gave them both a fierce stare. 'Protect them with everything you have. This is what we have been fighting for.'

'Aye aye, captain!' Alfie sarcastically replied with a stern face, the small twinge of a smile cracking from his stiff lips. Both saluted their commander and rushed to find ways to better defend the barricade and reinforce it.

'Let's go,' I said, nodding to the Kraznian.

The twists and turns we took weren't familiar to me, giving me a glimmer of hope that it wouldn't be Sylvie's tavern. We turned down alleyways and back entrances to avoid the onslaught of swords, spears, and bullets from both sides in an effort to get to our destination not only faster, but in one piece.

Gradually, the appearance of every house and building changed as we zoomed past them; every time we passed a building, the wood and the way it was being maintained worsened. Their appearance began to change from reasonably decent residences to sagging timber dwellings and occupied holes.

That was when I knew we were in the same area. I recognised the houses sinking into the sludgy earth thanks to the tower of homes stacked atop it, connected by ladders strapped to the decaying walls. It seemed quieter than usual though, perhaps due to the people being out fighting—it may have stirred something in everyone.

All of us slowed down, almost tumbling over each other, then stopped abruptly by the corner of a dangerously precarious pile of houses. Firth turned and waved her hands around in odd gestures none of us understood, and I felt myself getting annoyed because of it.

'What?' Kole asked.

'This is where he is being guarded!' Firth whispered as softly as she could.

And there, just as I'd dreaded, was The Drunken Willow. The lights were lit in every window, including the rooms above, but not a sound could be heard from it, not an ounce of drunken merriment to be consumed by. Out front, four outfitted guards stood like statues, eyes sharp, prepared for anything. They were fitted head to toe with armour made from mismatching metal plates welded to match their owners' form comfortably.

In the window above, I recognised the shadow of a man, one of power and greed, with a heart as black as coal. I glared at his silhouette, boiling with rage. I wished I could just mentally kill him, like one of the creatures he tortured and forced experiments upon. It would be so much easier, but not as satisfying as watching him die slowly.

Just then, his shadow moved ever so slightly, the head shifting in our direction, as if he could feel my sadistic desires. His eyeline stared straight back at me, presumably sensing what I was thinking, as if to say 'welcome to the other side'.

Flashes of what that disgusting sadist had done to me, made me suddenly fall into them, drowning out my surroundings. The idea of even seeing him again made my dry mouth fill with sour tasting, burning saliva. My body shook from his phantom touch. Pursing my lips and cursing those memories and terror away, I balled up my fists and forced myself to think of a Plan.

'What's the plan?' Kole loudly whispered.

The front of the line huddled back around to help form a circle.

While the others were muttering amongst themselves, I caught a glimpse of the wires and cables that crisscrossed between the rickety buildings and an idea began to form. I smiled, then turned to my team.

'Guys, I have a plan.'

A few minutes later, I was walking straight towards the entrance of the tavern, hands raised. I attempted looking innocent and non-threatening, but it was hard to hold back my smug smile.

'You! Halt! Stop right there!' one guard shouted, alerting the others and making them raise their weapons in defence.

'I believe I am expected,' I said calmly, still approaching. 'I'm Farrah. The person who began this whole uprising. I would like to hand myself in. No tricks.' I paused a few feet in front of the guards, who didn't seem sure what to make of the situation.

They shared looks of uncertainty, speaking in low tones. The palest of them finally stepped forward, eyes glued forward as he cautiously stalked closer to me, spear raised high.

As the man began patting me down, I looked towards the anxious soldiers still watching by the door. I couldn't help but notice that the soldier wasn't just patting me down, but he also took the opportunity to feel me up—going over the same areas three times, making triply sure that I didn't have a knife shoved up my ass or down my breasts. Until he was happy with his slimy work, I had to keep my composure; one slight movement could send my head flying. No matter how much I wanted to viciously attack the greasy-fingered man, I couldn't.

Not yet, at least.

The pale soldier gave a nod of approval to his comrades, who all now had growing smirks smeared upon their faces. The unwanted touching had turned their fear to arousal. The man beside me hooked his tensed arm through mine, entrapping me in a firm grip, and prepared himself to walk his prize to his master's hideout with a proud smile on his face.

Glued together and with his mates in tow, we marched into the lifeless tavern as one entity. Looking around, I saw broken tables and splintered chairs, shards of glass bottles and mugs, and splashes of deep red strewn across every surface—even the walls and ceiling. A big fight had broken out here, and judging by the fact that there were only bodies of courageous patrons and no uniforms, it was clear who stood victorious.

And there he stood, as if he'd been waiting for us—Lord Cowan. His feet were parted and arms held behind his back as he consumed me with glinting eyes that paired well with his ominous smile of wet, hungry canines.

'Well, well, well, look who we have here... The great Farrah, saviour of the people!' he spoke, raising his hands to the sky and forming a large smile. It quickly dropped, turning into a darkened scowl. 'And destroyer of my empire.'

'Did you come to offer yourself to me? Miss my warmth?' He asked, cockishly smirking. A fire of hunger burned in his lowered confident eyes.

I couldn't help but let out a tiny giggle. I tried to cover my mouth with the back of my hand, but it wasn't as concealing as I'd thought. His eye and corner of his mouth twitched with ire, offended by the unexpected response.

'What, may I ask, is so funny?' he asked through gritted teeth.

'It's just that... Well, come on. This isn't an empire, it's a mud pit. One you didn't seem to really care for. Especially when it comes to your people,' I answered honestly.

'Would you like to say that in front of your little friends that have made themselves at home here?' He smiled, raising his left arm to the direction of the back door.

Out appeared Sylvie, battered and bruised, followed by her father, whose eye was either gone or completely covered by a dark layer of blood. They were both pulling and pushing between a pair of soldiers whose arms were linked so tightly through theirs that it looked like their arms were about to pop off. Sylvie looked at me, tears in her eyes and lips quivering. I could tell it was her fear that kept her wild impulses at bay; if she weren't afraid, she'd have been dead by now.

Her mane of hair was pulled tightly back, apart from a few straying strands that revealed a patch of blood on top of a wound where she was likely struck and knocked out. The tears in her eyes made it appear as if brilliant emeralds were glinting in my direction.

'Farrah? What the hell are you doing here!' she cried, voice jumpy and filled with fright. 'Get out, you idiot!'

'I want to make a bargain,' I declared, causing Cowan's brow to raise with intrigue.

'My life for theirs. I will do as you say and won't speak against you,' I offered firmly.

Instead, an uproar of laughter erupted from the surrounding soldiers; luckily covering the thudding sound from the floor above, signaling that Lucius had made it across the cables and onto the second-floor balcony.

Just a little longer.

'And what makes you think you are worth two lives?' Cowan asked smugly, folding his arms.

'I know I am worth ten times what I am offering. I found out who my father was, what secrets my parents held…I found out what you did to him,' I finished, tilting my head down as I scowled at him.

A lump clearly got stuck in his throat as he swallowed, and he stared back, his appearance becoming pale and less self-assured.

He couldn't risk letting those secrets and plans out, especially when they can be linked back to him; he would be burned alive if the others found out it was because of his incompetence.

'Very well,' he agreed.

With a wave of his hand, he ordered his captives to be let go. The soldiers stepped away, and with that, Sylvie helped her father outside the best she could, sharing with me one last sympathetic look.

'Bring her upstairs,' Cowan commanded as he trudged upward, stomping his muddy boots one after the other, alerting Lucius— who was most likely already upstairs—to hide.

We turned into one of the tavern rooms, which looked to be a lot nicer than I'd previously imagined. My nerves a wreck. Cowan took a seat and I was forced down into the seat facing him; he still seemed confident that he was winning blowing me a kiss, making my blood boil and desire for revenge grow and fester. Out of the two of us, which one has a highly trained group of allies itching to attack?

So there we were, both sitting opposite each other, staring, waiting for the other to make the next move. It was almost time to take down the king.

The guards that came with us waited for the show to begin.

'Leave us,' Cowan ordered, waving his hand.

They both looked at each other before doing as commanded, albeit hesitantly.

'You think you know secrets, hm? I love secrets, tell them.' He seemed confident that I was lying.

'If I told you, they wouldn't be secrets, would they?' I replied with a smug smile that clearly irked him.

'You don't have anything. You're just trying to save your own skin,' he hissed, leaning over and holding his fists to his tightened face.

'If I were trying to save my own skin, why would I be sitting here in front of the Lord of the city I am trying to take down?' I replied again, making his face twitch under his knuckles.

I leaned closer to him, egging him on.

'I'll tell you *one* little secret,' I whispered, waving my fingers to beckon him closer. He reluctantly leaned forward, and I lowered my voice even further.

'I brought a few friends along with me, and they would love to say hello,' I finished, a victorious grin spreading across my lips. When I pulled away, his face was pale, but he let out a nervous chuckle.

From outside came the sound of steel bashing together and the gurgling cries of his men dying. This caught his attention, and he launched himself from his relaxed position to see what was going on.

'What the hell is happening?!' he said, his voice booming and brows arching as high as they would go. He looked at me and my smug smile and raised face, turning his relaxed palms into fists, growling with a low resonance, as he gritted his teeth and strode towards the door. Before he could open it, the door swung open and viciously unhinged itself from the frame. Lucius stood before him in all his glory. The large, muscled man filled the entrance, towering above the stiffened man half his size, smiling down upon him forebodingly, a glimmer of pleasure glinting from his eyes. The door downstairs slammed shut with an almighty power, and the sound of fighting entered the tavern. It did not last long, and the commotions of battle were quickly replaced by an eerie silence.

'What is this?!' he yelled, panicking.

'I told you... my friends want to say hello,' I said calmly, satisfied with his reaction. Lucius stepped closer to Cowan, almost cornering him, breathing heavily, and scowling so much that the space between his brows began to fold and form a ridge above his nose, making him look even more threatening.

'A few of them wanted to thank you personally for doing such a good job at ruining their lives and killing their loved ones,' I said dryly. 'You remember Lucius, don't you? Cut off his arm, killed his wife...' I lightly patted his arm, smiling at the pants-wetting look

Cowan returned. I then placed my hand on my friend's bulging shoulder.

'Remember, don't kill him,' I whispered. 'Just maim him a little while I ask the questions.'

Kole appeared shortly after. His clothes were sprayed with blood, a tiny cut was neatly placed on his lower lip, his cheek was swelling, and his burnt-orange eye was dulled with weariness. He mindlessly strode in, scuffing his heels slightly, as he carried a small chipped table that the tavern's customers used for card games. He placed it at an equal distance between Cowan and me. I watched my opponent's face, my legs spread, physically displaying my freedom. Kole shut the door behind him without a word, leaving the grinning jackals to their frightened prey behind the red door.

'So, shall we get down to business?' I asked sarcastically, leaning forward and placing my elbows on my widened knees. 'I am going to ask you some questions. If you don't answer them or lie to me, Lucius here will give you a reason to tell us the truth.' My pleasure was almost too unbearable to contain.

'Like what?' he replied, acting stupid.

'Perhaps you can give us some pointers. This is the first time we've ever been forced to torture someone, whereas you do it for fun. Tell us how you'd hurt someone to get what you want.'

He didn't answer. I smirked.

'Shall we begin?' I asked. 'Why did you wait all this time to take me away from the Drakes?'

No response. Lucius circled around him like a hungry beast, his muscles growing and teeth grinding in anxious anticipation.

Cowan didn't seem willing to talk, so I gave a nod of approval to Lucius, who grabbed the back of Cowan's head in one whole hand and slammed it down rapidly into the table between us. Jerking his head back, a gush of blood already began spewing out his nose down his chin.

'Aah! Fuck! I think you broke my nose! You're gonna pay for

that, you fucking cunt!' he howled, his eyes watering from the pain, causing me to snicker.

Lucius stepped forward, readying his fist for another strike. I raised my hand, signaling him to stop.

'Answer the question,' I said calmly.

'All right, fine…,' he answered, holding his bleeding nose. 'I waited for so long because others were looking for you, and I needed to take care of them first. Once I knew there was no one left searching, I went in and bought you. I knew exactly who you were and that you were placed right under that idiot Drake's nose—he didn't even notice who you were, just another person he could order around. The others wanted to kill you; I simply had other things in mind. I knew you would grow up as you did. So beautiful.'

Behind his cupped hand, his eyes turned to slivers as he ogled me. Lucius's face mimicked mine, cringing at that disgusting comment, and he raised his large hand, slashing it across the back of Cowan's head, causing him to slump over from the impact. As his crunched body slumped over, a tiny dribble of blood mixed with saliva trailed out of his grinning mouth.

'All right. Who else is in the group you belong to?'

Again, he refused to answer, tightening his jaw as hard as he could, causing his chin to stiffen. I gave another subtle nod to Lucius, who grinned at the approval for further harm.

He viciously grabbed Cowan's free hand, which quickly turned into a fist. One by one, Lucius pried his fingers open. When they were splayed out, Lucius grabbed Cowan's pointer finger and bent back. Cowan screamed as it snapped, writhing under Lucius's firm grip. But even still, he refused to answer. Another snap and a similar scream escaped his lips, and soon he began to cry. His tears mixed with the blood that had dried from his broken nose.

Lucius moved onto the third finger and started to pull.

'Hold on! Wait! No! No! No!' Cowan pleaded, begging for Lucius to stop. Lucius looked to me, waiting for my answer. I pretended to think about it for a moment. Crossing my arms whilst holding my chin with a curled finger, then nodded.

Cowan took in a shaky breath.

'There are many of us. A hierarchy, the twelve lords who, like me, are in high standings across the new world... Lord Karn is considered the elder...the leader. He is the messenger for a mysterious master he speaks to. No one has ever seen him. Only Karn is allowed to, and that's only when he is summoned.' It felt like there were more secrets to this Company than I'd anticipated. But there was something I cared about more than greedy men. Who are these other lords? Where they all at the Drakes' dinner party? And who's this mysterious 'master'? I leaned in. 'Is my mother still alive?' I asked, looking him straight in the eye, my own like sharpened daggers, intensely watching for any sign of a lie.

He began to snicker, which turned into a laugh, then escalated into a roar.

'Is that what this is all about? Seriously... Little girl wants her mummy?' he mocked.

Lucius's hand wrapped around his throat like a serpent, squeezing it.

'Answer the question,' he said through gritted teeth.

'If your mother were alive, she wouldn't want anything to do with you. It's your fault your father's dead, and your fault she got taken away!' His mouth grew as wide as he possibly could make it, blood smeared his teeth and covered his lips as he cackled maniacally. I continued to stare at him, blank-eyed and unresponsive.

With a lightning quick snatch, Lucius grabbed the back of Cowan's head, grasping onto a clump of his clean golden hair, and slammed him into the wall closest to them. Cowan hung there like a picture frame, cracks creeping out past his chest showing the force Lucius used to do it. Lucius then forcefully turned his stiff body, grabbed the frightened Lord's neck and squeezed it until veins began to raise all over his face and neck as the skin turned from pale to a pinkish hue. As he did so, I jumped up, scared of the strength he was showing and worried that he would actually kill him before we had finished. Lucius's face was snarling, cheeks rippling in furiousness as he stared down his prey. Cautiously stepping closer to the volatile situation, I gently rested my hand on his outstretched arm, rubbing it softly to soothe.

'Lucius, put him down… Please, Lucius. We need more information from him.' I spoke softly, looking him directly in the eye.

His eyes changed and became brighter, and his muscles began to relax from his face to his arm and finally his hand, allowing him to slowly let Cowan down. The pitiful Lord rubbed his neck gingerly as the redness in his face died down.

I grabbed his arm and forced him back to the seat.

'Now, tell me this… how is it you know my parents?' I asked more calmly than before, waiting for the tension in the room to die down.

Still shocked at what had just occurred and slightly grateful for still being alive because of me, he continued to rub his worn neck as he spoke in a raspy tone.

'Your father… was once the Lord of Erast, sister city to Prona… considered to be a very innovative Lord of the people… and beloved among many… My dearest of friends… I considered him a brother before he betrayed us. Your mother… that whore… was a princess and daughter of the Frey… the only beings who were strong enough to fight against us… skilled assassins who, like you, sought to fight back for the people… Your father, along with his men, were charged with destroying the Frey and ridding us of their annoying abilities…long story short, they fell in love and ran away… But you can never run away from the Company. Once you are a Lord, you can never be free,' he answered, scowling intensely towards his inquisitor.

I sat, staring straight ahead, not looking at anything in particular, hiding how shocked and surprised I was at the answer I was given.

I needed time to absorb it all before returning to reality.

So my mother was… is Frey? That means I'm part Frey. When my instincts take over… is that just my Frey blood protecting me?

'Farrah?' Lucius's muffled voice called me out of my mind, making my eyes refocus.

'Sorry… One final question, then you can do as you wish with him.' I whispered, gifting Lucius what he has been craving for all this time. I turned back to the evil creature before me.

'All right, Lord Cowan… Where is your partner? Where is your wife hiding?' I slowly asked, anticipating he wouldn't freely give this answer away, but leaned forward with my elbows digging into my knees.

No response. He leaned back and continued to match my stare.

Obviously, he won't tell me. At least he has a sense of loyalty.

I met Lucius's waiting, confident gaze and signaled him to commit one final act, but only to scare him into answering.

Forcing his palm down on the table, Lucius readied his echobriome arm, forming it into a curved, chisel-like weapon. He hovered it over Cowan's squirming wrist, slowly edging it closer until it was almost touching.

'Oh, please, god, no! No! No!' Cowan began to blubber, tears and snot and blood dribbling out of every facial orifice as he looked at my blank gaze.

'Is that what Agnes and the other maids said before you mercilessly killed them for your own amusement?' I answered, already knowing I was right.

'You bitch! You won, okay!' he shouted, bloody dribble spurting out at me as his face turned bright red. 'You will never find her! She's far away from HOME!' He answered in a desperate attempt to save his sadistic love, but he shouted the last word louder than the others, unknowingly giving me the answer.

'Thanks. I'll be sure to say hi from you.' I finished, surprised at how smart I actually was, confusing both Lucius and Cowan in the process. Cowan looked at me with shock and fear as Lucius drove down his chisel weapon right through Cowan's hand, hitting the table and causing it to split from the force. I was still sitting in front of him, oblivious to the fact that Lucius was actually going to cut his freaking hand off, with my mouth gaped open like a fish. I recoiled into the seat, feeling Cowan's filthy, corrupt blood splashing me and entering my unwelcoming mouth.

'What? It slipped,' Lucius lied, smirking as he did so.

I remained coiled and disgusted at what had just happened and afraid to swallow. It took a moment for me to calm down and stand up. Quickly spitting out the bit of blood that pooled in my mouth, I looked at Lucius in revulsion before storming off out of the room.

Exhausted and mentally drained, I softly stepped over and around the fallen bodies of Cowan's so-called 'elite' soldiers, and into the somewhat-ashy cold air, the taste of his dirty noble blood still clinging to my tongue. Looking up at the night sky, the endless number of twinkling stars paled in comparison to the amount of thoughts and emotions that spanned within my head, all swirling like a rampaging tornado that could not be stopped.

I could hear footsteps echoing from afar, but they were quickly closing the distance. At first, I thought there were only two, but their numbers grew as they approached with an unnatural speed. I turned to face the outlines of the figures and recognised the face at the front. It was Adam, and following closely behind were the Garudans he took with him on his mission.

He halted abruptly a short distance away from me, and it seemed as though he were about to keel over and collapse.

'You're still alive, then… Are you okay?' I asked sincerely.

'I'm… fine,' he answered, hunched over and gulping in air between words.

The Garudans seemed unfazed, even relaxed from their journey; it was like they'd just been on a leisurely stroll instead of sprinting across the city after having just liberated their people.

'Were you able to complete the job?' I asked, still cringing at the subtle metallic taste that remained.

Adam nodded, unable to speak. He was drenched, his golden hair slicked back with sweat as if he had used his fingers to comb it back.

He finally stood upright, now able to slow down his breathing, and began to stretch out his sore muscles. He smiled half-heartedly at my worried face.

'Well… where are they?' I asked, slightly concerned.

'They wanted to fight as well. They went off to join the others. You've got more soldiers on your side,' he answered, calmer and more composed.

A startling noise from the room above pulled his attention away.

'You left Lucius in there alone with him?' he asked, eyes wide.

I slightly nodded, biting my lower lip, unsure if it was the right decision.

He responded with a hiss behind gritted teeth. I looked away. Part of me enjoyed hearing Cowan's cries of pain, but his words kept clawing at my brain. When I didn't comment, Adam cleared his throat and tried to be heard over the screams from above.

'What's our next step, boss?'

'Well. If Lucius hasn't hurt him too much, I'd like you and the Garudans to take Cowan to the top of the gate and wait for us there. I have some trash to take care of in the upper part of the city,' I commanded, giving them all a slight nod.

And with that, we separated. Leaving Adam and his new friends to handle our new prisoner.

I waited for what seemed like at least an hour before Lucius appeared. He was drenched in cold sweat and blood, wearing a worn face and slightly huffing. He looked at me, briefly, but stayed silent. Whatever he did to Cowan, he wasn't going to tell anyone. He was going to have to live with it for the rest of his life.

Chapter 19

We had taken back the city, but there were many more things to take care of; one of them being taking back what was mine. My book was in the clutches of that wicked witch, Mistress Cowan, and all I could think of was the pleasure of tearing it out of her cold dead hands.

The thought of her death sent electrifying excitement through my body sending it into motion, a smile already spreading across my lips. This was something I'd wanted to do for a very, very long time.

Behind us, a platoon of our allies were carving a path through the wreckage and bodies of both our comrades and enemy soldiers. When they reached us, they must've recognised the bloodlust on our faces because a few readied their weapons.

Desperate city soldiers burst forth from the cracks and crevices of the rubble, flailing their weapons, intent on killing—or at the very least badly wounding—all of us.

Their nostrils were flared and ready. The thought of being the general of a now fallen city caused many of them to salivate with greed and desire. Because of their blind, impulsive rage, they stood no chance against us. We struck them down like irksome flies, one blow at a time. Nothing was going to stop me from my goal, nothing was going to get in my way. Blood boiled and swords clashed, like savage beasts we fought with no remorse and were driven by the power of courage and bravery into every battle. Even

Tiery fought as hard as she could with Lucius as her guardian angel. Without paying attention to my own surroundings, one of the city soldiers managed to break off from his squadron and began to race straight for me, sword swinging above his head and, viciously growling like a wild animal, his yellow eyes didn't budge from his target. Launching himself into the air almost two feet away from me, landing in an impressive dominating stance of readiness, surprising me as we tangled together, the both of us desperately trying to kill the other and become the victor. I managed to jerk his sword away before accidently dropping it into the bloodied sand—whoever got to it first would be the victor. I scrambled towards it as fast as I could whilst the beast of a man on top of me did the same, all the while trying to slow me down. I closed my eyes as he flung sand at them, squirming faster and blindly searching for the sword until the hilt of the blade found my fingertips and, as quickly as I could, I twisted around and stabbed him straight in the chest without even a second thought. Finally, our battle was almost won. We stood victorious once more with a new sword for myself as the prize.

Before us lay the courtyard of the upper city, where all the wealthy and powerful people lived. Broken vases, shards of crockery, and other shattered decor were sprinkled over the cobblestones amongst the broken furniture and torn-up floorboards. Every door had been stripped off its hinges. The once-fine houses that lined the courtyard were hollowed out and destroyed, with streams of smoke billowing out a few of them. But there was something else that silenced us.

Hanging in front of every house were the former residents and their families. All were strung up like rag dolls, mangled to different degrees. The men were bloodied and carved up the most out of all, some even missing eyes or jaws, the women had strange runes carved into them from head to toe, but the children were left bare— as if the perpetrators did not want the guilt of hurting an innocent.

I could sense a collective sorrow fall upon the group, a sting of regret. Seeing fighters die was one thing, but to see defenseless families strung up so unceremoniously had reminded us of our compassion.

Swallowing hard, I forced myself to focus only on acquiring my target's hideout. I steeled my nerves and soldiered on, and the others followed at a staggered pace.

Looming before me, the great yellow-and-white pillared lair stood proud and unyielding, daring me to step inside.

A still, deathly silence consumed the interior of the disheveled house. Around us lay broken plates and cutlery, splintered furniture, and ravaged floorboards. I unsheathed my knife and new sword, prepared for anything or anyone. Lucius, Kole, and Tiery followed my lead, as well as our trusty platoon, causing everyone to be on high alert as we crept through the house. Every room had already been ransacked, and there was no sign of where the she-devil had hidden herself. That was until a slight rattle from behind a familiar door drew my attention.

The meeting hall. Her favourite room of all, the place that held her most prized possessions—her beloved raunchy novellas.

I nodded to Lucius, and the both of us straightened, standing in front of each door. With a swift, powerful kick of our heels, the double doors crashed down with great force, revealing what I'd predicted. Mistress Cowan, the woman I had the most unebbing rage for, stood at the center of the room as master of her fallen kingdom. She was guarded by two nerve-racked and sweaty sentries, and it was clear in their eyes they knew that this was where they were destined to die. They simultaneously darted towards us with warrior cries, weapons raised high.

The two tagalongs behind us pushed past and energetically killed both pathetic soldiers, one after the other, looking back at me as if for approval. I gave them each a slight nod. The mistress simply stood her ground and raised a single brow of slight surprise.

'Well. Looks like I had the wrong idea about those sweaty weasels,' began Mistress Cowan as we circled her like wolves. I could feel myself growing impatient with every second that ticked by. She didn't turn her head, but her eyes flickered to me.

'I'm impressed, Farrah. I never knew that these people would be able to work with one another—street rats and the like don't usually have this sort of relationship. They're too stupid, only having a mind to help themselves and that's all.' I continued circling her as the others took a step back. 'You should be proud. These people wouldn't have been able to pull enough brain cells together to think of what you did. Forging bridges between outcasts; your own personal legion of thugs and miscreants.' Her eyes darted around the room, clearly uneasy.

I gave another nod to Lucius, causing him to pounce like a panther atop our target, pinning her down to the floor. As the mistress squirmed against his firm grip, I casually walked closer and closer, eating up as much satisfaction in the moment as I could devour.

'Boy, are we going to have some fun,' I whispered with a smile of pure evil, the same one she'd once given me.

And with that, I raised the butt of my dagger and slammed it as hard as I could into the side of her skull. A creepy cackle began to escape her bloodied lips. Lifting the butt of my weapon higher once more, I struck down harder to shut her up, causing her to black out in a slump.

'Kole, you and the others set the explosive charges on the gates; I'll meet up with you guys there. I just need a moment here first,' I instructed, keeping my eyes on my prey.

'Will do,' he rapidly responded, rushing out the door with the tagalongs close behind him.

'Do you want us to wait for you?' Tiery asked, voice shaking slightly.

'No. Go with him,' I replied, more focused on ripping my

captive a new one than anything else.

'Don't be too long,' Lucius urged, eager to get out of this hellhole.

I moved quickly, and found that the blood-red sex dungeon had been completely untouched, meaning that even the thugs and miscreants she looked down upon aren't as twisted as her or her husband.

I gathered as many diverse objects I could hold and displayed them all nicely on the floor behind her. Then I tied her as she did me, with the same rough ropes and filthy shackles, making her resemble a creepy mannequin.

A low groan escaped Mistress Cowan when she finally came to, her groggy eyes looking this way and that. When the realisation hit, she became more lively, desperately pulling at the restraints with rekindled strength.

'Good, you're awake. I'd hate for you to miss out,' I said calmly, weaving through the shadows as I passed back and forth.

I paused. 'I feel so bad that you never got to experience the same fun Agnes and I had when you and your husband watched on as we screamed.' I pressed my lips against her shaking face, my voice dropping to a whisper. 'As we begged.' I straightened, slowly, looking down at her.

'I thought you would love to know how it felt. So I figured we should reverse the roles. You, the plaything, and me, well…' I smirked.

'Look, I'll give you anything you want,' she pleaded, forcing her voice to quiver. 'I'm sorry I… It was his idea. He forced me to contribute. He was the sick-minded bastard who wanted to do those things to you. I was just another tool… I—'

'Shhhhhh…' I pressed my finger against her lips as hard as I could and patted her head to calm her, just as she did me.

'You remember Agnes, don't you? The sweet maid that worked for you for so long? The one that put up with your bullshit and disrespect for years as you stepped on her and treated her like shit… Then you decided "Hey, you know what would be fun? Let's murder her and pin it on her friend." Do you remember that?' I asked, picking up a riding crop off the floor. I slapped it against my palm as I stepped around the room, keeping my eyes on the begging, weeping heap on the floor.

'Who was the one that did it? Who was the one that murdered Agnes?' I asked, already knowing the answer.

'Cowan did it,' she started yammering, her eyes darting back and forth. 'He said to me, "Wouldn't it be funny if we killed Agnes and framed the other one for the murder?" I told him no, that it was a crime to commit such a thing. The next thing I know, he was standing before me, bloodied.'

'Really, that's an interesting story…but that's just it, isn't it? A story.' My face grew menacing as red consumed my vision. Looking into her eyes, all I could feel was fury, and a hunger for vengeance I'd never known.

I tore her shirt to reveal her breasts as she had done to me, basking in the sounds of her weeping. Her cries flooded the room as she pleaded to her executioner for mercy, but I'd long since passed judgement and the punishment had already been elected.

'Mistress Cowan, wife to Lord Cowan, as punishment for your countless acts of murder, torture, and endless other crimes, you are hereby sentenced to death by my choosing. Pray now if you wish… but let me tell you this…,' I grabbed her by the jaw, my teeth bared. 'No one will answer.'

I strode to the weapons, hands hovering over each, and stopped when my fingers brushed against something familiar. The same exact spiked whip she used on me, in this very room, still caked in blood from its last meal. As I held it in my hand, electric pulses of bittersweet revenge coursed through my body; my hunger reaching its apex.

The half-naked canvas in front of me was prepared and yet shaking, just as I was the last time. I scrunched my nose, gritted my teeth, and launched my arm forward. The lash struck true, and the first droplets of blood coloured the polished floor.

The sight of it caused me to let out a puff of excitement, whilst the corner of my mouth slid up my cheek, pleased with the outcome.

Again and again, I struck over and over, my anger and frustration growing thirstier and thirstier. I was overcome with memories of the pain I felt and horrors I'd witnessed inflicted upon my loved ones out of simple amusement and pleasure. My own screams of fury drowned out her cries of pain as I struck as hard as I could, countless times, and each time the flashes of memories appeared with every strike and made me more and more bloodthirsty. Blood and muscle painted me and splattered against the walls of the room, coating everything in bright reds. It even reached the painting of the judgmental man, whose face seemed to turn into a subtle smile with the blood streaked across his lips.

My arm began to deaden from the force. I'd struck so hard into the flesh that white flecks of bone began to peek out.

Still somehow alive, yet barely breathing, my artwork grew limp and exhausted, but my hunger for blood had not subsided. Picking up my knife, the same exact blade that they used upon my dear friend, I circled my masterpiece. One after another, I began to carve and cut, slashing and slicing icons and images that came to mind.

'Hmm… It's missing something,' I muttered to myself.

And then it came to me. Knife in hand, I chopped off her hair— all the way down to her scalp. When nothing was left but a patchy, bloody skull, I moved the blade down to her lips; the same lips that smiled softly and hungrily at every one of her innocent victims that were just like me. The lips that spoke the words that killed and tortured other women. Even now, I felt that she was still smiling, still softly instructing her partner to hurt and maim us. Yes, they had to go.

I stood before my masterpiece as she sat limp. Sad wheezing

noises passed through her raw throat and bloodied torn lips as saliva and blood trickled out, forming a small pool of blood on the floor below her.

I crouched down to her slumped figure, tilting my head as I stared patiently at the dying woman. I lifted my dagger to her chin, forcing it up so that she could see me.

'What's with that face? Don't be so sad… You'll soon be well looked after.' I end with a devilish smile of pure joy, which was met with the frightened look of realization from the former mistress and black-hearted Queen of Buson.

Without taking an eye off her slashed and battered face, I carefully touched my blood and flesh tipped dagger to her dark red caked chest and drove it in as slowly as I could. Her head lifted and she gasped in agony and terror at the thought about what was next to come. The blade slid into her heart with ease, in turn her body slumped over once again, lifeless.

With her finally dead and quiet, I stepped back, taking it all in. Slowly, the anger and evil that coaxed me into committing such a disgusting killing drifted away. The blood drained from my head and my eyes became clear, and I truly saw what I'd done.

Fear and disgust stirred in my stomach; my heart racing at the atrocity, each beat banging louder and louder in my head. I backed away, breathless and speechless at my actions, and the sudden need to vomit overcame me. I raced outside and released all of the horrid rancid feeling and taste of darkness from my tongue, expelling it from my shaking body.

'What have I done?! What did I just do?!' I wheezed as the image seared itself into my memory.

I took a slow breath, my heart starting to quieten. It was then that I heard a voice.

'It's all right, this means you are not like them.'

'DeeDee…' Tears fell down my blood-painted face as I struggled to breathe.

'This means you still have a soul; they never cried out of fear for theirs. They were born dark and soulless. Not like you or me,' she continued, soothing my mind.

I started to cry for a whole other reason.

'You have a job to do, Farr. You need to continue on the path you've taken. Your father and I are so proud of you. He's here with me, cheering you on… We will always be by your side…' I took in a big breath, wiping away the tears and blood.

'You're right, Dee. I need to finish this.' Swallowing my sadness and shame, I lifted myself up and stepped back inside, avoiding the room of blood and death.

The master's office was the first place that came to mind; if I took things from my maids, that's where I would keep them.

I'd never been into his office before. Standing on the threshold of the grand, dimly lit room, I still felt as if there were an invisible force-field blocking my path. I knew my fear was the thing creating the barrier, fear that he would catch me and beat me, that he would turn the corner at any second and punish me horrendously. But this time my rationality kicked in, reminding me that we had him; he was imprisoned elsewhere, and would soon be killed for his crimes.

I took a deep breath, pushing down my illogical reluctance. I took the first step into the velvet-carpeted room. A sigh of relief blew my fear away as I casually strolled towards his large wooden antique desk. There were two locked drawers, both with intricate key holes. Behind his desk hung an oversized imposing picture of himself in a throne-like chair, showing the viewer exactly what he thought of himself.

On a hunch, I felt behind the heavy gold frame and, funnily enough, found the cold edges of a wall safe that was slightly smaller. I tossed the painting to the side, revealing the silver door. It was locked with a large central circular mechanism, which normally would have put me off if I hadn't seen the hinges and rusty nails barely holding on. I grabbed my bloodied and jimmied the nails free from the hinges, loosening the safe's door until it gracefully swung open.

Within it were stacks upon stacks of money—not just Buson currency, but every other currency there was. There were also heavy coin bags being used as paperweights for the stacks, and next to one of them a small ornate box which held a key.

Turning around, I smiled as it easily slid into his desk drawer. Unlocking the first one, I discovered a single piece of paper with a series of numbers: 467757

Interesting.

Thinking this seemed important for some nefarious scheme the Lords were cooking up, I took it thinking would be useful information to look into, either that or a good piece of leverage for bargaining.

The second drawer held a small stack of papers and envelopes, which gave me an idea. I pulled out a blank page and writing supplies, setting them on the desk for a moment. I knew, though, he wouldn't lock a drawer of just blank pages. I felt around the wooden frame and found a small hole just behind the handle of the drawer. I tugged at it, revealing the bottom to be a fake, and lifted it slowly to reveal a secret compartment. Inside were my message books. Dad's and Cowan's, together—he was stupid for not separating them. Slipping the paper note into one of the books before searching around more for anything else that could lead to more information about the mysterious numbers.

Before leaving, I wrote a letter, using one of Lord Cowan's golden-tipped quills.

Dear Lady Farrow,

I know we don't know each other personally, but you knew my good friend DeeDee. She spoke of what you promised to her and your promise to us, her family.

DeeDee has passed on. Her brother and his companions have hopefully reached you and given you this letter. They are good people, as are most others like them. They need a new life and a new friend to help them. My hope is that it is you, that you are not like the others and you will help them. If so, I will be in your debt.

Sincerely, Farrah

Chapter 20

Happy with collecting my spoils, I stuffed them in a polished brown leather satchel that hung over the coat stand by the door. Reaching the threshold of the once grand manor, a feeling of anxiety fluttered in my stomach, my breathing began to stagger. The knowledge that, not only have I forged a new path for everyone, but also an uncertain and precarious one for myself, was overwhelming. Eventually the other Lords would find out what happened, therefore placing a big target on my back. I've not only made myself an outcast, I have also turned myself into a fugitive; but if this is the cost of freedom for all, I wouldn't have it any other way.

Let them come for me.

I left, surer of myself than ever before and filled with happiness and relief knowing that we had won, and I was free.

People had already arrived at the gates and were ready to be set free, just as I was. Lord Cowan was at the top, slumped over, beaten and bruised, and drained of any sort of emotion. His lone hand tightly gripped on by Lucius's echobriome arm, displaying him from the great gates of Buson as a symbol of hope that helped give people confidence, seeing their oppressor torn down to a mere purple and lumpy sack of human skin.

Walking up the spiral staircase of metal and iron, I realised I needed to say something to them, but what? Something inspirational, something that will give their humanity back, and build up their will to keep fighting. I needed to show them they still had worth as individuals.

It didn't take me long to reach the top, and that meant I didn't get enough time to think. As I looked ahead, Tiery stood by me, then Kole. Lucius and Adam stood on either side of the snake, and Pip occupied the opposite spire, looking triumphant.

Tiery gave me a nod as she saw my nerves rise. I clenched the strap of my satchel, anxiety skyrocketing as the crowd below became a sea of eyes looking towards their rescuers. I was nudged forward, roughly, and I turned back to snarl at Tiery. She simply smiled and mouthed 'go on'.

As I walked precariously to the middle so that all below could see me, my mind was rushing a mile a minute of all the things I could say, but nothing seemed right, nothing was perfect for this once-in-a-lifetime moment. And then my mouth opened, and the words just spilled out.

'For hundreds of years, his people thought of themselves as gods!' I pointed to my subject viciously. 'They wanted you to think of us as lower than them! That you weren't worth the life your mothers and fathers gave you! That you were less than the dirt you walk upon! Long ago, your ancestors built great buildings that touched the heavens; they built empires and communities. They were the ones that fought wars declared by his people, thousands dying for their petty causes. Our people learned to make names for themselves and to create their own worlds. They worked for *themselves*. His people destroyed a beautiful world with their greed and selfishness. Our ancestors are the people who built this world once! And I know that we are the people who can build it again!'

Silence hung in the air, and my heart started beating quickly. I began to second-guess what I'd said. And then...

A slow clap started, then spread, becoming infectious, and soon every single person below me was roaring and cheering and applauding as loud and as hard as they could. I looked at Lucius, who was smiling like a proud father, and Adam was left gob smacked. I quickly whipped around to an applauding Tiery who was blubbering so much that snot, blood, and dirt mixed into a disgusting combination that rolled down her plump, smiling cheeks. Kole simply clapped as a gentleman would, whooping with joy a little when he thought no one was looking.

'What do you want us to do with the prisoner?' Adam shouted over the roars of the city.

I didn't even need to think twice as a fun thought popped into my head. Walking over to the captive of the people, I crouched down close enough for him to hear my sadistic whisper.

'The fun I had killing your mistress is nothing compared to what you are about to endure. All those people down there want a piece of you… Do you hear them? They sound hungry, don't they? As our ancestors used to say… What was it? Oh, yes, 'can't keep the people waiting'.' I rested my hand on his dislocated shoulder, causing him to wince. I pushed his weak body ever so slightly off the sheer wall of iron and into the raging sea of angry citizens. His scream of fear was short-lived as he landed in the mass of the eager hands of his former people. He was quickly consumed and violently killed by his own creation.

Lucius, Adam, Pip, Kole, and Tiery stood watching on at the horrendous chaos I had created. Their smiles seemed to disappear, and I had a feeling it wasn't from horror, but the longing to be down there as well. To be honest, I wished the same, but murdering the mistress for Agnes, killing all those soldiers, and pushing Lord Cowan off the gates had all finally made me blood sick.

'Blow the gates, Kole,' I finished, walking off the top and down the spiral staircase, followed by a silent Tiery and Lucius.

After the people had had their fill of their own vengeance, the men who fought for their freedom began a chain barricade and backed the crowd to a safe distance. Once the crowd was pushed back, the ground where the Lord's body had supposedly landed was stained with blood—there was nothing to be found. Perhaps some of his goons were still alive and took the body, or maybe the crowd tore him to shreds.

'Wow… That was quite a speech!' a familiar voice spoke.

I turned around casually to meet the gaze of its owner and his trusty partner beside him.

Alfie and Sonny stood together, smiling ear to ear, the both of them brimming with pride. Sonny's eyes even seemed to be moistened with tears.

'What are you two doing here? I thought I told you to stay with the others at the wellness centre,' I scolded, trying to seem annoyed, but I couldn't help my smile.

'We know… but since we couldn't hear any guns or anything, we figured it might be over. We thought we would come and help if it didn't turn out so well,' Alfie explained, the both of them slowly walking closer. 'But good thing we won, otherwise we would have had to save you. And that wouldn't be a good look for our fearless rebellion leader.' Alfie nudged Sonny, who was wiping away his tears.

'Yes, well… It's a good thing you're here, anyway,' I replied, letting what he called me slide with gritted teeth. I cleared my throat, holding my crossed arms tightly to my stomach. 'There's one last thing I need the two of you to do for me, that is, if you accept it.'

'After what you've done for us, I owe you my life. Anything you need, consider it done,' Alfie answered fiercely. Sonny nodded in agreement with the same look on his face. Both of them leaned in, their curiosity peaked.

'I have a friend in Prona. She is connected to powerful people and cares for those like us. I have written a letter for her.' I raised it up before handing it to Alfie. His mouth gaped at the envelope as he held it, eyes intense.

'I would like you to take whoever you can from the wellness-centre to her,' I continued. 'I don't care who else you take as long as you get Mino, Margo, and Francis out of here. Here is a bag of coins I took from Cowan's safe. It should be more than enough to get all of you there.' My hands were sweaty handling the large bag of coins and discreetly forcing it into Sonny's hand.

'But what about you?' Alfie asked, concerned.

'I'll be scouting new allies wherever they may be. People and species alike who wish for the same thing we do. I believe my mother can help with that. I plan to try and find her,' I replied, confident in my decision.

'All right, we will do our best to protect them,' Alfie promised on behalf of the both of them.

'Oh, and tell Francis... Tell Francis I will see him again soon,' I added, reminiscing on the image of him and DeeDee as children together. Happy.

It was time to blow the gates and a countdown commenced. Everyone in the fallen city joined in, including myself.

'Three...two...one!'

Ear-splitting explosions ran along the seams of the gates, popping and blowing apart the supposedly indestructible structure. And then the iron and steel behemoth that kept us locked away began to crumble like a delicate pastry. It created a great dust cloud as it smashed into the ground, revealing the golden rays of the magnificent sunrise and the freedom that awaited all of us.

Another triumphant cheer erupted throughout the crowd, this time more hopeful and louder than before. Women fell to the ground just as the wall did, clasping their hands together in prayer, tears rolling down their grateful faces. Garudan men jumped high into the air above everyone, pumping their fists up in joy. Every creature of almost every land rejoiced together in their salvation and their freedom.

The rumble of an engine erupted from the large cement building that housed the vehicles of the soldiers. Nearby bystanders scattered, frightened, watching as the ground shook.

Bursting out of the building's locked iron doors was a moss-green vehicle fitted with an impressive bumper bar and machine gun on the roof. It drove straight through the freed people, who quickly dodged it however they could. As it sped past me, time stopped, and the man in the driver's seat was clear—there, wearing his uniform, his combed-back blonde hair flicking in the wind, and sporting the same gritted expression of anger I could recognise anywhere, was James.

He zoomed this way and that, clearly making a beeline for the exit. A few of the rebel soldiers began a barricade of guns and spears in an attempt to stop the person behind the wheel.

'No! Let him go! He's an outlaw now,' I shouted, raising a hand in the air.

Confusion rang out through the barricade, but they did as they were commanded, and made a path for the vehicle barreling down the street and out of this god-forsaken city.

'Why did you stop them?' Adam asked, clearly annoyed as he stomped over.

'He can't return to his family. He has brought shame upon them, and even if he does, they would have no choice but to hand him over as a man who fled his duty and be executed,' I explained. Adam's face softened, understanding.

'Good one. He'll have no place to go. An outcast of his own people,' he replied approvingly, clearly impressed.

'Farrah! Farrah!' Marta yelled, waving ecstatically as he bounded towards us. Sorra was in tow, smiling as much as she'd allowed it.

His long arms wrapped around me like a snake as he lifted me up and jumped for joy.

'I can't believe we did it! Thank you so much! You have freed us from that tyrant and his bitch!' he exclaimed, slapping me on the back as his happiness overwhelmed him.

Sorra stood beside him, bowing slightly in respect, showing her own kind of gratitude.

'Yes, we are forever in your debt,' she added on softly as she continued to smile. It quickly disappeared when her keen Garudan nose caught the scent of their natural enemies.

Voge-Norse and Firth silently joined, both wearing soft smiles of appreciation as well; which was surprising, being known as vicious unrelenting killing machines and all.

'Yes, we thank you as well,' Voge-Norse added. 'Our people are so grateful for your arrival. We will tell our chief about this day and it will always be remembered as the day we revolted against the evils of man… Whatever you need, we will be at your side.' He placed his fist on his bloodied chest and bowed, as did Firth, both with a grateful smile.

Marta seemed a bit annoyed at this, with his squinting eyes showing the rivalry that burned there.

Sorra's knuckles turning a brilliant pinkish white ready to strike.

'And the Garuda tribe of Firingar will be at your side as well. Not only that, but I wish to offer you my son's hand in marriage. He is but a child now, but one day will be the leader of the—'

'That's all right, Marta, just your support will be plenty,' I quickly cut him off, begging him not to continue. 'The Garudans and Kraznians are strong in their own ways and have skills in many areas of battle. I assure the both of you I will call when I need you as long as our bond holds.' Taking a final bow in respect, both the Kraznian and the Garudans took their leave and joined their fellow companions as they got ready to finally venture home.

'Wow… What an honour… and you just shot him down like that. Being married to a chieftain's son, and a *child*, no less. Are you sure you made the right choice?' Adam snickered under his hand, giving me his usual poor sarcasm, to which I slapped back with a death-stare I had learnt from Ms. Turner.

'Farrah hasn't got time for marriage, she has a rebellion to lead,' Lucius commented as he walked through the crowd of bustling city folk. They were all eager to leave their cage as they pillaged and scrambled for valuables and anything else they could find to sell.

The biggest smile stretched across Lucius's face, causing his cheeks to ripple. A great big bear hug was happening, and I'd already had my fill of rough break-your-back hugs from Marta today. This time, though, Lucius was different. He was tender as he rubbed my back in gratitude and elation. The humble, kind smile and warm, dark eyes looked down upon me as he patted me on the shoulder as a proud father would.

'And with me by your side as your right-hand gal, what would you need marriage for?' Tiery added, pushing her way through the crowd and resting her arm over my already aching shoulders, standing on tip-toes to comfortably meet my height.

'I was the one that poisoned the guards at the mine! Shouldn't I be the one getting praised!' a mousy little voice squeaked from below as Pip appeared out of nowhere, roughly squeezing her way through Adam and Lucius's legs. Tiery scooped her up and nuzzled her roughly, which Pip unsurprisingly squirmed away from.

'Of course, I wasn't the only one. Everyone played a part in this. I couldn't have done it without the strength and courage of everyone else in the city. I simply showed you that there was another choice, not just following their rules,' I admitted.

'Don't be stupid, you were the one to bring every creature together, even the Kraznians and Garudans—which I didn't really think was going to work, considering their rivalry and past,' Kole interjected, casually strolling in with crossed arms. 'Don't put yourself down so lightly. You were the only one able to bring everyone together; I don't know how, but you did. It was impressive.'

We were all together again, the six of us.

'So what now?' Tiery asked, breaking the peace between us in the middle of people buzzing past.

'What do you mean?' I asked.

'I mean, where do we go from here? What's our next adventure?' Excitement spread across her face as she waited impatiently.

Before I knew it, everyone's eyes were on me, waiting for an answer.

'You guys want to come with me? I don't even know where I'm going,' I bluntly answered with a chuckle.

'Well yeah, we're a team,' answered Adam, looking surprised I'd even ask.

'And we're all outlaws now. It's not like we have anywhere else to go,' Kole reminded me, casually waving his hand about.

'Okay. So I'm supposed to decide where to go from here?' I begrudgingly concluded.

How did I become the leader?

'Well, I do plan on finding more people like us who desire freedom and a choice in how they live their lives. My mother is Frey. I've never met any other Frey, but I'm hoping we can find some to help us and join us in our crusade,' I offered, nervous about their reaction.

They became frozen statues of shock and awe, all of them with gaped mouths and widened eyes, their pupils dilated. All apart from Lucius, who seemed more grim than shocked as he looked at the ground.

He's holding something back. Why is he hiding things from me?

'Wait... Your mother's Frey? That means you're part Frey... Oh my God... My best friend is a kick-ass magical assassin!' Tiery squealed and jumped excitedly as she wrapped her arms around my neck, totally fan-girling.

'This is so cool. I'll get to meet the most badass assassins of all time and speak to them and learn from the Masters!' Pip cut in. 'And then I'll be able to become a captain of my own squadron! We shall be named the Shadow Clan! Avengers of the Night! And we—' she stopped herself, realizing she had lost her cool and was speaking aloud, fighting invisible bad guys while we watched, shocked and amused.

'More like the Fighting Fleas,' Adam cruelly corrected her,

gaining deadly death stares from everyone, forcing him to swallow his tongue.

'Look. I'm not sure about this idea,' Kole said, a worried frown crowning his eyes. 'Some factions of Frey that left their clan and homeland also abandoned their teachings and laws. They have become corrupt and blinded by greed. I've heard terrible stories.'

'We won't know if we don't try. Besides, if anything goes bad, we're all here for each other. We're a team.' Tiery calmly said, placing her hand on his tensed shoulder.

'I've heard whispers of sightings in a place called The Forest of Belle, which is next to East Haven—an outcast and Fugitive colony. If we travel to a coastal town called Dert, we should be able to catch the barge there and get to East Haven under a week,' Adam suggested optimistically.

'Really? You're suggesting we go to a place called *Dert?*' Kole scrunched his nose in disgust.

'Really. You were beaten and lashed, forced to mine rocks for years, but a town called Dert is where you draw the line? It's incredible that your stuck-up personality has stayed intact after all this time,' Adam snapped.

'Okay, that's enough,' I intervened. 'As the unofficial leader of our group, I say we go to Dert and take the barge to East Haven.' My decision put smiles on most of our group's faces, apart from a concerned Kole, and Lucius, who seemed to be putting on a false show of acceptance to appease me.

'Are we sure about this?' Kole asked, agitated by our free-minded group decision.

'Not scared, are we?' Adam poked with a devilish smirk on his face as he elbowed poor Kole.

'It's okay, Kole. Like Tiery said, we are in this together. As one.' I attempted to reassure him with a gentle smile.

'Fine. But if I die, I'm going to kill all of you!' He said, reluctantly agreeing.

'Then it's unanimous,' Lucius concluded.

Tiery was right. We were together as one, a strong team of rebels, thieves and outlaws on a mission to change a world that had become rotten. I was in search of answers to the hundreds of questions that ravaged my mind, determined to find the truth, and maybe with that truth reach a better and brighter tomorrow.

The end.

The Last Resort

Author's Note

Within these pages you will find hidden worlds and ancient forests frozen in time for thousands of years, bizarre creatures that have evolved differently to the ones above them with their own cultures and religions, thriving on disease, no cancer, illness, or plague. Everyone of them dying peacefully at a very old age. This incredible find of health and prosperity is thought and hoped to be humanities salvation but, in the end, will our own self preservation and greed lead to the destruction of not only one but two worlds?

Before the world grew dark and the land turned against its people, humans were on the verge of annihilation—countries once again on the precipice of turning on each other. None of them knew, however, that it would be for the final time.

Many years before the Great War of Humanity, scientists had discovered large objects under the earth's crust, roughly the same size as the surface's continents. What was odd were the shapes and materials that surrounded them.

A team of geologists and scientists led by a man named Richard Tannor wanted to drill into the earth's crust to the centre of one of the masses. To satisfy the United Nations' curiosity at what valuable materials may be found, they approved their proposal, and an expedition was launched.

'How much longer till we hit the field?' Dr. Tannor asked.

'Twenty kilometres. Preparing trajectory change for 15.748 degrees. Centre of the thinnest part of the metamorphic rock barrier,' alerted the youngest recruit of the team.

'All right, alter our speed so that we can prepare the equipment for the sediment samples. Major, get your men ready and double-check the breathing apparatuses,' instructed Dr. Tannor, ignoring the rolling eyes of the meatheads, which unfortunately, he was forced to let come along as protection.

'Actually, sir, I don't think we need them…' Dr. Thorpe interjected. 'Assuming my readings are correct, the atmospheric conditions seem to be similar to the surface. It's slightly different from what we are used to, but it is breathable.'

'Are you sure?' he responded, only to receive a raised eyebrow and an odd look back.

'Okay… Dr. Yeung, could you please stop the drill? I can see we are about to breach the barrier. Before we do, I want to go through some things again.'

'Yes, sir. Stopping now.' With a flick of a switch and a slow pull of a heavy lever, the drill gave a loud rattle and squeak before stopping completely.

'Gather around, please. Before we embark on this journey, I'd like to remind you of the dangers we may face inside of the field we're about to penetrate—' Tannor paused due to the giggles and chuckles coming from the huddle of green bodies in the back. 'Yes, well, remember that the samples recorded suggests that the atmosphere will be unlike our own; if you have any difficulty breathing, tanks will be provided for you. It will be difficult to walk the first few hours, so don't journey too far. The primary reason for being here is to harvest samples of the dirt, but since we suspect there are underwater rivers and reservoirs, we'll need to get samples of possible vegetation too.'

'Nice speech, doc,' interrupted the captain, 'but you do realise that we're only here for three days—so no one wander off to look at dandelions, and every one of your people must stay within view of one of my men. Oh, and no one take stupid risks for one another. We don't know what's down there.'

'Right,' Dr. Tannor nodded. 'Quick and efficient, everyone.'

A grand forest loomed before them, illuminated by bioluminescent moss that covered almost everything from the cave walls to the ceiling. Long arms seemed to grow from their clusters like slim vines, glowing a beautiful green and shining down on trees that stretched above us like giants. The sound of rushing underground rivers echoed around the team, and sometimes Tannor swore he could feel them coursing inches beneath his feet. But it was not just the allure of vegetation that enamoured him. He could hear creatures cooing and rustling further in, and he felt his curiosity drawing him closer and closer. The pull was so strong it was borderline involuntary, as if the life in this bizarrely beautiful forest was bewitching him with its sweet melody.

'Wait!' Captain Warner's ape-like arm stopped Tannor in his tracks, snapping him out of his trance. 'We don't know what's in there. This is a hostile environment, and therefore the situation has changed.'

'We can't just leave,' Dr. Francine Thorpe challenged. 'This is a new environment and there might be other ones like it. And besides, we just got here!' She thrust her arms out, frustrated.

Richard Tannor admired Dr. Thorpe; she was an abrasive, yet determined and bright woman—almost as bright as himself.

'I'm not saying we're leaving, Doc. I'm telling you that you will be supervised under my team's protection; one of my men partnered with yours at all times. And if any of you nerds wander off, you also get a weapon, just in case.' The burly Major gave her a reassuring wink.

'Are you kidding me?' Francine's hands flew outward, face reddening. 'This is not a war zone! Not everything is done with muscles and guns!'

'Dr. Thorpe, he's right,' Dr. Tannor said calmly. 'We don't know what's out there. It's best to be safe.'

'Wise words, Doc!' Captain Warner said, slapping Tannor on the back hard enough to make him cough out his lungs.

'Y-Yes...' Tannor wheezed.

'We'll set up camp here for the night,' Warner declared, turning from us.

'And how do you know it's night time captain?' Dr. Thorpe snidely retorted. 'If you haven't noticed, we're underground.'

The captain shot her an equally snarky glare, holding up his wrist. 'I still have a watch on.'

As the others were arguing, a soldier walked to one of the rivers with a bottle.

'What do you think you're doing?' asked Dr. Thorpe.

'I'm thirsty; I'm getting some water. Chill out, Doc.'

'But we don't know what's in that water. For all we know, there could be poisons and harmful bacteria,' she said, crossing her arms. 'We need to analyze it first. Besides, there's water in the drill tanker we came in.'

The soldier rolled his eyes. 'You're being para—'

'What's that?' Dr. Tannor interrupted.

A small ripple disrupted the water. Then a larger one, closer.

The crew stood by, watching, shocked and scared.

'Don't move, son,' the captain warned the soldier, fright in his eyes and palms out.

No one could see into the murky depths, but as it came closer to the shallows, a strange shape started to form.

A brilliant spray of water burst from behind the poor unsuspecting soldier, and from it, a creature emerged. No one would have believed. It had large yellow eyes, bright against its pale green skin, and in between them was a strange oval-shaped lump, and from its snarling mouth protruded multiple rows of razor-sharp teeth. With its webbed fingers, it violently snatched the soldier, who still had his back turned. As quickly as it emerged, it disappeared with the soldier in its grasp, splashing down into the dark pool.

The captain was the first to snap out of the paralyzing shock, running towards the still-rippling water.

'We need to save him!' he said, whipping out his gun.

'Wait, you'll shoot your man!' said Dr. Yeung, racing after him and forcing the captain's raised gun down.

The water began to ripple, then thrash against their legs more violently than before; signs of struggle between man and beast. Not moments later, blood bubbled up. Then the water became calm. It was as if the soldier had never been there.

They all stood, silently watching the waters, comprehending what they'd just witnessed.

Dr. Yeung finally broke the silence, 'I'm getting out of here!' He then made a frantic beeline for the unguarded drill tanker. Yeung jumped in, slamming the door behind him and locking it.

He hears small twitching like creature noises coming from all around him. Slowly reaching out to turn the light on, he flicks the switch and screams bloody murder when faced with yet another terrifying creature. This time, it was like a reptilian rat or mole-like creature, and there were dozens of them. They must have crept on while no one was looking, shredding apart the metal of the inside of the vehicle and were interrupted by the terrified geologist which didn't faze them. Just as they shredded apart the vehicle, they got to work rabidly shredding the geologist in a frenzy. His blood-curdling screams permeating the windows until nothing could be heard but silence.

'Holy fucking hell,' whispered Matherson, the youngest soldier—which pretty much summed up what everyone else was thinking.

'What the fuck was that?' another terrified soldier spat, raising his gun slightly in readiness for whatever the hell else was going to attack.

'We need shelter; let's go further into the jungle,' Captain Warner piped up, regaining control. 'Roberts and Hamburg, you'll take the rear. Matherson, John, and Mckoy—you'll flank us. The rest will be in the middle.'

'Woah, woah, woah, hold on—You can't be serious.' Dr. Thorpe said, exasperated. 'Are you crazy? Did you not just see what just happened by the water!'

Dr. Thorpe bickered with the captain again, who seemed to have already shaken off the horror of what he'd just seen. After a few minutes, it was clear Dr. Thorpe was getting on the captain's last nerve.

'Let's just get in the drilling tank and go back up,' she attempted to reason, battling the rising panic that froze the other men in place.

The captain put his hands on his hips and rolled his eyes at her. 'Dr. Thorpe, take a look at our vehicle.'

She didn't need to; she knew what he was getting at.

'Those things destroyed the insides of it, and in case you didn't hear it, Dr. Yeung had the decency to lock the door from within so that we were left out here to be killed. Even if we could get in, there's no way we are going to be able to fix it.' His eyes were as wide as he could make them and his face was as cold as stone.

They all hated to admit it, but he was right. There was no way to fix the machine and keep each other safe from these creatures; the group was too small.

Once everyone hesitantly agreed, they trudged onwards, leaving their poor fallen comrade behind. Leading were Roberts and Hamburg—both large men, and the most well-trained—then Captain Warner, who'd volunteered to go next in line. After, the group of scientists scurried close, ending with a shaking young Brandell, Dr. Tannor, and Dr. Thorpe.

Exploring the unknown wilds of the dark jungle proved just as difficult as the thickest rainforests in the world. As they only had two men clearing a path ahead, making a dozen steps took about forty-five minutes.

It felt like they'd stood in the same place forever, all exhausted and panting from the outrageous heat and humidity. Looking back at our progress, Dr. Tannor realised he couldn't see the river anymore. Which seemed impossible, because not five steps ago he looked back and he could still see the muddy waters clearly through the giant trees.

'Captain, I think we should stop…' Dr. Tannor said, shouldering through the other scientists to the front. 'Something isn't right.'

Without even looking, the captain said, 'We aren't stopping until we find an open area.'

Too exhausted to argue further, Tannor simply gave up. It probably wasn't as bad as he thought.

Hour after hour, and it still seemed like they barely moved. Tannor no longer bothered looking back—what would have been the point? Something odd was happening either to them or around them, and no one else seemed to notice.

Exhausted and drenched in their own sweat, they walked like zombies—drained of their energy and not really caring about the curious creatures watching them amongst the shrubbery.

The man leading the depleted pack pushed aside large fanned fronds and disappeared beyond them as usual, but then there was silence. As the rest of them passed the same plant, they realised that their front man had vanished into thin air.

'Where's Roberts? Hamburg, where is Roberts?!' demanded the captain.

'I…I don't know, sir. He was just in front of me, and then—'

Something rustled in the shrubbery that surrounded them.

'Circle formation! Prepare to fire!' yelled a terrified captain.

But that would not stop whatever it was to strike from above. First the defenceless scientists, who were snatched within seconds, and then a furious strike down onto the armed soldiers, who no longer guarded anything—disarming them with shock and speed. The forest fell silent once more, as if no one was ever there.

It wasn't long until the crew was dropped at an unknown destination. They were placed on a small plot of land surrounded by large, pod-like structures. Each pod seemed to be made of material similar to what the American Indians used to construct their homes—an extremely flexible material that mimicked straw. Most were firmly tied to the ground, but there were many others that were strung up in the monstrous trees, as if they were the latest victims of a ginormous spider.

It was incredible to see such similarities between vastly different cultures and species.

Odd-looking beings were scattered throughout the surrounding area, either on top of the suspended huts or roaming around at a safe distance. They were large humanoids with crimson-coloured skin and double-jointed legs—standing almost like mythical fauns. Their elongated arms stretched past their naked knees, each bearing white markings that climbed from their wrists and across their chests like tribal symbols. I noticed long tails trailing behind as they moved, a black tuft of fur like a lion's tail at the end. Where feet would normally be were paws like a big cat. Looking closer at their faces, their noses were flat, with pricked ears like elves, and each had two enormous eyes that were currently focused on the strange animals they brought into their home.

The crew sat, waiting. They were bound tightly to a long staff of wood, each behind the other, and were being prepared to move out of the camp. Judging by the amount of tribesmen coming along, Tannor suspected they were likely going somewhere considered special.

A horn blasted sharply, awakening the rest of the jungle and signaling the time to move out.

The surface-dwellers were led onward into the dense jungle, once again trudging into unknown danger; but this time they moved faster and more efficiently because of the worn path carved over the years. Dr. Tannor felt more at ease that they were in a larger group—granted, they were captives in that larger group, but their captors were natives of this unusual land. Finally stopping to rest by a large tree, no one anticipated the crewmate that was more afraid than the rest was about to snap. Mckoy, fidgety and shifty-eyed, had had enough. Once the creature had pulled his hands free, he bolted through the low shrubbery as fast as he could, not looking back. With a swift movement, a large spear skewered him through the chest, causing him to drop like a fly, dead.

'Tie them to that tree! We cannot allow another to escape!' barked the leader.

A shout from up ahead signaled that they'd reached their destination. The lead guardsmen shouted in response and yanked at the wooden pole to hurry the humans along. A clearing opened before them, but it wasn't clear where they were heading. Looking above, Dr. Tannor wondered at the gigantic stalactites hanging above with small holes in them.

Climbing to the apex of the ridge, they were greeted with an astonishing sight. There was a cluster of gigantic stalagmites and stalactites, which seemed to grow bigger and bigger; honestly the smallest ones looked to be as big as a skyscraper. A natural white light bathed the stalactites in the centre, refracting it and bouncing the beams to the rest of them. Creatures flew high above, in and out of the city carved in stone, though it wasn't quite clear what they were.

As they walked through the mighty structures, it became obvious that this was another larger home for even stranger creatures. The question was: were they friendly? The closer they got, the more impressive the internal infrastructure became—there were carved railings, doors, windows, and even pathways that wrapped themselves around the great rocks.

The group finally stopped at the monstrous stalagmite in the middle, which looked like a magical castle, with beautiful carvings and chiseled grand staircases that weaved in and out of the structure.

The crew were untied from the wooden pole before they entered, each being led by their arms.

Up the stairs they stepped, one foot after another, until everyone reached a grand, polished floor with tall walls and a ceiling so high that it was virtually non-existent.

The crew was confronted with three tall and extremely lanky beings sitting before them. Each creature's large eyes studied the surface-dwellers' faces, interested in the strange things they'd never seen before. The one in the tallest center chair wore a see-through garment that glittered ever so slightly. Around its neck hung a large oval blue-green gem, and a smaller one seemed to protrude from between its eyes. It spoke, its melodic voice using the same language as the red creatures.

They started a lengthy discussion of the group's capture, surmising their origin, and formulating ideas of going to the surface. They believed that the crew would be able to help them get to the surface if they aided in reconstruction of their vehicle.

However, not all the creatures seemed to agree. Not that the crew had a say in the matter, being mere prisoners; before anyone could object, they were taken out of the room and ushered into a prison cell. There they waited anxiously, hardly speaking to each other.

They jumped at the squeak of the door opening.

None of them expected to see the tall, elegant creature from earlier, its sheer outfit glittering in the dim light. It stood by the ajar door, waiting patiently for something. Then it spoke.

As fluently as if it was its own language, it murmured, 'Dr. Daniel Tannor?'

Speechless, all of them just stood where they were, disbelieving what just happened.

It spoke again. 'That is your name, right?' This time, it looked straight at Dr. Tannor.

'U-Um…yes?' The doctor's mouth was wide open in astonishment.

'May we speak?'

He nodded, inching towards the creature and out of the cell holding his comrades. All without taking my eyes off the being.

They found themselves wandering around in silence. So many questions roamed through the doctor's head. One, more prominent than the rest.

Before he could even ask, it broke the silence.

'We are called Aurelian, the creatures that captured you are Garuda. We Aurelian have the ability to read other creatures' minds and learn what their cultures are and what knowledge they may hold, thus gaining the ability to use it as if it were our own.'

That answered one question. 'Your species and the…Garuda, as you call them, are similar physically. Can they do anything like your species?' he asked, pretending like this whole thing was normal.

'We are—how do you say? The more evolved species. Garudans have the skills to hunt and are very agile.'

'What do you want from us?' It was a deadly question, but it had to be asked.

'For centuries, we have desired to go to the surface. To feel real air and the heat of whatever brilliant light shines down above us, and to see what the world looks like.' Its face was dream-like, smiling as it spoke.

Acknowledging its expression, Tannor prodded, 'You want it more than the rest.'

It smirked. 'Is it that obvious?'

They found themselves roaming around a natural fountain in the middle of a large aqua-coloured pond. The space helped ease Dr. Tannor's emotions and made him feel almost tranquil.

'You're their leader?'

A gloomy look seemed to fall upon its face. 'I am what you would call the Priestess of both Garudans and Aurelians.'

'A heavy burden.'

'Yes...one I take seriously for the sake of my people. As you do with your title.'

'My title?'

'Yes. You are their leader.'

Tannor chuckled. 'No, I think you have me mistaken.'

It paused where it stood. 'No. I don't. People look to you for guidance. Perhaps not with words, but with their thoughts and feelings. They look to you more than their assigned leader.'

Tannor burst out laughing, something the Priestess clearly wasn't used to by her look of surprise.

He forced himself to refocus, remembering his team was counting on him. 'We don't belong here. Can you help us go back to the surface? Is there a way?'

'We can help you, but in return, we only ask one thing.'

'Of course, anything!'

'You will allow us passage to the surface.'

'Ah...well, that may be a difficult request.'

'It is the only one we ask.'

'I know, but that decision isn't entirely up to me.' His reply left a confused expression on the priestess's face.

'There are far more of us than you could ever imagine. We decide worldly things as a team, and vote what is best.'

'This is all we ask..'

'Very well. I will do my best,' the doctor said, finally admitting defeat.

It didn't take the Aurelians long to start work on the damaged machine. The minerals and metals taken from the mantle below us worked just as well as the original materials. Patching the pierced frame was the easy part, the hard part was getting it started again. But in a few days' time, the humans were back on the surface, and Dr. Tannor found himself in front of the most important men in the world.

'Their resources and minerals are far more than you could ever imagine,' Dr. Tannor said to the President and his trusted advisors with rapturous enthusiasm. 'And their cultures are similar to some of our own. Their medical resources and materials have the abilities to cure the diseases we have been fighting for decades!'

Murmuring echoed around him. Richard Tannor watched with optimistic eyes.

'We don't know what their true intentions are. What if they want to take over the surface?' argued one representative.

'I'm sorry, Dr. Tannor, but we cannot afford to bargain with creatures for their supplies. We cannot risk the lives of this earth for the wealth of our own governments.'

Tannor could feel his jaw clench. 'You didn't have a problem with that sixty years ago.'

'Dr. TANNOR! I am going to let that one pass purely on the fact that your father is a close friend of mine, but let me warn you that you're walking a very fine line,' one of the council members said sternly, wagging his finger.

'Very well. Thank you for your time.' Dr. Tannor turned away slowly, knowing that he wasn't giving up that easily.

That was the pinnacle moment in time that would change the world forever.

Dr. Tannor wasn't able to sway the government to give passage to the creatures that lived down there. He would not back down on his promise. During his scientific career, Dr. Tannor managed to acquire certain 'tools' that his superiors and the government did not see as legal by means of the underground market. Whilst acquiring these objects, he also managed to gain new friends that knew powerful people—people who were not friends with his country, who could help him in his ambitious venture of freeing the creatures. He left his country and home believing in what he was fighting for. Unbeknownst to him, those he was working for would use his trust and knowledge to invoke a war of insurmountable proportions.

The world is now a blank page. The past is forgotten and lost, only remnants remain. The present is dark and evil rules. But the future is still unwritten. What we do now sets us on a journey with multiple paths; we must choose the right one.

Love's Final Embrace

Author's Note:

Farrah is out looking for that stupid little dog! Leaving DeeDee distraught thinking the worst could happen at any given moment. Miles puts it upon himself to save Farrah going out alone in the storm to find her. DeeDee want's to help not giving any notice to Miles's clear annoyance pushing him and pushing him until...

In this short story scene, readers will find out if DeeDee and Miles truly do get together and find out how each other feel, damn the consequences and the Drakes!

'I'm worried,' DeeDee exclaimed, breaking the silence that had befallen the mansion since Farrah left. 'It's been way too long.'

'I know. It's been twenty minutes,' Miles whispered. 'What should we do?'

'Our Farrah is a smart girl. She'll find that stupid little rat and seek refuge somewhere,' Ms. Turner said reassuringly.

'But who could survive out in this?' DeeDee protested.

'What's going on?' shouted an annoyed Mr. Drake, frightening everyone with his sudden appearance. Fraya continued to look at the door with big, round, hopeful eyes.

No one answered, everyone too unnerved by what was happening outside.

'We're sorry, sir,' Miles finally spoke up. 'We couldn't stop her.'

'Who's out there?' he repeated, sterner than before.

'Someone's outside? In that weather? Ha! Well, aren't they stupid?' snipped Mrs. Drake, who was listening from the stairs.

'You see, Miss Fraya's puppy was missing, and we couldn't find it anywhere inside,' continued Miles.

'I am the master of this house! I ask again, WHO IS OUTSIDE?'

'Farrah, sir. Farrah is outside.'

'Oh, that's it? She's easily replaceable,' Mrs. Drake snidely remarked.

'What?' DeeDee's face went pale as a sheet.

Ms. Turner rubbed the young girl's arm in comfort, not realising she was just as pale.

'Yes, slaves are very easy to get. We can ask Mr. Anderson for a better one. Right, dear?' She looked up at her husband with wistful eyes.

Drake glanced down to his wife, then to poor DeeDee, who was on the verge of collapsing from grief. The distraught girl looked straight back at him with big sorrowful eyes, making Mr. Drake slightly flushed. Unfortunately, Mrs. Drake caught the exchange and shot a mean scowl in DeeDee's direction before turning her eyes back towards her husband. Her claws quickly latched onto his thick arm, pulling herself closer.

'Right, dear?' she repeated, puckering with what little lips she had.

Shaking his head, Mr. Drake's gaze returned to the woman at his side. 'Yes. We can easily get a better one.'

Pleased with his response, Mrs. Drake smiled. Unclasping one of her hands from his arm, she reached for his face and pulled him into a selfish kiss. Everyone turned away, having absolutely no desire to watch her display of desperation. During the kiss, however, Mrs. Drake shot DeeDee's slumping figure a look of warning.

'Daddy! Daddy!' a familiar voice screamed excitedly from outside the dining room. 'Daddy! Guess who I found!'

Running inside with the biggest smile on her face was little Fraya. Standing on her toes, she showcased the scared furry rat who started it all, being strangled by her owner's chubby little arms.

'Oh, God, no!' DeeDee shrieked, then promptly collapsed.

Miles barely caught her before she hit the floor, lifting her limp body into his toned, muscular arms. The Master watched on with a controlled, yet worried face as he took a step towards her.

Mrs. Drake still had hold of his arm and squeezed it.

'There's no need for dramatics. Take her to her chambers,' Mrs. Drake instructed. Miles carried poor unconscious DeeDee to her room, followed by a worried and sad Ms. Turner.

***

Once they were in the servant's quarters, Ms. Turner patted DeeDee's furrowed brow with a damp cloth as Miles held her hand.

Awakening drowsily, she wept.

'Please don't cry, dear. Everything will be fine,' Ms. T said reassuringly, as she gently played with her soft hair.

A shadow appeared in the doorway. Clearing his throat, Lord Drake entered the room. 'Leave,' he instructed sternly.

Miles's body refused to move. For the first time, he stared down his master, but a slight brush of DeeDee's cold, pale hand knocked him out of his trance. He looked at her weary face, and she gave him a nod of assurance that she would be okay. He left, reluctantly, meeting Ms. Turner by the door who guided him out.

Sitting up slowly, DeeDee looked at the ground, stomach churning at the idea of being alone with the Master.

Mr. Drake sat beside her, leaving barely an inch between them.

'I'm sorry,' he began. Shocked by an apology—from her master, of all people—she looked at him, confused. 'I know she was a dear friend of yours, but you have to know it was suicide for her to go out into the storm.' He grabbed her clenched hand and encompassed it within his. She met his gaze. His face was genuinely remorseful.

'I promise I will find one just like her. A new friend. It will be like she never—'

'Her name was Farrah,' she interrupted, 'and... I'll never get to see her smile again, or hear her laugh again, or get to brush her beautiful brown hair again...'

A hand rested on her shoulder, and she felt herself being pulled into his chest.

'I know. I'm sorry, my love,' he whispered, soothingly stroking her arm.

DeeDee heard him sniffing the top of her head. She trembled.

'Sssssshhhhh,' he said, trying to calm her. 'I promise… soon you will be my mistress, and our baby will be safe.' DeeDee could feel his hand brushing across her hip, making its way over to her stomach, rubbing it gently. 'I have to go. My wife will be wondering where I am, but I'll be back.' He kissed her head as he stood. Before leaving the room, he gave her one last creepy smile.

***

'Stop it.' Ms. Turner snapped at a silent, yet agitated, Miles. 'What?'

'I know what you're thinking.'

'She could still be alive.' Miles was chewing the inside of his mouth, regretting not going with his friend.

'I know, but we can't help her. You can't save her without putting yourself in harm's way.'

'I'll be careful.'

'The Master will find out what you did.'

'I'll use the old servant's entrance to the backyard.'

'Okay—let's say you make it outside. What if you die out there? DeeDee will never forgive you. And you haven't even told her how you feel yet, have you? You are so blind. You can't even see the way she looks at you. How stupid are you? Or are you just a coward? How do you expect to have the courage to save Farrah when you aren't even brave enough to speak what's on your mind?!'

'Fine, I love her! Is that what you want me to say?' he snapped, throwing himself into a pace as he spoke, 'I love the way she smiles, how passionate and caring she is, and the way she makes me feel like I'm more than just, well, you know.' He turned to Ms. Turner, who had the biggest smile on her face.

A clattering sound came from outside the kitchen's entrance.

'Who's there?' they said in unison, anxiously looking toward the doorway.

'Um—I'm sorry. I didn't mean to.' A red-faced DeeDee shuffled into view. Miles's eyes became as round as frying-pans and his face turned as crimson as hers. Neither of them said anything for a solid minute.

'DeeDee! It's so good to see you up and well, dear!' Ms. Turner said, breaking the awkward silence to give her a hug.

'I gotta go,' Miles said, briskly walking past them with his palm up to his face.

DeeDee watched him disappear with desperation in her eyes.

'It's okay, dear. Everything is going to be fine. Come, have a seat.' Ms. Turner said, comforting DeeDee with a gentle pat on her shoulder. DeeDee's eyes were still glued to the door Miles had walked through.

'I'm fine, Ms. T, I think I just need to walk around for a bit, if that's okay.' Giving her a smile, DeeDee followed the flustered groundskeeper.

'Stupid idiot. What were you thinking?' Miles mumbled to himself while he fumbled around with what little possessions he had and what his parents had left behind.

'What are you doing?' a voice asked.

Miles jumped, startled by DeeDee's appearance.

'Sorry, I didn't mean to frighten you.' She chuckled.

'No, no, it's fine. I'm just...' Their eyes met, making Miles stop and blush just as red as before. He continued looking down. 'I'm going to save Farrah.'

'I'm coming with you,' she replied.

He didn't respond at first, only continued to rustle through his dirty clothes.

'The Master won't allow it. He cares for you too much.'

'So? She's like a sister to me.'

Again, no answer.

'It's my choice, anyway. You can't make me stay.' Agitation curdled inside her as she stomped away from him and towards the door. She felt a tight grip on her arm as he tugged at her, making her stop in her tracks.

'You're not going out there, DeeDee!' he said, his face fierce.

'And why not? I care for her more than you do!' she argued, returning his scowl.

'Because—You just can't, okay!'

'You're not the boss of me! I'm going!'

'You can't go because... because!'

'Because why? Just spit it out!'

At the top of his lungs, he screamed, 'Because I'm in love with you!' As looked at her, his face slowly softened, returning to the kind, handsome face she always cared for, the one that was always anxious of what she was going to say next, but all she did was look at him with shock. His tight grasp on her arm slowly released, and he turned his face away. She took a small step forward, an awkward smile on her lips.

'Umm… I know… I kind of heard you and Ms. T earlier.' She blushed, her heart racing. She couldn't believe that all this time he loved her too. Warmth spread throughout her body and her smile widened. Tears of relief and pure happiness streamed down her flushed, freckled face, and enriched her beautiful golden eyes, making them seem like gems.

She stepped closer to him, slowly and nervously. With a gentle hand, she softly grabbed his chin and pushed it up so that he could see her gorgeous, smiling face. He looked into her eyes, taking in all her feelings laid bare, and understood.

Grabbing her arms, he pulled her into his thick, muscular, warm chest. Their faces inched closer and closer; so close that they could feel each other's breath. Finally, they kissed. Timid, at first. Then his soft tongue slipped into her welcoming slender mouth, deepening the kiss. It grew to be passionate, desperate; as if they'd never see each other again. Lips squeezing together even tighter until their teeth clicked, their tongues danced and meld with each other as the both of them sought the timeless sensation in a singular passionate moment. Heat rose in DeeDee's cheeks as Miles's tongue gently slipped in deeper; her taste was delicious, like warm honey and berries. The feeling between them was electric, the both of them seeking to chase down the elusive liquid lightning that ignited between the both of them. Their bodies became one and the world seemed to stop. Aroused by each other's movements, neither one wanting the moment to end.

'Ahem!'

The young lovers pulled apart, startled.

Ms. Turner was there, watching with a big smile of acceptance and happiness for them.

'We were just—' Miles started, face flushed.

'Never mind. Are we going to save Farrah or not?' she asked.

'You're in?' Miles said, surprised.

'She's like a daughter to me; of course I'm in! What kind of monster do you think I am?'

Both of them smiled at her.

'Yes! We are going to save Farrah! As a family!' DeeDee jumped in excitement and raced to give Ms. Turner a great big hug.

'All right, all right! Keep those hormones to yourself!'

'We need to get to the old passageway so that Drake doesn't know what's happening,' Miles explained.

Both women nodded. It wasn't long before they gathered the supplies needed for the rescue. 'Ms. Turner, you will need to stand by to make sure no one is coming to look for us,' instructed Miles.

'Okay, I'll do my best.'

'DeeDee, you'll need to open the door. It locks automatically when it closes, so you'll need to unlock it when you hear me knocking.'

'Okay,' she said with a concerned expression.

'Don't worry, I'll be fine.' Miles assured, caressing her cheek.

She held the hand caressing her and smiled lovingly at him.

He strapped his father's old workman's gas mask onto his face tightly and tied a rope around his waist—it would act as a tether if he were to get lost in the storm.

DeeDee grabbed his hand. 'Come back to me.'

He looked at her and smiled under his makeshift mask. 'You have to leave when I open the door or the toxins will come in.'

'Okay.'

Once DeeDee was at a safe distance, he opened the creaking passageway door. Toxic air gushed in, nearly toppling him over. Miles pushed through the unforgiving gusts, struggling to close the door behind him.

Once the toxins had dissipated, DeeDee left the room she was hiding in, looking around to make sure it was safe.

Twenty minutes had passed and still no knock or sign that Miles was back. She started to fidget; nibbling at her already stumpy short nails and shaking her leg to the point where it was nearly vibrating. All of a sudden—

BANG! BANG! BANG!

It was Miles! She took in a large breath of fresh air, covered her face with her hanky, and opened the door as fast as she could. The gritty air blinded her, and she scrambled backwards when she knew Miles had made it inside. She heard grunts and thuds and something big being dragged across the floor. Could it be?

'Close the door!' Miles yelled over the wind.

Doing as she was commanded, DeeDee pushed her whole body against the door, but with all her might, it still wasn't enough. Large hands appeared on either side of her as Miles got up to help from behind. Together, they managed to close the rusty old door.

They had to wait a few agonizing moments for the toxins to disappear before both Miles and DeeDee could take off their masks. DeeDee cleared the sand from her eyes, hoping to see her dear friend safe.

'Did we do it? Is she back inside?' Ms. Turner asked from behind a wall.

Miles knelt down over a familiar form, her once smooth face now scratched, grazes and cuts covering her body. Her soft brown hair was now tangled in massive knots with twigs and small spiky balls. It was as if she had been flung around like an old rag.

'Is she...?' DeeDee whispered, fearing the worst.

Putting his ear to her chest, Miles prayed and listened for a sign of life.

Everyone held their breath as they waited.

A short cough emerged from Farrah's weak lungs.

'Yes! She's alive!' Miles said with a sigh of relief. Tears ran down everyone's faces.

Shawline Publishing Group Pty Ltd
www.shawlinepublishing.com.au